Taken by Tuesday

CATHERINE BYBEE

Taken by Tuesday

BOOK FIVE IN THE
WEEKDAY BRIDES SERIES

Text copyright © 2014 Catherine Bybee

Published by Montlake Romance, Seattle

www.apub.com

Amazon, the Amazon logo, and Montlake Romance are trademarks of Amazon.com, Inc., or its affiliates.

ISBN-13: 9781477823774
ISBN-10: 1477823778

Cover design by Crystal Posey

Library of Congress Control Number: 2014900810

Printed in the United States of America

To Aunt Joan

Simply because I love you.

Chapter One

Judy pressed the red *raid* button and hoped she hadn't misjudged her opponent in this stupid online game. She only needed five more valor points to make the next level, and the battery on her tablet was flashing a 20 percent warning.

"What the hell are you doing?" Meg, her roommate of four years, stood in skimpy workout shorts and glared from the doorway.

"Avoiding!" Damn it, her math was off and the raid failed, putting her behind for at least half an hour. "Stupid game."

Meg tossed her gym bag on the floor and moved into the small kitchen they shared in the off-campus apartment. "You told me you weren't joining *hell* with me because you needed to study. I walk in . . . and what do I see? You, on that waste-of-time game and not studying."

"I needed a break." *Hell* was their code word for James and his boot camp workout at the local gym. James constructed his workouts in a series of obstacles that worked every possible muscle in the human body . . . hence the term *hell*. It was H. E. double L. when you couldn't sit in a chair or on the toilet without cursing James. Yet they went back day after day.

Not today . . . at least for Judy. Her take-home final for advanced architectural design was kicking her ass. So what that it was due tomorrow at seven in the morning. Or that she'd all but told herself she was a fool for adding an additional major to her senior year. Who cared that she'd tossed fifteen thousand dollars onto her student loans? So what!

She buried her head in her hands. "I'm screwed."

"You're fine." Meg kicked the refrigerator door closed, a cold water bottle clenched in her hand.

"I suck. The design I'm working on doesn't make any sense. There's nothing dynamic about it . . . nothing that says 'I'm the best structure in the world, build me,' nothing."

Meg waved away Judy's concern. "You're overthinking it. Stressed. What you need is a night out and a good lay."

Judy rolled her eyes. "It's due tomorrow, Meg, I don't have time for a quick anything." Besides, she'd given up the quick mean-nothing guys in her junior year. Even the young, attractive professors seemed less interesting since . . .

Since . . .

"Well, you need to do something to relax," Meg told her. "You're all clogged up." Meg always said things like that. Her parents were throwbacks from the late sixties, early seventies. They had Meg late in life and were completely burnt when they conceived. Hence, Meg's *free* feeling about sex and *screw the establishment* agenda. It was amazing she'd made it through a formal education. Yeah, she was leaving the University of Washington with a degree in business, but just barely.

The fact that Meg studied business had confused Judy when they first met. Meg seemed much more likely to major in art. According to Meg, students graduating with an art major waited tables their entire lives and seldom had any security when they grew old. Judy still questioned if Meg would be happy in *any* business setting. Time would tell.

Judy had finished her business requirements early in an effort to tack on architectural design as a second major. Her father wasn't happy but couldn't bitch a whole lot when he learned that Judy had taken online courses during the regular school year as well as her last summer to complete what she needed in order to graduate with a double major.

Only now, she was sitting in her apartment playing stupid online war games and avoiding her final.

"Some of us are getting together at Bergies. A drink could clear your head."

Judy tossed aside the tablet that housed her video games, her e-mail, her life . . . and stood. "I need to shower first."

———

"I'm on assignment," Rick whispered to himself once he hit the campus of the University of Washington. Didn't matter that he'd started his trek en route to Boise State, the college where Karen had told him Judy studied. He only wasted one plane ticket to the wrong destination.

He scouted the auditorium where graduation ceremonies would take place . . . looked at the location he'd been told the VIPs were going to stand while they watched their sons, daughters, or in this case, sisters, walk.

Michael Wolfe, the celebrity and friend Rick was there to protect, was the Elvis of modern film . . . minus the guitar and voice. Michael's entire family—parents, siblings, and even his ex-wife—would be present for Judy's graduation. The paparazzi were the most likely obstacle to overcome, but Rick knew he couldn't be too cautious.

He envisioned the tiny pixie that had held adventure and fire in her blood, and smiled.

The arena was fine, he decided. Two main exits were the only places the media could breach. It would take less than three men to manage, and Michael and his family could watch Judy's graduation in peace. On second thought . . . maybe he'd add a fourth man to the job so *he* could watch Judy graduate.

"Does everything meet with your approval, Mr. Evans?"

Rick had nearly forgotten about the administrator of campus security who had joined him.

"How much security do you have on hand on graduation day?"

"A dozen are scheduled."

"Trusted? None can be bought . . . right?" It wouldn't be the first time a security guard earned a quick buck by letting the media slip in.

"Of course." Pete, the head of security, looked offended.

"So, where do the graduating seniors hang out two weeks before graduation?"

Rick hadn't gone to college. He'd joined the Marines shortly after high school. Formal education or pushing paper around all day wasn't in the cards for him. No! He wanted adventure. So much fucking adventure that his buddies had been killed and parts of his own body were damaged and scarred thanks to his time in the service. Yeah, once a Marine always a Marine, but at thirty-one, he didn't have a strong desire to go back.

He didn't regret his time, but it did seem as if he had simply put his life on hold while everyone else passed him by. Now that his last remaining Marine colleague was married and had a kid of his own, it felt like maybe Rick was missing a key element in life.

When the nights were long, and sleep evaded him, Rick's thoughts moved to one person . . . Utah.

God, she was piss and vinegar . . . sexy and smart all rolled into one. Not that he should pollute her world, but he couldn't stop thinking about her.

———

Bergies was a dive off the college row of trendy joints where most of the kids hung . . . this was for the slightly older students blowing off steam during their last days of carefree college life.

A slow, steady sprinkling of rain fell outside but the windows were open to the outside to let the air circulate. It was only nine but the bar was packed and the music was loud. The perfect combination for forgetting or hooking up. Somehow, he didn't think he'd see Utah inside.

But she'd surprised him before, so who knew?

Rick stepped into the bar and let the door behind him shut. The mat under his feet was soaked, so wiping was a joke. He moved past the first booth and the burnt bouncer that sat close to the door. The man wasn't attentive enough to realize that Rick, wearing more than one weapon, had breached the walls. Not that Rick had any intentions of showing anyone his guns. Well, not the bought and paid for ones, in any event.

"Hey, handsome? What can I get ya?"

The cocktail waitress, who was too skinny and too needy, zeroed in on him before he could smell the stale beer. Her invitation was more about showing each other their body parts than offering him a beverage.

Rick stuck with a drink.

"Heineken."

She winked. "You got it." She disappeared with a shake of her hips and a flick of her bleached blonde hair.

Not his type.

The smile that always sat on his lips pivoted a couple of heads in his direction, but when he glanced beyond the eyes following him, the women twisted around in their seats and returned to the conversations they were having with other patrons.

Blondie balanced the lone beer on her tray and licked her lips while she handed it to him. He fished a ten from his wallet. "Keep the change."

The ten disappeared in the tiny pocket of her short skirt. "I'm off at midnight."

"And I'm here looking for someone."

She offered a small pout. "If you change your mind . . ." She winked and walked away.

Not gonna happen, sweetheart.

Rick moved to the back of the bar, where players held cue sticks and waited their turn by a few pool tables.

A throaty laugh made him pause.

He knew that laugh.

The smile on his face suddenly felt more genuine. His gaze slid across the room when she laughed again. Her back was to him, but it was her . . . Utah. She held her cue stick and pointed at a corner pocket. "Watch 'em and weep."

She sank the eight ball like it was her bitch and the guys around the table groaned. A short-haired blonde lifted her hand and made a grabby motion with her fingers. "Pay up!"

Utah laughed, laid her cue on the table, and grabbed the bottle of beer at her side. All the while Rick just watched the interplay. She wore tight jeans, a tucked-in tank that hugged her waist in a mouthwatering way . . . over the ensemble was a jean jacket that he could easily picture draped over the handlebars of his motorcycle.

"I think we just got hustled," one of the young college kids said as he shoved his hand in his wallet to pay his debt.

"I tried to warn you."

Judy's friend shoved the bills into her pocket faster than the waitress had. "Anyone else? Twenty-buck minimum with a round of drinks."

This might be fun.

Rick took a step forward and lifted his voice above the crowd. "A hundred bucks."

Utah froze, but didn't turn around. He wondered if she recognized his voice. Had she thought about him in the last year? With the exception of her brother's divorce party, he hadn't seen her . . . not outside of a wet dream or two.

The blonde swiveled her head like a snake to prey and her eyes did that sweeping thing that happened to him once in a while. Rick knew he wasn't hard on the eyes, knew he filled out his shirt like a Marine should. His thick shoulders and neck screamed military or linebacker. He did play a little football in high school.

"Who the hell are you?" the blonde mumbled.

Rick chuckled.

Judy slowly turned and had to tilt her head back to look at him. "Green Eyes."

"Hey, Utah."

"You know this guy?" The blonde shoved in next to Judy and nudged her arm.

God, she was even more adorable than he remembered. He didn't let her eyes go, just matched her stare. A blush rose to her cheeks and a few freckles peeked through. Her snarky remark about his presence was a heartbeat away. He'd lay another hundred bucks on the table as a bet that the next words out of her mouth would shock everyone within earshot.

"Did the steroid train stop in town when I wasn't looking?"

The blonde started to laugh.

Rick stepped even closer so barely an inch separated them. The smile never left his face. "I hear steroids shrink dicks."

As if she couldn't help herself, Judy glanced down, and it was Rick's turn to laugh. He brushed the edge of her body with his and removed the cue from the table. "What do ya say, Utah? I'll even let you break. Ladies first and all that."

Rick knew they were drawing a crowd, but the interplay between them matched the sparks that hovered over them like a damn rainbow, and he was powerless to care what anyone thought.

"A hundred bucks is steep, Judy."

"S'OK, Meg . . . Rick's a big talker. Besides, he doesn't know what I'm capable of."

Rick shook his head and clicked his tongue. "Now, now . . . don't want to show all your cards."

"She's really good, dude," the guy she'd relieved of twenty bucks said from across the table.

Rick lowered his voice. "Will you go easy on me, babe?"

Judy regained some of her lost composure and pushed away from his personal space. "Not on your life. And I'm not your *babe*!"

We'll see about that.

He couldn't stop smiling.

I'm not going to smile. I'm not going to smile. OK, inside she was smiling. Though the man could be quite aggravating, he was so yummy to look at. Made the men in the bar look like boys. Compared to him, they were.

Meg lowered her lips to her ear. "Who is he?"

Judy chalked her cue stick and whispered, "Mike's security."

"The guy from last summer?"

Yeah, the guy who helped find Becky Applegate and bring Becky's abusive father to justice. Rick might have the nickname Smiley, but that smile would vanish in a heartbeat if someone screwed with him. She'd seen him in action, and he was a tornado without a weather warning siren. Though if her own heart beating in her chest was any indication, she was being given a warning or two about this man.

"Grrr!" Meg growled under her breath like a freaking cat.

"You should go for it."

Meg snickered. "Hon, he's not here looking at me."

Judy glanced up and noticed Rick's intense stare. She finished her beer and signaled the waitress. "The bet is a hundred bucks and a round of drinks."

"Whatever the lady wants."

"Another round, Cindy . . . and whatever he's having."

Rick waved his beer in the air, leaned back, and crossed his arms over his chest. Too bad this dive didn't have Dom Pérignon or she'd see if Rick's wallet could handle her. Not that she'd had a lot of experience with expensive wines . . . well, when she visited her brother there always seemed to be pricy bubbly.

"Anytime you're ready, babe."

Around her, there were side bets taking place. Not that she had any earthly clue of Rick's ability, but she had to guess some of the guys thought his very stature was enough to bet on. She had to admit, his confidence shook her . . . a little.

Judy placed the white ball on the table and leaned over. Directly in front of her, Rick stood, just on the other side of the colorful balls all racked up and ready to fly. Pool was nothing but angles and lines. Things she worked with every day in school. Once she pictured the table as a big grid with a multitude of possibilities, she started sinking balls and raking in some spending money for her and Meg to blow. She didn't have to hustle pool. Her friends at the bar did it for her. Newbies were warned, and the bets were never high . . . just drinks and pocket change.

It was fun, and in the end, everyone had a good time.

She pulled back on the cue a few times, lining up the balls. "How many times do I have to tell you . . ." She slammed the balls together and both a solid and a stripe managed to disappear in opposite pockets. One glance at the table and she set up three more shots . . . solids. She walked around to Rick's side of the table, leaned over, and finished her sentence. "I'm not your babe." She sank the four and stood with a grin. With her index finger, she pushed Rick out of her personal space, and offered him her ass as she banked the one ball into a corner pocket.

She couldn't remember flirting this shamelessly, especially when she had no real intentions of making good on her sexual vibes. Flirting with Rick was fun, but the man screamed danger and she just didn't do danger. Not even for one night.

The next shot wasn't a given, it would take a bank and it would probably hit the striped ten ball on its way in . . . but if she hit the ten at ninety degrees, it might just work. Judy lined up her angles while everyone around the table grew silent.

She felt the weight of Rick's stare as she tapped the ball and watched as it slowly hit her target and nearly stopped before sinking. She sighed and grinned.

"Damn, Utah . . . you *are* good." Yet Rick's smile didn't waver.

"Warned ya, dude." Jerry was the resident killjoy, making sure every opponent knew the risk of betting against her.

There wasn't a decent shot on the table, so Judy made sure the white ball wasn't in an optimal position for Rick to make an easy target.

Rick walked around the table, studied the balls. "Wanna up the bet, babe?"

Judy's back teeth ground together. The term *babe* just wasn't one she'd ever liked.

"What do you have in mind?"

"If you win, I'll stop calling you *babe*."

"And if you win?"

"A date . . . anytime, anywhere I choose." He wasn't even looking at her when he suggested it.

"A date?"

He chalked his cue. "Anytime, anywhere."

"I have finals and graduation."

"Those dates are exempt."

Judy glanced at the table . . .

"Seems like a win-win to me," Meg chimed in from the stool she sat on while sucking on her vodka tonic.

Judy rolled her eyes.

"OK, bad boy . . . you have yourself a bet."

Noise from the bar caught her attention. A couple of guys were arguing about a game on the massive TV.

She turned around and focused on Rick.

"So." He leaned over and without any real focus, sank the eleven, a shot she hadn't seen. "You really don't like being called *babe*."

"I prefer Utah over *babe*."

The fourteen was an easy hit, but he managed to bank it and shove the nine in an opposite pocket on the other side of the table.

Those around the table started exchanging dollars.

Rick's next shot missed.

Judy pulled off her jacket and handed it to Meg. So he wanted to play hardball?

The seven practically took a protractor to line up, but down it went and up went Rick's eyebrow. Her next shot missed, but so did Rick's.

She managed the two ball and was feeling confident when Rick sank two in one shot . . . again.

The hell!

"So, they play a lot of pool in the service?" she asked.

He laughed. "Not really." He lined up his last ball on the table. It went in with ease and Judy's heart rate shot up. She didn't really have a hundred bucks on her. They'd only been in the bar for a couple of games before Rick managed to make an appearance. And then there was the date on which she just knew he'd call her *babe* the entire time.

"So where did you learn to play?"

He paused . . . made eye contact. "Hustled pool when I was seventeen. Made a ton of money, too."

Ahh damn.

Noise from behind them caught both their attention. Seemed the resident drunk didn't like the ref's call and was getting in someone else's face about it.

Judy focused on the table, noted the position of the eight ball. In all its black glory, it hugged the side of the table. Rick would have to be a moron to miss the shot. She might as well have the name *babe* monogrammed on her towels now.

"What's the matter, *babe?* You look upset."

"You don't know me well enough to know if I'm upset."

Rick chuckled, leaned over, and pulled the cue back.

From the bar, glass crashed to the floor. Judy swiveled in time to see a chair sailing in the air. She was about to duck when strong arms wrapped around her waist and pulled her out of the line of fire.

Her lungs exploded and all the air inside pushed out and had her head spinning.

Rick tucked her head into his strong, thick shoulder at the same time she felt his body jerk. Around him, wood splintered and she heard Meg yell.

Judy dared to look and noticed the bar erupt in a full-blown fight. This had happened once before, right after she'd turned twenty-one, but that had been a couple of years ago.

"You OK?"

Green eyes accompanied a stern face . . . so different from the laughter that always seemed to dominate Rick's expression. His entire body covered hers . . . from head to knee. She felt every hard edge of him. Every edge.

"Fine."

Rick suddenly turned his face toward hers, and shoved her even farther under him. Glass splattered over them both.

From the corner of her eye, she noticed Meg and their friends fleeing through the back door.

Noise filled the room and the sound of fists meeting flesh made Judy cringe.

Rick practically lifted her off the ground at the same time he pushed off the floor, his arm a vise grip on her waist.

The minute he was on his feet, someone threw a punch and was met with Rick's elbow, followed by his foot, tossing the drunk aside.

"Back door?"

Judy pointed in the direction her friends had just exited and Rick ran with her out the exit.

They stumbled into the damp alley, and the cool spring night smacked up against her face.

Without meaning it, she found a smile on her face despite the sting to her arm where she'd met the ground with Rick's tackle. His blow to the ground was better than a chair across her head.

"Are you all right?"

She started to laugh.

"Judy?"

She leaned forward, hands on her knees to catch her breath and stop her laughter. "Ever notice how every time we see each other something crazy happens?"

It took a minute, but Rick started to laugh along with her. "I'm going to blame you."

"Easy to do since I live here and you're visiting."

She straightened and placed a hand to her sore elbow. Then she remembered her favorite jean jacket inside the bar. "Oh, damn."

"What?"

"Nothing . . . my jacket . . . whatever." It wasn't worth going back in for.

"Judy?" Meg called her name from the street.

"We're here."

Two patrons exploded from the back door, and Rick once again pulled her away from the fists flying as the fight moved onto the street.

They jogged away from the chaos and met with Meg and two of their male friends.

"That's one way to end the night!"

Judy blew out a long breath. "I have my final to work on anyway . . . what time is it?"

"Not even ten."

Judy cocked her head to the side as her eyes met Rick's. The man was such a contradiction. Soft green eyes, thick muscles . . . easy smile, fierce protective gene.

"That's it!" That's what her project needed. Soft lines and thick wood. God, it was in front of her the whole time. It was going to be brilliant. OK, maybe not brilliant, but over-the-top unique and nothing that had been done before . . . or so she hoped.

"Utah?"

Judy didn't consciously realize that she'd lifted her hand and traced Rick's arm. Soft and thick . . . she snapped her hand back when he reached to steady her.

"Did you hit your head?"

It ached, actually . . . but that was probably the noise from the bar spilling out and the excitement of knowing exactly what she needed to do for her final.

"No . . . I'm good. Meg?" She turned toward her friend. "We gotta go. My final . . . I know what I need to do."

Meg shook her head and laughed.

Rick grasped her hand before she could sprint away. "About that date."

Judy tugged away, pointed a finger in his direction. "You didn't win, Green Eyes."

"I didn't lose, *babe*."

Judy laughed. God, he annoyed her in a perfect kind of way. "Until a rematch then." As Meg was pulling her away, Judy said, "Thanks for keeping my head from being kicked in."

Rick stood in the alley, rain drizzling all around him as the fight from the bar moved into the street and sirens started from somewhere east of the alley. "Anytime, Utah."

Judy turned and ran down the rainy street to the apartment she shared with Meg, all the while knowing that Rick watched her from behind.

Chapter Two

Michael rented a small reception hall and cased in the Dom Pérignon for Judy, her friends, and their families.

Judy floated on a cloud. She'd aced her finals, had the well-earned honors cords around her neck, and a smile on her face that no one could knock off.

Meg stepped into the reception hall, her parents at her side.

Judy ran up and once again that day, threw her arms around her best friend. "We did it."

"You're a geek, Gardner. You knew we did it last week." But Meg was smiling just the same.

"Hello, Mr. and Mrs. Rosenthal." She kissed Meg's parents.

"You make me feel old, Judy."

Judy shrugged, refusing to call Meg's parents by their first names. "It's the way I was raised. Have you met my parents?" She flagged over Janice and Sawyer and introduced them to Meg's parents. Once the four of them started talking, Judy pulled Meg away.

"C'mon, we need some pictures."

She started with Mike, but first she needed to drag him away from her other friends, who zeroed in on the celebrity and were asking for autographs.

She hugged her brother and let him lift her and turn her in a circle. "There's the graduate." He kissed her cheek.

"Thanks for the party."

"What's a rich older brother good for if not a decent graduation party?" Mike knew he was so much more than that.

"This is Meg, by the way."

Unlike any of her other friends, Meg oozed coolness and none of that fan-girl crap. "I've heard a lot about you, Mike."

Mike raised his eyebrow, probably because of the use of his name. Everyone other than family called him Michael. "I heard that the two of you were in a bar fight that may or may not have involved hustling pool."

Meg shrugged. "Well, there was a bar fight, but we never *hustle* pool."

The memory of that night had Judy looking around the room. She'd seen Rick in the back of the VIP box at graduation, but she'd not seen him since.

Judy stopped one of her friends as they walked by. "Can you take our picture?"

Judy sandwiched Mike between herself and Meg and blinked when the camera flashed. The second picture was perfect and she immediately posted it to Facebook.

"We need to get all of the family before anyone leaves," she told her brother.

"I doubt Mom will let us leave without it."

The waiter walked by, offered tall flutes filled with champagne, and the three of them toasted the day.

"You sure it's still OK that Meg and I stay in your place when we get to LA?" Judy had lined up an internship at Benson & Miller Designs, and Meg wanted to see if California had anything to offer. The first couple of months would be easier to handle in a new city with a home base. Her brother's Beverly Hills home was anything but tiny. Not that she planned to stay there long, just long enough to find a part-time job and for her and Meg to get their own place.

"I'm never there, Judy. I'd appreciate someone I can trust watching over the place while I'm on location. Ask Karen."

Karen was Mike's ex-wife, and Zach, their other brother's new wife. It was a complicated script, and a family secret. Apparently, Mike married Karen as a paper marriage when the studios wanted him to look like he'd settled down. Karen and Mike had never been anything but friends. When Karen and Zach met, apparently, there were some serious sparks and they hooked up. That was a good thing, because Judy liked Karen. She didn't want to hate the woman because she broke her brother's heart . . . either of her brothers.

Hannah, her younger sister, snuck up behind them, her cell phone in hand. Meg took pictures of all of them, and before Judy knew it, someone was dragging her away.

She'd shed her cap and gown and danced when the DJ started playing. Seemed everyone enjoyed a good party, and Mike knew how to keep it rolling. Zach and Karen had shown up along with her older sister, Rena, and her husband. The family picture was taken before every hair managed to get out of place.

After an hour of nonstop dancing, Judy stumbled outside to catch her breath and some fresh air. The sun was nearly gone, only a few remaining strands of orange and pink with a scattering of clouds. Seattle had been good to them on their graduation day, and that was rare. Mt. Rainier stood in the distance, a sight she knew she'd miss when she moved to LA. But that's where her internship was taking her.

Footsteps behind her made her turn around.

Rick, wearing a suit that belonged on a secret service agent, loomed over her. He tilted his head and spoke into a mic she couldn't see. "I found her. Everything's fine."

Judy put her hands up in mock surrender. "Was there a kidnapping threat when I wasn't looking?"

There was no humor in Rick's stern expression. "There's no telling what someone might do to get to your brother."

Wow! Who knew Rick took his job so seriously? Seems he always had a smile and laughed in the face of adversity.

"Just looking for fresh air, Green Eyes."

His shoulders relaxed. Even in the suit, he took on the laid-back posture of the man she'd grown used to. "I haven't seen you all night. How is it you knew I walked away?"

"Just because you haven't seen me doesn't mean I'm not there . . . watching."

Lord, if she didn't know the man . . . or kinda know him, that line might have made her squirm. "Stalker much?" she said even though she knew Rick wasn't the twisted stalker type.

"Private security is a license to stalk." He smiled now, as if he was enjoying his own private joke.

"So . . ." She paused, took a breath. "You were on duty . . . or assignment the other night?"

She expected a safe retort, not the truth.

"No. That was personal." His lips actually lost some of his smile and his eyes peered into her in a way she'd never seen before.

"P-personal?" The cool air around her actually heated.

He tilted his head to the side, as if he was debating what exactly to say. "I take it you passed that final."

"Hard to graduate without passing your finals. Now, back to that personal thing . . ."

Rick rocked back on his heels. "I wanted to see if the girl I met in Utah had the same amount of fire in her as she did last year. Then I find you hustling pool—"

"Playing for money isn't hustling. You're the one who said you hustled pool."

Rick nodded. "I guess that's true. Though bets over a hundred usually constitute a hustle."

She pointed at him. "You're the one who suggested the hundred bucks. I didn't even have that much on me."

Rick closed his eyes and dipped his head. "Welching on a bet? So bad."

"I didn't welch. You didn't win!"

"I would have."

Yeah, he would have . . . they both knew it, but she sure as hell wouldn't let him know she knew it. "Gee, ego much?"

Rick walked to the side of the open veranda while Judy leaned against the pillar.

"I hear you're going to stay at your brother's while you find your own place in LA."

"Mike tell you that?"

"I do monitor his place when he's in town and come to events like this with him."

Judy laughed. "I don't think his sister's graduation party is a high-risk event that requires a bodyguard or security."

He turned to her now and ran a hand over his chin. "You'd be shocked at some of the crap your brother puts up with because of his fame. Living in his home will put you center stage."

"After last summer, I don't think I need to worry."

"Last summer was all about someone else and had nothing to do with Hollywood's leading man that everyone wants a piece of."

Rick had her there.

But her adventure with Rick in locating Becky had made her feel alive in a way she'd never felt before and gave her confidence. Becky's parents had kidnapped her, and Rick and Judy drove over half the state of Utah searching for the girl.

"I'm a big girl. I can handle it."

Rick's eyes lost their laughter as he turned his head to the side. He placed a finger to his ear. "Moving inside now." He closed the space between them and placed a hand on her waist. "Time to go inside."

"What?" She moved alongside him, looking over her shoulder at the darkened sky.

"Paparazzi spotted on the south lawn looking for a photo op."

"I doubt they care about me."

Rick leaned in. "Anonymity is your friend."

Inside, the music seemed even louder, and before she could say his name, Rick was walking away. His parting words were, "See you in LA, Utah."

At least he didn't call her *babe*.

———

The apartment she and Meg shared in Seattle had come furnished, perfect for college students who didn't have money. Only now, they didn't have anything! They had their cars, their clothes, and boxes of personal stuff that didn't need a home outside of an attic for a while. Moving into Mike's home was a blessing and also brought to light that she and Meg had a lot to accomplish before they could move out and do more than sleep on the floor.

Two guest rooms sat on the opposite side of Mike's room in the massive house. Both Meg and Judy piled boxes into them, using the closet space and cluttering up the en suite bathrooms.

"I can't believe your brother is letting us stay here. This place is amazing."

Meg's enthusiasm matched her own. Mike's taste was off the charts. His Spanish-influenced palette of colors and textures complemented the rambling mission-style home and stucco walls. The massive great room opened up to the chef's kitchen and dining room. Double glass doors opened to a courtyard that spread for at least a quarter acre, complete with fountains and a view of the city below. Judy couldn't wait to explore every inch of the house and property.

"And we have our own bathrooms. Do you have any idea what it was like growing up in a house with so many people and only two toilets?"

"Not a clue," Meg said. She was an only child and didn't have to share a Barbie, let alone a sink and commode.

Now the light in the bathroom actually turned on when they walked into the room, no need to adjust a switch or anything. Both of them were about to embark on a style of living neither of them had any experience with.

The sound of Karen's voice rang from the front of the house.

"Back here." Judy brushed her hands together, removing some of the dirt that had accumulated from the stacks of boxes.

Karen's blonde hair and bubbly personality moved with her into the guest room. In her hand, she held the foam board that Meg and Judy had laughingly placed in the back window of Judy's car on the drive down. *California or Bust* sat in bright green letters with stars and smiley faces surrounding the text. It was juvenile and perfect for their postgraduation trip to LA.

"Look who made it in one piece." Karen tossed the foam board on the bed and accepted Judy's hug.

"I swear it took longer to get from Santa Barbara to here than it did from San Francisco to Santa Barbara."

"Welcome to LA traffic. Might want to get used to it if you plan on staying."

"My internship lasts six months . . . from there, who knows."

Meg walked into the room and offered a wave. "Hey, Karen."

The two greeted each other with a hug before Karen dragged them from the guest rooms. "I think you both need to know what it's going to be like living in this house."

Karen had lived there for over a year as Mike's wife. Only she and Mike were never really "together," no, their marriage had been arranged in order to make Hollywood and the producers of the films

Mike starred in think he was happily married. The ruse was meant to last a year and then fade away. It did fade, but not in the nice, calm manner Karen and Mike wanted. Karen met Judy's other brother, Zach, and the two really fell for each other. Needless to say, the media had a field day with the entire affair and littered the tabloids for months after the divorce.

Something Judy realized during those few months was that Hollywood, and the plastic lifestyle that followed her older brother, was nothing but an illusion. She still didn't think she knew the entire truth about her brother and Karen's brief marriage, but living in LA in her brother's home would probably bring her up to speed.

"It's going to be great," Meg said as they stepped onto the back patio and took in the view of the city below.

"The house . . . the grounds . . . all this *is* amazing. The men showing up with cameras when you least expect them, and even when you do expect them, that is going to be a pain in your ass. You might think it's funny the first couple of times, and then you'll just be ticked."

"How bad can it be?" Meg asked with a laugh.

"It shouldn't be awful for the two of you, but you never know. After the first few times the paparazzi show up, snap a few pictures, and realize that Judy is Michael's sister, and that you're her friend, they will probably dry up. When Michael is back in town, they'll show up again. It's like they have a tracker on him. They hop the fence, risk being taken to jail for trespassing . . . you name it, they do it." Karen moved to the center of the courtyard and turned toward the house.

"Has anyone ever tried to get into the house?"

"Not when I was here. After the divorce, there was one break-in, but Michael wasn't home when it happened. That's when Neil and Rick upped the sensors and alarms."

Judy had used a key to unlock the door and an electronic sensor to disarm the house alarm.

"Cameras all over the place."

Judy twisted around and looked to the eaves of the house. There were a couple of domed cameras she recognized from those she'd seen in department stores. "I see them." Judy pointed above their heads.

"Yeah, but there are even more you don't see." Karen pointed toward a decorative light post that would illuminate a path to the back of the yard. "That one covers the back. There are others on the three identical posts on the side of the house and in the front. A camera watches every car that enters. There are motion detectors that hit the floodlights and can be a huge pain when the wind kicks up. You'll usually get a call from security when they sense any unexpected activity."

"Why not just shut off the motion detectors when the weather is foul?" Judy asked.

"Because that's when the camera-toting buttheads show up. They understand the security better than you do."

Meg shrugged. "So they snap a few pictures and move on . . . who cares?"

"I guess if you only had to worry about a few unflattering pictures in the tabloids, that would be fine. But there are fanatical creeps out there, too. Michael's fame comes with a price."

They moved around the yard, and Karen showed them more sensors, more cameras, and then moved back into the house. "There aren't any cameras inside the house. Michael refused them. Sensors monitor every door and window." The three of them moved to the control panel and Karen went through a few steps to show them how the security system worked. How to set the alarms when they both were away . . . when they were in for the night and didn't want the alarm going off when they walked into the kitchen for a glass of milk. There were panic buttons hardwired into the system and even a three-digit number that called security directly from the house phone.

"So who watches the cameras?"

Karen shrugged. "Depends who's on. Neil has a team monitoring twenty-four/seven."

Judy ran a hand through her hair and tugged it behind her neck. "Does Rick watch?"

"Sometimes." Karen's grin grew a little bigger.

"What?"

Karen laughed. "Nothing."

Judy glanced at Meg and noticed her larger-than-life smile as well. "What?"

Where Karen might hold herself back from saying what she thought, Meg did not. "We're here less than two hours and you're asking about Rick."

"I asked if he monitors the house, watches the cameras." The question was legit inside her head. "It's not a personal question."

"Uh-huh, sure." Meg shook her head.

"Was that a personal question, Karen?"

Karen bit her lip and shook her head. "Nope. You did not ask a personal question about Rick. A little word of advice, however . . . conversations outside have microphones that record them. Just so you know . . . in case you want to ask questions about Rick."

"You're kidding."

"Nope."

"That's just crazy."

Karen grabbed a cold bottle of water from the refrigerator and leaned against the counter. "So, what's first on your list, girls?"

Meg sat on one of the stools surrounding the kitchen island. "I'm starting my job search tomorrow."

"And I'm going to drive by the offices in Westwood so I know where the heck I'm going next week." Judy had a little more of a slush fund than Meg and wouldn't have to find a job the very week she started her internship.

"How many hours a week are you putting in with the internship?" Karen asked.

"I was told thirty to forty."

"That doesn't leave a lot of time to work for pay."

Judy cringed. "I know. Not in the business sector in any event. I waited tables in Seattle, I can look for something like that."

Meg groaned. "If I never wait on anyone ever again it will be too soon. I need to land something clean where I won't get my ass pinched."

Karen and Judy both laughed.

"You have a business degree, right?" Karen asked.

"Yeah."

"Hmm . . . well, Samantha's looking for help at Alliance."

"What's Alliance?" Judy asked.

"It's an elite matchmaking firm."

"A dating business?" Meg asked with a frown.

"No, much more than that. Very exclusive and only for the überrich. We match couples based on their long-term plans. Some executives need a temporary wife to land a position at their job, or a girlfriend to get their ex off their backs."

"Where do you find the women who agree to this?" Judy asked.

"Everywhere. Industry parties, fundraisers, there are plenty of women looking for a short-term contractual agreement with a payout when the 'relationship' dissolves."

Awareness slapped Judy upside the head. "Oh my God! That's how you met Mike!"

Karen wiggled her eyebrows and shot a glance at Meg.

"Oh, please . . . Meg is my best friend. She knows you and Mike were married in name only. It makes sense now."

"Michael needed a wife and I wanted to open up a safe house for runaway or abandoned kids. It was a win-win for both of us. More so for me since I met Zach." And Mike's career had just kept on skyrocketing after the divorce. Seemed her brother always had another starlet on his arm in the tabloids, but none worthy of introducing to his family. Maybe he just wasn't ready to settle down. Who could blame him? He had the world at his fingertips and few homelife responsibilities.

Judy understood that. She wanted to find herself before she invited anything steady into her world. The thought of a temporary and fake relationship in order to put some money in her accounts didn't sound half bad.

Meg must have been thinking the same thing when she asked, "How do you screen people for this service? My guess is there are a lot of wackos out there that might try and sue, or have issues that could really mess with a spouse, temporary or otherwise."

"Samantha places everyone in our directory through a very thorough background check. I don't care how hidden someone thinks their skeletons are, Samantha finds them. And in order to work for her, you have to be willing to go through her check. It's imperative that nothing in our files is leaked."

"Sounds very cloak and dagger," Meg said.

"Nothing so dramatic, but the people we deal with have serious money and expect complete secrecy. The pay isn't bad and with The Village taking more of my time and Gwen busy with the baby, we could use the help."

"Where is the office located?" Seemed Meg was seriously considering Karen's suggestion.

"Samantha started the business in a two-story house in Tarzana and the office is still there."

"How do you keep a house in a residential neighborhood secure?"

Karen laughed. "Oh, hon . . . first of all, Rick lives there now, and let's face it, he's a huge roadblock to anyone who might want to break in. And second, the security at that house makes this one look like a child's lock on a paper diary. Gwen and I lived there before I married Michael, and before I moved in, Eliza was there with Samantha. Seems like anyone who lives in the house is destined to get married within a year."

Meg cringed. "Remind me never to move in."

"Not interested in happily ever after?"

Meg shook her head. "Wouldn't mind happy for now with a paycheck, but forever . . . yeah, no . . . not for me."

Karen glanced at the watch on her wrist. "Well, I gotta go. Let me know if you're interested, Meg . . . and Judy, Samantha even pays finder's fees for male and female clients. You'll probably find yourself in some really flashy parties hanging out with your brother. Something to think about."

Chapter Three

It took five days for Rick to find an excuse to *drop by* the Beverly Hills residence. Never mind the paying client was in Germany filming his latest blockbuster, or that the use of the key-in code was probably nothing more than laziness on the end of the houseguests. Instead of fishing out the key fob from the bottom of a purse, they punched in numbers. Bottom line, the key fobs told him exactly who was coming and going from the home, and the key-in codes were meant for the groundskeepers and maid. Not Judy and Meg.

Rick watched the monitors on the Beverly Hills home more than he needed to, and listened in more than he should. Bottom line, he wanted to see how Judy was settling in. The paparazzi had yet to clue in to the fact that two very attractive and desirable women now occupied Michael's home. Rick thought for sure pictures would fill the tabloids the moment the girls moved in. They hadn't. The girls had been painfully silent outside, and Rick was no more privy to their lives than the neighbors were.

That sucked.

The second chime on his alarm told him that someone had entered the Wolfe home. Michael's stage name was how he labeled the Beverly Hills estate. Rick glanced at the monitor and noticed that Judy actually used the electronic device this time . . . but her roommate hadn't. It was time for a tutorial and he was more than happy to deliver it.

The Ducati made the ride from Tarzana to where Hollywood's elite lived a breeze. The motorcycle had been a gift from Neil. His friend had serious taste and knew how much Rick missed his Mustang, which had been destroyed not long ago.

The two cars in the drive had become familiar over the last week, Judy's economical Ford and Meg's beat-up Toyota that should have been put out of its misery several years before now.

He let himself in and hoped the noise of his arrival would alarm the girls.

Unfortunately, neither Meg nor Judy noticed the alarm of the gate to the home opening or even the noise of the powerful motorcycle idling in the drive.

Rick wiggled the lock on the front door, found it open, and let himself in. "Hello?"

Music from the east end of the house caught his attention.

He stepped inside and closed the door behind him. "Hello?"

Irritation brewed on the surface. It was one thing to use the wrong key-code to get in the house . . . it was something completely different to have a would-be stranger standing in the foyer . . . an armed stranger with two young women in the house, alone.

"Judy?" Fuming, Rick started toward the music, ready to read the riot act.

Outside the first guest room, he heard Judy's voice from inside. She was singing, off-key, to the music on the radio.

He paused and listened.

God, she was awful. Couldn't carry a tune to save her life, but damn it, he shouldn't know that about her by just walking in the door.

Noise from the other bedroom made him shift his direction and head into the main living room of the house. As much as he'd like to see his little pixie naked, he wouldn't do so by sneaking up on her in her own bedroom.

He walked around the main living space of the large home for several minutes, checked out Michael's side of the house and the garage before returning to the living room.

The women still hadn't noticed his presence.

Eventually the water turned off and the music was turned up. Rick made himself comfortable on the couch and opened an *Architectural Digest* magazine.

"Good Lord, Gardner, how many times do I have to tell you, you can't sing!" Rick heard Meg yelling at Judy down the hall.

"You can say that again," Rick muttered.

Meg rounded the corner, looking behind her, and before Rick could say hi, she twisted, saw him, and screamed.

Rick placed his hands in the air, but it took Meg a few seconds to realize who he was.

She finally stopped screaming and grabbed her chest. "Shit. Holy . . ."

"What is it?" Judy ran into the room, water falling from her hair and a towel covering her naked body.

Meg sucked in air and seemed to have trouble catching her breath. She pointed toward him and Judy followed her hand.

She grasped the towel tighter. "What the hell?"

Meg was still doubled over. Suddenly, Rick's brilliant idea of showing up unannounced felt entirely wrong. Before he could explain his presence, Judy knelt beside Meg. "Do you need your inhaler?"

Meg nodded and Rick heard her wheeze. *Oh, damn!*

Judy ran down the hall and returned seconds later. He managed to move to Meg's side right as Judy thrust the medicine in Meg's hand. She sucked in two deep breaths and closed her eyes as if savoring the oxygen.

"You OK?" Rick asked.

"No thanks," she sucked on her inhaler again, "to you."

Judy glared at him and managed an indignant pose even wrapped in a towel. "Think you can get her some water while I find some clothes?"

Rick ran his hand over his short hair and moved into the adjacent kitchen. He returned to Meg's side with a bottle of water while she sat on the arm of the couch.

"You scared me to death."

"Wasn't my intention." Well, it was . . . kind of. Had he known what Meg's reaction would be, he would have waited outside. He handed her the water and watched as she slowly brought her breathing under control.

"You're asthmatic?"

Meg rolled her eyes. "What was your first clue?"

Yeah, that was a stupid question.

"Comes on like that when I'm *scared to death*."

"Sorry," he mumbled.

"You should be!" Judy heard his half-ass apology as she walked in the room. She'd managed a tiny pair of shorts Rick was sure were illegal in a few states and a tight knit top. Her hair was still wet, her skin still pink from her shower.

He swallowed, hard.

"You both have slipped into some bad habits since you moved in."

Meg glanced at Judy and they both glared at him.

"The fact that I walked in and made myself at home should stand as a warning. Not that I thought you'd react like that."

Meg shrugged.

"You have keys," Judy told him.

"Keys I didn't need to use to get in here. This isn't Utah, Judy. Lock the doors and use your sensors to get in and out of the gate and to disable the alarm on the house."

"I put in the key code," Meg told him.

"Yeah, I figured it was you, but the codes are meant for the hired help, not you two. It's important that we know who is home. And unlocked doors are just sloppy."

"Paranoid much?" Judy asked him.

"There are more people that live on this block than everyone combined in Hilton, Utah. The days of keeping your doors unlocked are over, babe."

Judy bored holes in him with her glare. Maybe *babe* wasn't the best choice of endearments.

"You know, Mr. Annoying, we're not children."

Rick flashed his dimpled smile and let his gaze move down her frame. "I can see that, Utah."

She actually growled at him.

"What would you have done if it was anyone else sitting in here?"

"I would have hit the alarm."

He paused, smiled. *This could be fun.*

"All right." He stood and grasped her hand, ignored the heat of her palm, and placed her in the hall in the spot from which she noticed him the first time.

Meg watched from the other side of the living room while Rick moved back to the sofa and sat.

"Meg, on your call. Judy, let's see how quickly you can get to that alarm."

Rick picked up the magazine again and sat back on the sofa, not that any would-be attacker would be as relaxed as he was. Still, he wanted to give Judy a chance.

He thumbed through the pages . . . waiting.

"Go!"

Rick was up, over the coffee table, and had his arm around Judy's waist, her backside pressed against him before she managed four steps. She struggled in his arms, attempted to elbow his ribs.

His steel grip kept her from landing any punches as he pushed her against the wall, immobilizing her. "Your towel would have already fallen, babe," he whispered.

She relaxed in his arms and he loosened his grip. "Your foreplay needs some work, Rick."

He laughed and drew in the floral scent of her shampoo before letting her go.

"Well that was entertaining," Meg said from her perch.

Judy moved out of his reach and smoothed a hand over her torso. *Lucky hand!*

"Wouldn't be a bad idea for the two of you to take some self-defense classes," he told them.

"I doubt we'd stand a chance against a Marine, regardless."

Rick lost his smile for a moment, not liking the thought of Judy at the mercy of one of his old mates.

"Still not a bad idea."

Meg pushed off the chair. "How about we just lock the doors and use the right keys?"

"What about when you're not home?"

"Wow, Rick . . . don't take the job as hospitality ambassador for the city."

"It's a shitty world, Utah. No reason not to be prepared."

Judy placed her hands on her hips. "I think Meg and I will be just fine, thank you very much. Now if you don't mind, we were getting ready to go out."

"Out?" *Where?*

"Yeah, and before you ask . . . no, you're not invited."

It killed him not to ask, but he accepted her dis and moved toward the front door. "Lock the doors and use your key fobs, ladies."

Judy gave him a mock salute. "Yes, sir."

Rick narrowed his eyes and walked out of the house. Behind him, he heard the lock click into place.

His motorcycle had a small compartment where he kept a few toys. He found a small tracking device, removed his cell phone from his pocket, and synced the two together.

He moved to Judy's car, opened the driver's-side door, and tossed her jean jacket in the front seat. Then he placed his hand on the underside of the steering column and stuck the device where no one would see it.

"I take my job seriously, Utah. Get used to it."

On a map, Westwood wasn't a long distance from Mike's Beverly Hills home. Driving there at seven thirty in the morning, however, would test the patience of a saint.

Wearing a pencil skirt, a silk blouse, and sensible heels, Judy hustled from her car after finding a parking spot near the top of the structure. Her excitement over her first day as an intern was clouded by the mad dash to the elevator and the realization that she was going to be late if there was anyone else attempting to get to the lower floors.

At two minutes after eight, she walked up to the receptionist at Benson & Miller Designs and waited while the lady on the phone finished her call.

"Hi, I'm . . . ah, I'm Judy Gardner. The new intern."

The blonde behind the desk looked to be in her early twenties and seemed to have a genuine smile. "Is it that time again?" the woman asked.

"Excuse me?"

"Intern time. Seems we just did this." She picked up the phone and dialed. "Mr. Archer, your intern is here. Great."

The receptionist hung up the phone and pointed down the hall. "Go down the hall, take the first right, and you'll see offices lining the left side of the building. Three down and you'll find Mr. Archer's office."

Judy hiked her purse higher on her shoulder and started down the hall.

The phone rang behind her. "Benson and Miller Designs, how may I direct your call?"

The greeting alone brought a smile to Judy's face. She was here. Chasing a dream of becoming a world-class architect. The soft brown and taupe color palette of the office soothed the space and highlighted some of the more recognizable designs of the talented staff. Each photograph had a spotlight from above, giving the hall a museum quality. She didn't have time to study the buildings. That would have to come later.

She found Steve Archer standing over his overburdened desk with a phone in his hand. Judy stepped into his office with a smile. "We haven't heard back from engineering on the soil report, Mason." While Steve spoke into the phone he had poised between his shoulder and his ear, his hands dug into the pile of paper to the left of his phone. "As soon as I have it I'll send it to your secretary." He glanced at his watch. "It's five minutes after eight. I haven't even had my coffee yet, let alone checked my e-mails. I know . . . I got it."

Mr. Archer hung up the phone. "You're late."

Judy froze. She really had hoped he wouldn't have noticed. "Uhm . . . the off-ramp—"

"Is messed up. Yeah, I know, has been for months. Leave fifteen minutes earlier. Interns are expected to be here on time, if not early." He still fumbled on his desk, searching for something.

"I'm sorry."

He tossed his hand in the air. "Never apologize and never give any excuses, Lucy. I only want to hear how you'll fix it so you won't do it again."

Right. "I'll leave twenty minutes early tomorrow."

"Perfect."

"And it's Judy."

Mr. Archer had to be in his midthirties, but his hair was thinning and though he wore a nice suit, it looked like he'd been in it for several hours. "What?" he asked, never taking his attention off his desk.

"My name, it's Judy, not Lucy."

"Right . . . OK." He found the paper he was looking for and whipped it in front of his eyes with a smile. "There you are." He moved around the desk and out of his office with swift, determined steps. Judy had nothing else to do but move out of his way and follow behind.

In the center of the office were several cubicles along with a dozen light-table workstations. "You can put your purse here," he told her, pointing toward an empty cubicle.

Judy tossed her purse under the desk and nearly jogged to keep up with her mentor.

"Coffee's in here." He pointed toward a small kitchen. "The fridge is for lunches. It's emptied every Friday so don't leave anything there over the weekends."

"OK."

He kept walking, rounding another corner and down a dark hall. He opened a door and they stepped into a well-lit room with several copy machines.

Steve opened the lid of one, clicked in a command, and waited for the copy to come out the other end. "As you can see, we have paper size, drafting size, and even a blueprint copy machine in here. Did you work on these in school?"

"Not this new, but—"

"There are guide sheets on the side of every machine. If something about the instructions doesn't make sense, ask someone. You don't want to be responsible for jamming these machines. It will take you half the day to find the problem and we can't be without them that long."

She wanted to ask if they had someone who fixed them in the office, but he was already walking out of the room.

The next door they moved through was the mail room. It was Monday, and the Saturday mail had been delivered and sat in a large bin right below the massive slots with several dozen names.

"This is where you're starting."

Judy actually stumbled. She knew being an intern meant she'd be doing a lot of the busy work at first . . . but the mail room?

"Everyone expects their mail ready by nine. If you're smart, you'll jump in here again before you leave for the day to get a head start on the next day." Steve turned to leave her to the daunting task of sorting. "I expect you in my office at nine fifteen. I have a nine thirty meeting and I'll need a few minutes to tell you what you need to do next."

And then he was gone.

A blur as he pushed out of the mail room without so much as a *Welcome to Benson and Miller.*

"Holy shit." *How much coffee did he have this morning?*

Chapter Four

"I'm going to find out everything about you, Meg. I do mean everything."

Meg looked across the table at Samantha Harrison, who looked nothing like Meg had pictured when Judy told her Samantha, or Sam as she liked to be called, was a duchess. Her red hair exploded from the clip holding it back, and even with four-inch heels, she was barely five and a half feet tall. Yeah, she was in casual but expensive clothes and her makeup suited her features perfectly, but she was about as down-to-earth as any of Meg's old college friends.

"I don't have much to hide."

Sam raised one eyebrow and waited.

"Got caught smoking pot in high school once, nearly got tossed out but never bothered to party in school again so they let me stay."

A slight smile met Sam's lips and Meg's confession kept rolling.

"Partied a little in college but my asthma kept me from smoking anything."

Sam made a note on her pad of paper. "Anything I should know about your parents? Your family?"

"They voted in cannabis for recreational use and grow their own up in Washington. Total throwbacks from the sixties. Dad's family is Jewish, Mom's is Catholic . . . never was sure what that makes me."

Now Sam laughed. "So no strong religious tendencies?"

"More like confused tendencies. Mom would bless the bacon like she'd been taught by my grandmother and put it on everything."

"Siblings?"

"Only child."

"What's your Facebook profile name?"

Meg gave it to her.

"Any other social media platforms?"

Meg's palms started to sweat. Not that she had any naked photos hanging around out there, but she wasn't sure of every picture taken over the last four years. "I deleted my MySpace four years ago. Never have figured out Twitter, but I'm on there."

"How did you meet Judy?"

"Freshman dorms. She was two doors down from me. We often met in the lobby while we waited for our roommates to move their dates along. Didn't take long for us to switch rooms."

"Did you know Michael was her brother when you met?"

The questions struck Meg as strange, but she answered them anyway. "Not a clue. She talked about her brothers, but it wasn't until the rumor mill started up and people were lining up to be her best friend that I was told that Mike was Michael Wolfe."

Sam made another note.

"So why that question?" Meg asked.

"I need to know how you respond to the rich and famous. Many of our clients are beyond loaded and nearly all of them are famous in their own world."

That made sense. "Seems everyone in this city thinks they're famous. I've never met so many aspiring everythings in my life."

Her future boss laughed. "What about you? Ever want to be an aspiring anything?"

"Not enough to pursue it."

"Not even a singing career?"

Meg shot her eyes to Sam. "How did you know I sing? Did Judy tell you?"

Sam shook her head. "I haven't talked to Judy . . . yet."

Shivers ran up Meg's arms. "What else do you already know about me?"

Sam placed the pen and paper on the table and reached for her coffee.

"Let's see . . . your student loans top seventy thousand, and as much as your parents would like to help you out they've never planned for the future and have less than ten thousand in their savings account."

"Financial information can't be terribly hard to discover." Meg knew there was very little that couldn't be found out with a click of a mouse.

"Dane Bishop was your high school squeeze."

Meg froze.

"Kind of an ass from what I could tell. What did you see in him?"

She hadn't thought of Dane in years. Tried hard not to. "I was young and stupid."

"And he was a couple of years older and a user."

Boy was he.

"Like I said, Meg, I will find out everything. My business is rooted in secrecy and trust. There can never be a breach in either if you work for me. So far, everything you're telling me pans out. If you weren't looking for a job, I'd attempt to recruit you as a client."

It was Meg's turn to grin. "Can't I be both?"

———

This is a stupid game, **Judy** typed into her tablet. I've hit the boss six times and still haven't won once.

She clicked out of the chat room and hit the boss again. The image of Steve Archer and his endless tasks of meaningless shit fueled her desire to win the game in her hands. For five days, she'd played secretary, postman, and useless runner. This was not what she thought an internship meant.

The voice on the house intercom let her know that Meg was home.

She pulled a swig from her beer and hit the boss one last time with the energy level she had in the game.

Match lost.

Damn game.

She moved back into the chat room when Meg sailed into the house, tossing her keys and purse on the coffee table. "I see you're being as productive as ever."

"Don't judge," Judy scolded, even if her best friend was right. "I've had a shit day."

"Again?"

All Judy could do was growl.

"Well I've had a fabulous day."

Judy closed her tablet and tossed it aside. "I take it you met Sam today?"

Meg opened the fridge and grabbed a beer as she spoke. "I can't believe she's a duchess. Are you sure about that?"

"Ask Karen if you think I'm lying."

"I don't think you're lying . . . she just seems, I don't know, normal."

Judy laughed. "People say the same thing about Mike. Being a celebrity or royalty doesn't make you less than normal. Just makes people think you need to be some kind of cartoon character of a real person. So Sam shows up in normal clothes and treats you like a potential employee and suddenly she's not a duchess?"

Meg tilted back her beverage and then sighed. "Yeah. I guess. She's so . . . I don't know, normal."

"A real person."

"Right."

Judy pushed off the sofa and tossed her empty bottle in the trash. "I wish my boss was as real as Sam."

"Is he still calling you Lucy?"

"Yes! Every damn time he does, I tell him my name. I laugh." Judy demonstrated with a dramatic toss of her hair. "It's Judy, Mr. Archer." She paused, then said in a lower voice to mimic her boss, "What? Yeah, yeah . . . file this. Fix this. Do this."

"Sounds awful."

"I haven't seen a blueprint since I walked into the office." Well, she'd managed to see a work in progress on one of the drafters' desks. Other than that, she'd seen nothing. Filing, paperwork, and bullshit.

"Sounds like you need a night of confidence. I've scoped out the local pool halls."

Suddenly Judy felt a little more like herself. "Did you say pool hall?"

Penthouse Pool was a dive. Something that would fit in with the college crowd. Too bad the college crowd wasn't anywhere near Hollywood. The beer was cheap and it only took one round to find someone to buy them their drinks.

"I'm actually really good," Judy warned the thirtysomething guy and his friend who challenged her to a game.

"I can stand losing twenty bucks," he told her.

Judy racked up the balls and let Meg hold the money. It took less than five minutes to relieve Phil, or maybe it was Bill, of twenty dollars. Phil/Bill doubled his bet and lost in four minutes. "I warned you."

Phil/Bill scowled and moved back to the bar, leaving Meg and Judy sitting on the side of the table. If it wasn't for the music in the jukebox they probably would have left the minute the guys left. It didn't take long for a couple of other men to take their place. Only these guys were looking to get into something more than a corner pocket, and Judy and Meg both knew better than to challenge them to anything.

"I can sink that ball in your hole," the scuzzball managed.

Judy laughed, not willing to meet the guy's gaze.

"We're lesbians," Meg announced.

The blond actually seemed turned on by the idea.

"And we don't share," Judy told him. To add to the effect, Judy slid a hand around Meg's waist and pulled her close.

"Fucking Hollywood," the man mumbled under his breath as he walked away.

Judy turned toward her friend. "This is a bust."

Meg scanned the bar with a nod. "Cheap beer and cheaper pool. I thought it sounded great."

"We managed sixty bucks. Not that bad."

Behind them, someone laughed. "That was classic."

Judy and Meg both twisted toward two guys who stood shoulder to shoulder. They were about the same height as Meg, which rivaled five nine, and they both looked enough alike to make Judy think they were brothers. Only the auburn-haired man placed his hand on his friend in a way that told her they were much more than friends.

"What was classic?" Meg asked . . . the music in the pool hall changed and seemed to get louder.

"Putting those guys off."

Judy laughed. "Not hard to do when they come on that strong."

"You guys play?"

"She does," Meg told them.

Lucas had short blond hair that fell in his eyes with every shake of his head. His friend, and if Judy had to guess, his lover, Dan, had an easy smile and an open wallet. "You girls want another drink?"

"You go ahead," Meg suggested. "I'll drive us home."

"Not to mention I've had a crap day."

Lucas racked the balls while Dan sat across from Meg at a nearby table.

"Bad day at work?" Lucas asked.

"You can say that."

Lucas pulled the triangle away and hung it on the nail sticking out of a beam. "We playing for money?"

"She's good," Meg warned him.

"I'm good," Judy said at the same time.

Dan laughed. "You guys suck at hustling pool."

"We're new in town," Judy told him. "It's never a good idea to hustle anything until you know the players or have backup."

Lucas pulled a twenty from his back pocket and set it on the table with Meg. "I'm not half bad either. If you kick my ass, it will be the only twenty we ever play for."

Meg placed a twenty on top of it, solidifying the bet.

Judy broke, sank a solid, and missed her second shot.

Lucas followed with two stripes before she had another turn.

"You guys aren't really lesbians." Dan wasn't asking a question.

"Not even in my diary," Judy said as she set up her shot.

"And you guys aren't straight." Meg called them out.

Dan laughed. "According to my mother I am."

Lucas leaned next to his friend and watched Judy take out two more balls.

"So is this place always so lively?" Judy asked, letting the sarcasm drip from her voice.

"This place is a dive, but the drinks are cheap."

"Hence the term, dive." Meg glanced around. "Even the jukebox isn't turned up enough to drown out the burps from the bar."

Lucas cleaned the table on his next turn, putting Judy to shame. Once he sank the eight ball, she handed him the forty bucks and shook his hand. "And that will be the last twenty you get from me."

"Fair enough," he said as he slid the forty bucks in the back pocket of his skin-tight jeans.

"There's a dance club up a block. Wanna blow out of here?"

From anyone else, Judy might be a little concerned, but Lucas and Dan were obviously into each other and about as safe as anyone could be outside of her brother.

Meg nodded when Judy made eye contact. Ten minutes later, Lucas was using the money he won from their match to pay the cover charge.

Judy wasn't sure if walking into the club with two good-looking guys kept men away, or if there just weren't that many single guys in the room, but she and Meg didn't have to brush off one hand all night.

Lucas was a wannabe actor who waited tables as a day job, and Dan worked in research with a small newspaper. They'd dated each other for nearly a year and had just moved in together to make life easier.

"So how come you girls don't have dates?"

"We just moved here," Meg told Dan.

"And I really don't need to complicate my life right now."

"Is that why you keep blowing Rick off?" Meg asked.

Before Judy could open her mouth, Meg leaned into their new friends and said, "Rick is seriously hot, and boy is he ever trying to get her to go out with him."

Lucas leaned forward. "What's wrong with Rick?"

His never-ending smile, his huge arms and thick everything? His alpha self was just too mind-numbing to actually ever consider in a real relationship. Getting wrapped up in Rick would distract her from her goals. If she was ever going to prove her independence in the architectural world and prove how wrong her father was about her second major in school, Judy needed to concentrate. Placing Rick in her life . . . or, she sighed, her bed, would shift her off course. He was too intense not to. Just thinking about him made her smile and her palms sweat. He'd even returned her favorite jacket. Which meant he'd gone back into the bar fight to retrieve it. In her perfect avoidance fashion, Judy hadn't opened up a conversation with him to thank him. She figured she'd see him sooner or later and thank him then.

Meg waved a hand in front of Judy's eyes. "Earth to Judy?"

"Sorry . . . what was the question?"

Meg shook her head and answered for her. "There's nothing wrong with Rick."

"He calls me *babe!* That annoys me," she told them.

"He calls you *babe to* annoy you."

The guys laughed and they changed the subject to how they met.

The dance club was packed, and more than one person was taking pictures with their cell phone. It wasn't until a particularly close flash made Judy flinch that she turned around to see a long-lensed camera pointing their way. Her first thought was *why?* . . . then she remembered Rick's and Karen's warnings. "Must be a slow night," she said to Meg and nodded behind her.

"If they're searching *you* out, it must be."

"What's up with him?" Lucas asked while nodding toward the photographer.

"He must think you're famous," Judy told Lucas, who would love to have his face in a tabloid . . . any tabloid. She had to admit, the thought actually brought a smile to her face. Mike might have gotten over the attention he attracted, but as his sister, she hadn't really experienced it all that much. Yeah, the photographers showed up at her graduation, but they weren't searching her out. Her entire family had been plastered all over the papers shortly after Karen and Mike had announced their pending divorce. When news spread about her and Zach's relationship, it seemed the entire Gardner family was under the media glare. It didn't last long, however. According to Karen, the media had the attention span of a gnat.

"I don't think a few buried commercials have made me anything but a wannabe," Lucas said.

"Well you never know. Might as well smile and pretend you don't see him. Then he'll question who you are."

"You think?" Lucas glanced over her shoulder and quickly looked away. Beside her, Meg laughed.

The flash went off several more times.

"Don't most celebrities duck out a back door when they're spotted?" Meg asked.

Judy took a last swig from her beer and pushed away from the table. "Let's pretend we're famous," she told their new friends.

Dan and Lucas surrounded the two of them as they shoved through the bumping and grinding crowd on the dance floor.

A bouncer stood between them and what looked like a hall to the back of the building.

"Hey!" Meg smiled at the overly large man and gestured behind the four of them. "We need a discreet exit."

The bouncer looked over them as a flash from a following camera blinded them. He leaned to the side and the four of them ran down the hall laughing. They burst out the back door and kept running toward the street. They slowed when they reached the pool hall.

"You guys are crazy!" Dan caught his side as he leaned against Judy's car.

Judy opened the passenger side since Meg was driving and tossed her small purse inside. "This was fun. We'll have to hang out again." They'd already put their phone numbers in their cell phones earlier.

Meg hugged Lucas right as the photographer from the dance club found them.

Judy jumped in the car with a wave. "See you guys next weekend?"

"Sounds good."

Meg sped out of the parking lot while Lucas and Dan scrambled to their car. The photographer didn't give chase.

Judy met Meg's eyes and they both burst out laughing.

Chapter Five

The sound of a crying baby met Rick's ears as he stepped into Neil and Gwen's home. Neil was all about security and seclusion, so he knew Rick had arrived long before he entered the house. A must when your best friend topped two hundred and fifty pounds of pure muscle and had a Marine background that would hold no issue with taking out a trespasser entering his home uninvited.

Neil was fiercely in love with his lady wife and had nearly lost her over two years ago. The experience had changed the man. Now he smiled more than Rick ever remembered while they were on active duty, and he talked more. Oh, he was as silent as ever when he was working on something in his head, but Gwen had made the man open up since he'd married her.

"Neil?" Rick called out as he walked through the large home to the source of the sound. "Gwen?"

The crying grew louder as Rick walked up the back stairs to the nursery.

The explosion of pink and purple always made Rick smile. The room resembled a tower in a castle, complete with a mural of a turret behind the crib.

The smell hit Rick before he realized what his friend was dealing with.

Neil stood over his infant daughter, his back to Rick. "Not sure what you're crying about. I have to deal with the mess."

Emma cried harder.

Rick leaned against the doorframe and folded his arms across his chest.

After a few attempts at using those wet wipe things, Neil abandoned the traditional diaper-changing route, picked Emma up at arm's length, and turned toward the adjoining bathroom. "Are you going to stand there and watch or are you going to help?"

Rick chuckled. "Didn't think you saw me here."

"I knew you'd follow the noise. Or the smell."

Emma's tiny cry grew silent as the two men worked their way into the bathroom. "Where's Gwen?"

"Helping Sam with a new employee. Turn on the water," Neil instructed Rick while holding his daughter over the tub.

"Isn't she a little young for a bath in a full-size tub, Dad?" Rick opened the flow of water.

Emma's wide eyes blinked several times and a tiny smile lifted one side of her lips. At only seven months old, the girl had her daddy wrapped around her itty-bitty finger. Truth was, Rick was pretty wrapped himself. Blonde hair had barely started to fill her once-bald head, and her blue eyes always seemed to take in everything around her. She watched, just like her father, appeared to assess the world around her, then reacted to have her needs met.

"Grab that." Neil nodded toward the removable wand that doubled as a shower head.

"I take it you've done this before," Rick said as he pointed the spray away from all of them and checked the temperature of the water.

"How so much comes out of such a tiny thing is beyond me."

"Maybe you're feeding her too much," Rick teased.

Neil leaned farther over the tub. "I'll hold, you spray."

"Let the kicking begin, eh, Em?" Rick let the water hit her tiny feet first and slowly let the spray move up to the mess. Instead of letting out a war cry, Emma giggled and kicked at the water while Neil turned her around so Rick could get her backside. After a little soap and a washcloth finished the cleanup, Emma was wrapped in a fluffy pink towel.

"Seems you have diaper duty down," Rick offered while Neil redressed and laid Emma in her crib.

"Easier than scrubbing toilets with a toothbrush."

Rick would never forget his first few weeks in the service, when the joy of his ass being kicked by his commanding officer often ended with him scrubbing toilets.

The service had been one of his only options. His size, speed, and intelligence landed him with the elite. The Marines. He hadn't grown up with much so living out of a duffle bag wasn't a hardship. His dad was a broken-down dockworker, his mom worked odd jobs off and on his whole life to help where she could. Rick wasn't sure if their marriage was happy or just routine. The two of them fought more than he thought they should . . . or maybe they just fought when they were around him or they fought about him.

Neil paused for a moment and stared down at his daughter. A rare smile met his lips and he turned and led them both out of her nursery.

"That's it?" Rick asked. "No fussing or pitching a fit to go down for a nap?"

Neil shrugged. "It's nap time," he said as if the explanation was complete.

"Babies fuss."

"Emma cries for her mama, not for me."

Rick laughed. "I'll bet Gwen loves that."

Neil shrugged again and walked them into his security office. Monitors filled one wall with all the houses they monitored, including their own. A new set of monitors was dark and waiting for the next system to be installed.

"Looks like you're all set up for Karen and Zach's place."

Neil sat behind his desk and opened a file drawer. He tossed a manila envelope filled with papers across the desk in Rick's direction. "Everything you'll need is in there. Kenny will supervise his team at Parkview Securities while they fit the house with the new system."

Rick took the envelope, glanced inside. "What made Karen change her mind?"

"Combination of Zach and the courts."

Karen's safe house for kids had been an uphill battle with the courts. All she wanted to do was have a large home where kids from dysfunctional families or homeless kids could live without the fear of violence and hunger. The space had been the easy part. Getting Child Protective Services to license her was another story. At the current time, she had two teenage kids, one sixteen and one seventeen. The kids were brother and sister and had the emancipation of the courts after their mother was killed by their father and Dad landed in jail. The seventeen-year-old brother had left school to work full-time to try to keep it together for his sister. The kids came to Karen's attention through the Boys and Girls Club where she volunteered her time. They now lived full-time at The Village, the Victorian home with more rooms than occupants.

"I take it the court wasn't quick to grant them the ability to house a bunch of needy kids."

"Not at all," Neil replied. "The security system will help give the court a level of safety . . . or at least they think it will."

"Anyone wanting to get at the kids inside will breach the system."

"Not without evidence. And that seems to be all the court worries about. A trail of evidence if anything bad happens." Neil sighed. "Anyway. I need you to set everything up on this end. Gwen's mother expects everyone home for her birthday."

Everyone meant Blake and Samantha and their two kids as well as Neil, Gwen, and Emma, and *home* meant the estate at Albany, outside of London.

"I have ya covered, Mac."

Neil chuckled with the use of his nickname.

They both paused. Rick reflected back to when Neil was introduced to him as Mac. Back then, everyone on their team called Rick Smiley. Life was too short to frown all the damn time. He pushed away the memories that always threatened to remove the smile from his face and forced the smile again.

"How is the ol' mother-in-law?"

Neil grinned. "Linda's actually kinda cool."

The slang caught Rick by surprise. "How so?"

"Hard to describe. Just easygoing now that Emma is here."

"You won her over, did ya?"

"Sometimes quiet and stoic wins."

Neil's comment just made Rick's smile bigger. "Vain much?"

Neil glanced at the monitors, looked back. "How is everything with you?"

Rick found the question odd. "Great . . . fine."

Neil shook his head. "When we hooked up, you said you hated LA, yet you're still here. I keep expecting you to move on."

"Oh." Rick leaned against the desk, glanced out the window. "Trying to get rid of me?"

"Surprised."

"Working with you doesn't suck." It didn't. In fact, Rick finally felt connected with people, something he had only felt when he was on active duty. Didn't suck that some of those people introduced him to Judy . . . and she didn't suck.

"So you're gonna be around for a while?"

"I don't feel the need to move on, if that's what you're getting at."

Neil nodded. "Good. I'm going to be gone for two weeks. I need you to watch everything here."

"Not a lot here when both yours and Blake's families are gone."

No, there was a security team at Albany fit for a duke and his family. Not that anyone needed to worry with Neil among them.

"I need you ready to help Carter or Eliza if something happens. Michael will be back before the fundraiser." The fundraiser was a black-tie event at The Village to help raise funds for the kids there. Carter, the governor of California, had a security team, but when push came to shove in the real world, Carter knew he could depend on Neil . . . and Rick was an extension of Neil when he wasn't available to help. "How's the campaigning going?"

"I think a second term is a shoo-in. We need to keep ourselves open to any threats."

"So," Rick recapped, "everything should be perfectly boring while you're gone?"

Neil looked up and glared. "When is our life ever boring?"

Then, as if on cue, noise from the baby monitor interrupted their conversation and Emma fought her nap.

———

"There's a black-tie event at The Village right after we get back." Samantha handed a check to Meg and turned away. She glanced at the amount and nearly choked.

"What's this for?"

"It's a clothing allowance."

Meg hadn't spent that many zeros on clothes her entire life.

"For clothes?"

"Crazy, isn't it?"

The only thing Meg could do was nod.

"The rich sniff out cheap crap. I understand the need to pick up a bargain, but don't start at a big box store."

"But—"

"I expect receipts. Evening gowns go to your feet, keeping in mind your shoes. There will be alterations and accessories. I expect every image recorded in the tabloids to reflect wealth. Even those from a dance club."

Meg closed her eyes, swallowed hard. "You saw that?"

Samantha laughed. "Cute guys."

"They're gay."

"Still cute. Next time wear a silk shirt. The rich know all about the paparazzi. Most love the attention, but anyone watching us will expect a certain level of quality. And once you're here, they want you to be someone that can relate to their issues. Even if you can't."

"I don't even know where to shop."

"Not a problem. I have Karen stopping by tomorrow to take you and Judy out shopping."

"Seriously?"

Samantha laughed. "Seriously."

Meg sat back in her chair with a laugh. "This doesn't feel like work."

Her boss switched into a file on the computer. "No worries, what I'm going to show you next will feel like work."

Two hours later Meg's head was fried. Not only were there portfolios on women to match with men . . . but a few men looking for a longer-term selection of women. Memorizing the faces so Meg could match couples at a glance was imperative. Then there were the kinds of profiles of men and women she needed to keep an eye out to recruit.

Meg was clicking through pages long after Samantha had left the Tarzana house.

When the front door opened, Meg assumed it was her boss returning. When a male voice interrupted her thoughts, she jumped.

"Hey."

Meg swiveled in her chair, a hand to her chest. "Good Lord."

"Sorry."

Rick stood in the doorway, his lazy smile gracing his face. Why Judy wasn't jumping the man was beyond Meg.

Meg looked out the window, noticed the sun setting. "I lost the time."

"Happens to the best of us. So you're Samantha's new recruit."

Meg turned toward the computer, hit *print* so she could study the information at home, and turned off the computer when she was finished. "Samantha is the perfect boss."

"She's a nice lady."

"Agreed." She stood, looked around the office. "Does it bother you that I'll be around?"

Rick shrugged. "I'm used to it. Besides, I'm not here often. Just be sure and set the alarm when you come and go."

Samantha had taught her the drill. It mimicked that which she'd already learned living with Judy at Michael's home.

"Not a problem." Meg gathered her papers and lifted her purse onto her shoulder. "Well, I guess I'll see you tomorrow."

"I'll be gone most of the day."

"Oh . . . OK."

Before Meg made it to the door, the inevitable happened.

"So how are you and Judy settling in?"

A slow, easy smile met Meg's lips. The man was terribly transparent. "Judy thinks her new boss is a dickless putz."

How Rick managed to have dimples and hold back a smile was beyond her.

"Other than that, she's fine."

"And the tabloid fodder?"

"You saw that?"

The piece had been small, but it seemed to have made the rounds.

"Double date?"

Oh, now Meg got it. Rick was fishing for the real story. "We'd just met the guys." She left out the part about them being into each other and not them.

"You were all laughing."

"Evenings out do that." Instead of elaborating, Meg squeezed between Rick and the doorway. "Well, it's late. See ya tomorrow, Rick."

She would swear Rick grumbled as she sailed out the front door. *Men are so easy.*

Chapter Six

"I can't believe how great this place looks." Judy spread her arms in the middle of the living room of Zach and Karen's home and spun in a circle. "I love the high ceilings, the wainscoting . . . even the windows that had to be a pain to replicate."

Karen ran a hand along the drapes framing the windows that spanned half the length of the wall. "Zach was relentless in the effort to keep as many of the original fixtures or make sure a modern fit had an old feel." The Victorian home would have been drafty with the single-pane windows that undoubtedly came with the original structure.

"You must be happy."

"More than you can know."

Karen's smile laid claim to her happiness. Meg's shopping excursion was delayed until Judy could join them, and being a Saturday, Judy opted to help Karen out by staying at the house so she and Zach could sneak away for an overnight trip. Not that teenage kids couldn't keep to themselves, but with the courts watching every move while they worked on getting all the proper licenses to get The Village running full bore, Karen didn't want to take any chances.

Zach walked into the room with a small bag in his hand. "There you are."

Karen slid into his embrace and accepted the kiss he laid on her cheek. "You ready?"

Zach winked. "I pack light."

"Which means he didn't pack much of anything." If Judy had to guess, her brother and his wife wouldn't make it out of the hotel room. They really were in love.

"Devon's shift ends at nine, his curfew is eleven. Dina is in her room. She's been a bit moody lately."

"Everything OK?"

"I think so. The counselor said to expect more than normal mood swings."

"I guess that's to be expected in light of everything that's happened." Judy couldn't imagine how the kids coped with the loss of their mom and living with the knowledge that their dad murdered her.

Zach patted Karen's butt. "We're burning daylight, hon."

"OK, I'm done. Call if you need anything," Karen said.

"I will. Have fun and don't worry." Judy turned away as they walked out of the room.

They'd just stepped out of the room and Karen ducked back in. "Oh, by the way . . . Rick is coming by to work on the security system, adjust cameras and such."

With the mention of Rick's name, Judy's cheeks heated. "Rick?"

Karen waved. "I'm sure he won't get in your way. Have a good night."

If Judy didn't know any better, she would have sworn there was a dancing light in Karen's eyes when she wiggled her eyebrows and left the room.

Ignoring the flutter in her chest, Judy took her small overnight bag and walked through the hall and up the stairs to one of the guest rooms. The light blue and white color palette matched the seaside view from the window. The entire home screamed tranquility, and Judy found herself caught up in the view of a passing sailboat and wondering who might be on it.

"Hey?"

Judy turned to see Dina standing in the doorway.

"Hey."

The girl's dark skin and soulful eyes stood in contrast to the light, airy room. At sixteen, she had an extra twenty pounds on her frame than she really needed, which she tried to hide behind baggy clothes.

"I take it Karen and Zach left."

Judy moved away from the window. "Yeah."

"I really don't need a babysitter." Her defensive words matched the arms she crossed over her chest.

"Good thing. I never did like to babysit."

"It's stupid. Nobody cared that Devon and I were on our own for months. Now we're here and there are nothing but rules."

Judy sat on the edge of the bed. "And I'll bet your parents left you guys alone a lot."

"All the time. Nobody cared then, either."

"It's the overnight thing. I'm sure things will loosen up in time."

"Stupid."

"Oh, well." Judy stood and walked toward the door. "Might as well make the most of it."

Dina followed her down the stairs and into the kitchen. Judy dug in the refrigerator and removed a package of ground beef, an onion . . . a few eggs.

"You don't have to cook for me."

Boy, this girl was a hard sell today. "You don't have to eat it. I'm sure Karen and Zach will like the leftovers." She rolled up her sleeves and washed her hands. "Can you grab the bread?"

Judy watched from the corner of her eye as Dina stepped into the pantry and removed a loaf. She picked up the onion and waved it in the air. "Do you want onion duty or shredding the bread?"

Dina narrowed her eyes. "You're making meatloaf?"

"Yeah. I don't do gourmet. Meatloaf and mashed potatoes."

"What about gravy?"

Judy nearly smiled, but hid her excitement. Seemed maybe Dina was going to step out of her funk after all.

"I kinda suck at gravy. Do you know how to make it without lumps?"

Dina gave a tiny nod. "I think so."

"Great. I'll cry over the onion, you slave over the gravy."

Judy was crying over the onions while Dina removed a few potatoes and started to peel them. "Do you like to cook?"

When Dina didn't answer, Judy kept talking. "Growing up in a small town meant there weren't many options of restaurants."

"Even fast food?"

"We could go to the next town over for a burger joint, but we didn't go all the time. Conrad's has the best fries."

Dina actually laughed. "Your brother said the same thing."

"Our mom taught us all the basics. The first two years in college, I only cooked when I went home to visit. Then Meg and I got an apartment off campus and I cooked all the time. Gained a bunch of weight, too."

Dina scoffed at that. "You're thin."

"Yeah, well, doesn't mean I don't have to work on it. Meg and I went to an exercise class in Seattle but we haven't found anything that isn't crazy expensive here. I've been reduced to jogging after work."

"Karen jogs all the time."

Judy glanced out the kitchen window. "If I lived on the beach I'd be happy to jog all the time. In the city I have to dodge cars and suck in the exhaust."

"Why don't you pay for one of those fancy gyms?"

"Because unlike my brother, I'm broke."

"Didn't you say you worked?"

Judy slid the chopped onions into the big bowl of beef and cracked a few eggs into the mix. "It's an internship. I'm not paid and I'm overworked."

Dina squished her face in an expression of complete horror. "Why would anyone work for free?"

"I've been asking myself that question for two weeks." She cringed when her fingers met the cold meat and she started the process of mixing the ingredients. "Damn that's cold."

"Yeah, but it's the only way to mix it right." Dina peeled and kept the conversation going. "You really work for free?"

"It's a six-month internship. It's a way of gaining experience so someone will hire me."

"I thought college meant someone will hire you."

"Not necessarily. I guess with some professions it works that way, but not for me."

"Zach said you want to design buildings."

"I do. The only thing I've been doing, however, is filing and playing the mail lady. I shouldn't complain. It's actually not that bad . . . but I can't help but think I'm spinning in circles."

"It can't be any worse than high school. Like I'll ever use algebra."

Judy was about to correct her when a deep voice from behind them offered his opinion. "Amen to that. I never used algebra."

Rick. Her skin tingled.

Without turning around, Judy said, "I use it all the time."

"That's because you have a geeky desk job, babe."

Dina actually laughed. "A geeky desk job that doesn't pay."

"Even better. Hey, Dina."

Judy heard the giddiness in the teen's voice. "Hi, Rick."

Rick stepped up behind her, looked over her shoulder. "Aww, babe, you didn't need to cook me dinner."

"I'm not . . . and I'm not your babe." Judy turned the bowl over onto the counter and shaped the loaf.

"Seems like a lot of food for two tiny women."

"I'm sure there's plenty for you to join us," Dina told him.

"Perfect. I haven't had meatloaf in years."

Judy turned, found it difficult not to take in the man standing a breath away from her. "I'm sure you have something better to do."

Rick shook his head. "Nope. My work is here tonight. Should get done right about the time that comes out of the oven."

She glared but found a smile somewhere deep inside. "So you hustle pool and dinners."

"I do what I have to, Utah."

Damn he was too good-looking for her sanity. She found herself staring at his lips, and when he lifted an eyebrow, she snapped out of her trance, placed her sticky hand on his arm to push him away, and moved around him to the sink. "Whatever."

Rick moved beside her, took the washcloth from her hands, and brushed it against his arm before handing it back. "I'll start upstairs. If you hear the alarm going off, just ignore it."

"Fine."

He chuckled as he left the room.

Once he was out of earshot, Dina said, "That man is hot."

Judy fanned her warm cheeks and kept her comments to herself.

How an alarm could go off fourteen times in an hour was beyond her. Judy's nerves were fried by the time the buzzer on the stove told her dinner was ready. Then, as if Rick were standing in the hall waiting for the call, he showed up with clean hands and the easy smile that always graced his face, and sat beside her for dinner.

Dina actually carried much of the conversation. The teenager yakked about school, her lack of desire to study math, her crappy teachers.

Judy tried to concentrate on what Dina said and ignore the presence of all things Rick. Didn't matter that Rick's green eyes drank her in like water on the floor of the desert every time he looked her way. Didn't matter that every time his eyes collided with hers, her heart flipped in her chest. Didn't matter that the chemical sparks flying off them could ignite soggy maple leaves during a rainstorm. Didn't matter.

Rick was a distraction. And Judy wanted a career, a life where she met different people, experienced lots of life. Rick was danger-ous, which she admitted, if only to herself, was a complete turn-on. His devastating smile and his fascination with her could break her. She had learned early on she couldn't be a player in a dress. Flirt-ing was one thing, but the whole intimacy without emotion thing was difficult. She blamed the small town she'd grown up in for her inability to play and move on. It would be easy to give in to the temptation known as Rick if she could do so without latching on and not letting go.

"You know, babe, this is really good." Rick shoveled in a second helping of meatloaf.

"Dina helped."

Dina sat taller, liking the praise.

"And enough with the *babe*."

He pointed his fork in her direction. "One way to get rid of that."

Judy shook her head and rolled her eyes.

"Well," Dina pushed away from the table and grabbed her plate, "I have a stupid book report to finish tonight. You're going to be here in the morning, right?"

"I'm not out of here until Karen and Zach are back. They looked like they'd sleep in," Judy reminded her.

"Great, because solving for X isn't working."

Judy told her she'd help with the algebra; give her a different perspective than Karen was offering.

Dina headed toward the kitchen with her plate, and soon the sound of water running in the sink filled the silence in the dining room.

"I can do that," Judy told her.

"Rules of the house are everyone helps."

Judy almost told her to skip the rules for the night, then Rick placed his hand on her arm. "Routine and order are signs of stability. Something she needs," he whispered.

Judy glanced into the kitchen, noticed a grin on Dina's face. When she turned back to Rick, he was staring at her. "Then you can clear the rest of the table."

"I'm a guest."

"I don't think so, *babe*," she threw his endearment back at him. "Inviting yourself isn't the same as being invited."

They put a plate aside for Devon and cleaned up the kitchen within twenty minutes. Dina excused herself, leaving the two of them alone.

Rick was handing her the last of the dishes to dry while she put them away.

"How about some coffee?" he asked once he dried his hands.

"Inviting yourself again?"

He leaned a hip against the counter. "I know you'll find this hard to believe, but I need to stick around until after dark to check the outside cameras."

"It's hard to take you seriously with that smile on your face."

He winked. "I've heard that before."

His dimples were perfectly lethal, not that she'd tell him that.

"Fine." She went through the effort of brewing a pot of coffee, secretly happy he wasn't running off. *You're flirting with fire, Judy.*

She was removing coffee cups from the cupboard when he asked, "So, are you avoiding dating altogether while you're here, or just dating me?"

She hesitated, then said the first thing that came to her head. "You're dangerous."

"Only to an enemy."

"The first time we met you were swinging a gun around."

"Again, an enemy was involved."

That's true. "You're too cocky for me."

"Confident," he corrected her. "And so are you. I think it's sexy."

Judy squeezed her eyes shut and released a sigh when the coffeemaker beeped. "Something tells me you think a lot of things are sexy." She poured two cups of coffee, sugared hers up.

"I think meatloaf is sexy."

She couldn't help but laugh. "That's sad." She brought her coffee to her lips and turned toward him.

"Most of my home-cooked meals are heated-up frozen food from a microwave."

She blew over the hot java. "I don't think a microwave means home cooked."

Rick stepped close, reached to her side, and took the cup she'd poured but failed to hand him.

She looked over his massive chest and thick shoulders as he loomed over her. She grasped her cup with both hands to avoid the temptation of touching him. Because damn if he wasn't sexy.

Rick left his hand next to the coffee cup on the counter and stared down at her.

She squirmed under his stare, didn't trust herself to call him on it. Only when he reached for her coffee did she look into his eyes. Her nose flared and her breath caught in her throat. The smile he always wore wasn't there, in its place was something much more intense.

"W-what are you doing?"

He set her cup beside his and boxed her in, one hand resting on each side of her.

"I'm going to kiss you," he said over her lips. "Taste you."

Her breath caught somewhere between her lungs and her brain . . . the short circuit could bring the grid down. "I . . . I—"

"You want to taste me, too."

She licked her lips . . . knew he was right and reached for the words to prove he wasn't.

"There's been chemistry between us from the day we met." He voiced the thoughts in her head. He kept moving his gaze to her lips, his body so close but not actually touching hers. So many parts of her started to tingle she couldn't catalog them fast enough. "Don't you want to see if we fit, Judy?"

"You're dangerous." But she wasn't pushing him away. She was imagining that spark, and wondering at the same time what he would taste like.

"I am," he told her.

She licked her lips, knew he wasn't thinking of the same danger she was. Hooking up with Rick and lingering in his life could threaten everything she'd worked hard to achieve. "I-I don't do danger."

He slid both hands to her hips, the contact made her actually jump. "I disagree. You like danger, uncertainty, crave it even."

"No . . . I don't."

Without any effort, he lifted her onto the counter, left his hands on her waist. His strong fingers branded her, made her feel small . . . made her feel protected.

He smelled of pine soap and something so unique she thought it must be pheromones. The same scent filled her when she closed her eyes at night. Rick dipped his head closer to hers, but didn't touch her. Her breathing came fast now, his kiss so close.

His lips nipped at hers, the shock so complete she gasped and his contagious smile transferred to her. She leaned forward, tempting danger to touch her again. He did, this time lingering until her eyes drifted closed and his tongue licked the edges of her lips, seeking entrance.

Danger came in the form of a man, one so skilled at seduction she didn't even realize when he wedged between her thighs and pulled her body next to his. Rick left no part of her mouth untouched. The depth of his kiss stole her breath and shot stars into her head. His hands spread over her back and into her hair. There wasn't room to think . . . only to feel and taste.

Noise behind them made her freeze.

"Dude, sorry . . ."

Devon.

Rick pulled back but didn't leave her personal space.

Judy opened her eyes to see Devon retreating from the kitchen.

"Oh, boy." She sighed, looked into the laughing eyes of danger's son.

"We're not going to talk about this," he said against her lips.

She could still taste him, wanted more. "We're not?"

He shook his head. "We're not."

Rick backed away a couple of inches and Judy actually leaned forward.

"I'm going to finish my work and then I'm going to go home."

Disappointment resulted in a frustrated sigh. "You are?"

"I am. Because if I walk back into this house and see you looking at me like this again, I'm going to show you just how dangerous I really am. And I don't want to scare you, Judy."

She squeezed her hands, which had managed to grasp his waist at some point during their kiss.

Rick gave a throaty laugh. "I'm not going to call, but that doesn't mean I'm not thinking about you."

"You kiss me crazy and you won't call?"

"No."

"Why?"

"Because." He leaned closer, placed his lips next to her ear. His hot breath brought every needy nerve in her body on alert. "I'm not giving you a chance to blow me off over the phone. And in person, I'll remind you of this moment." She closed her eyes, felt the featherlight touch of his tongue on the lobe of her ear, and moaned.

Then Rick walked out of the room.

Chapter Seven

"He hasn't called."

"He said he wouldn't call."

Meg laughed at her over the phone.

"I can't concentrate at work." Here she was on her lunch break, eating a sub sandwich and talking to her BFF over the phone about a boy. "This is why I didn't want to go out with him."

"He's a sexy distraction. I'll give you that."

"I need to work."

"Because it takes all your brain power to file and play the mailman. Geez, Judy, it's not like you have some high-power, high-stress job."

"Even if I did, I'd be staring out the window thinking about him. I should just call him and tell him I can't do this."

"Oh, stop. If you called him, he'd just show up at your work and call you on the *sizzle*."

Why had Judy told Meg every detail of their kiss? She should have known it would all be thrown back at her.

"This is crazy."

"Isn't your brother coming home on Friday for the fundraiser?"

"Yeah."

"Doesn't Rick play bodyguard for Mike?"

"Sometimes."

"Then you'll probably see Rick on Friday at the house . . . or at the fundraiser."

Judy pushed her lunch aside. "Great, telling Dr. Dangerous that I need to concentrate on my career and not him in a room full of the rich and famous ought to be fun."

"You're not going to tell him that. You're going to take one look at him and melt."

"You're so not helping, Meg." The fact that Meg saw Rick almost every day since she worked in the downstairs office in the Tarzana house he lived in made everything worse. If Rick wanted to pass on something, he had a direct link. Yet nothing came from the man.

"Oh, you want me to help?"

"Isn't that what friends do?"

"OK, let me see . . ." the phone sounded like it was dropped, and then Judy heard Meg's voice yelling in the house. "Hey Rick?"

Judy's heart jumped. "Meg!"

"Yeah . . . Judy's on the phone. Says she wants to jump your bones—"

"Meg! Don't you . . . oh, shit." The people sitting on the outside patio of the sandwich shop were watching her as she lit into her best friend.

Meg's laughter filled the earpiece. "You're so freaking easy."

"He better not be there."

"I told you I hardly ever see him. I usually leave before he gets home. Relax."

When Judy felt her heart return to a normal beat, she cursed her friend. "I'm going to get back at you for that."

"I would expect nothing less."

After a few more complaints, Judy hung up and stared at her half-eaten sandwich. She really shouldn't have allowed his kiss. Because kissing led to dreams and dreams led to desire.

She cursed herself and clicked into her war game on her phone. For a couple of brief minutes she stopped thinking about kissing and scent and battled her cyber enemy. "Take that!" she told her phone as she raided Spike, an enemy who used to be on her cyber team. He'd jerked out during the summer-long online battle, bitching the team wasn't spending enough real money to win their faction battles. Now he popped up from time to time on her rotating list of enemies, and she had no problem sending him a game kiss by blowing up his buildings and taking his cyber money. In the notes, she wrote `waving` and placed a winking emoticon on his page. Judy turned off her game, tossed her lunch in the trash, and headed back to the office.

———

Mike was home by the time she got off work on Friday. The energy in the house completely changed with his presence. Blaring music greeted her as she walked in the front door. In the drive, his Ferrari had been pulled from the garage and evidence of someone coming by to wash it was left in the way of puddles. Judy didn't expect to see Meg since she was already at Zach and Karen's prepping for the evening. The entire event was set up and managed by Karen, but the opportunity for Meg to learn how to rub elbows with rich clients while mingling among all of Mike's and Zach's friends was too good to pass up.

"Mike?" Judy called through the house, attempting to raise her voice over the music.

"In here."

Judy followed her brother's voice and found him standing in his bedroom, his dress shirt open and his hair still wet from his shower.

She opened her arms to her brother. "So glad you're home."

Mike lifted her with his hug and kissed her cheek. "It's great to come home to a house with people. Where's Meg?"

"At Karen and Zach's. She went to work for Samantha."

Mike blinked. "With Alliance?"

She gave him a playful smack to his arm. "Yes, with Alliance. I didn't realize you used an actual service to hook up with Karen."

Mike offered a strange look. "Seemed practical at the time."

Judy stood back while Mike buttoned his shirt. "How long are you going to be in town?"

"I'm flying out Tuesday night."

"Geez, that's not a lot of down time."

"Not sure how much down time there will be. It won't be easy keeping my eyes open tonight with the jet lag."

"You didn't sleep on the plane?"

"Even private charters are bumpy."

She started to leave the room. "You can tell me all about your exclusive plane trips on the drive out. I need to shower and get ready."

Judy walked out of her room forty minutes later in a floor-length sequin job and three-inch heels.

Mike whistled. "Who are you and what did you do with my sister?"

Judy rolled her eyes. "Dork."

"You look amazing."

Even from her brother, the compliment made her smile. She ran a hand over her flat stomach and twisted. "I borrowed it from Karen. You bought her a ton of clothes."

"Took me four months to get her to break down and spend some money."

"I can think of worse traits in a woman."

Mike grabbed his dress jacket and swung it over his arm. "You don't have to borrow Karen's stuff."

"I can't afford this stuff. And before you can offer . . . no." They were walking beside each other and out the front door.

"No, what?"

"I'm not taking your money. You're already giving me a place to live."

"It's just money, Judy. I have more than I'll ever spend."

She hesitated as he locked the door behind them.

"I need to make it on my own, Mike. My own decisions, my own career."

"A loan then?"

Judy shook her head. "You don't loan money to family. Even I know that never works. Who knows, maybe I'll have Meg find me a temporary husband."

Mike narrowed his eyes. "I don't think so."

"Why?" Not that she would really consider the proposition, but why did Mike think the arrangement was good for him but not for her?

"Too dangerous for a woman."

"Oh, please." She walked away from the house and waited by the Ferrari for him to open her door. "They screen for anyone with malicious intentions." Mike gave her a hand into his überexpensive car, closed the door.

Mike glared at her from the driver's side and turned over the engine. "You're not cut out for a temporary marriage."

"How can you say that?" The double standard was kind of ticking her off. Why was it good enough for him and Karen but not OK for her? The life of a modern woman was something she was reaching for. Did her mere existence scream small-town woman living out of her element in LA? Did the people at Benson & Miller Designs see that about her and that's why they weren't taking her seriously?

"You're not really considering it, are you?"

"The fact you're worried I would is hypocritical, don't you think?"

"You're my little sister. It's my job to look out for you." He actually sounded scared.

"Relax, Mike. I'm not doing anything right now. I'd like to see where this internship goes before I make any decisions like marriage . . . temporary or otherwise. If I could just get my boss to ask me to do something other than clerical work, I'd be happy."

They talked about her job, her lack of exposure to anything she truly wanted to be doing. She complained and Mike listened. She talked nonstop, bending his ear and completely unloading on him. Her brother had always been a good listener.

"Want my advice?" he asked as he made the turnoff to Zach and Karen's place.

"Always."

"Take a risk. Do something that will gain their notice. What's the worst thing they can do?"

"Make me leave."

Mike pulled into the long drive to The Village. "Make you leave an internship that's highlighting your ability to file papers."

Cars were backed up down the drive. Limousines, sports cars, town cars . . . luxury like she'd never seen. "You're about to meet a bunch of very powerful people. Yeah, some will promise the world and deliver nothing. But I've seen some of your designs, sis. You're good."

"You don't know anything about design."

"I know what looks good. And if you lacked talent, you wouldn't have graduated with honors and some of your college professors would have suggested a different major. Aren't you the one who told me your last project landed a place on your teacher's list of exceptional achievements?"

That had been a sweet moment. "Yeah. I am good, damn it."

"Time you let your boss . . . or maybe his boss, know it."

She sighed, hating the feeling of defeat. "Getting noticed in that office is impossible."

They pulled up to the valet and someone opened her door. Mike jumped out, offered his Hollywood smile as the kid accepted the keys, and said, "Be careful with her."

The kid blinked. "I will, Mr. Wolfe."

Mike laughed, came up behind her, and draped his arm over her shoulders like he'd done forever. "Getting noticed is easy. Delivering on the promise of good designs, that's the hard part."

"You're a movie star, Mr. Hollywood. I don't have the same star power."

He laughed and bumped his hip into her, nearly knocking her off balance. She laughed and bumped him back right as a flash of a camera went off.

Rick saw stars. Judy's words echoed in his earpiece. *Maybe I'll have Meg find me a temporary husband?*

The conversation as Judy and Michael were leaving the Beverly Hills home started out innocent enough. Something Rick only planned to listen to long enough to know they left the house so he could estimate their arrival at The Village.

Judy wanted to make her own decisions, make her own money. Then the mention of Meg and a husband made Rick see red. "She can't be serious," he said to himself. She had to be pulling her brother's chain.

Wearing a tux and packing more than three pieces, Rick mingled with guests while keeping an eye on the door.

The silent auction in the backyard was heavily monitored with a security detail Neil had put in place. Rick's attendance was more about protecting Zach and Karen's inner circle, which included

Michael and Judy. Neil watched over Gwen, Samantha, and Blake. The only elite members of their group not directly under Neil's supervision were the governor, Carter Billings, and his wife, Eliza. Billings had his own posse following him around.

Rick heard some of the crowd talking about the new arrivals before he noticed Judy.

The gold glittery dress ran all the way to the tips of her toes. Toes strapped in delicate shoes that led to a slit up her dress. Her lean leg beckoned from under her gown and made his mouth water. Up her curves, he found the V of her dress dipping just enough to give a glimpse of her pale skin over her breasts. Judy wore her hair up in a messy style that looked as if it took only seconds to achieve, but he knew it probably took her an hour. She wore a little more makeup than she normally did, but instead of it looking fake, it looked hot.

He forced his gaze away before she caught him staring. His weren't the only eyes following her around the room. She was an attractive woman. If Meg wanted to find Judy a temporary husband, it wouldn't take long for someone to snatch her up.

That was not going to happen, not as long as he was breathing.

"Hello, Captain Obvious?"

Rick snapped his gaze away from Judy again, found Meg standing beside him. "What?"

Meg shook her head. "You know, Rick, I find it amusing the two of you are dancing around this attraction."

He thought about that for a second. "I didn't think I was dancing." No, he'd been asking her for a simple date for well over a month.

"I guess that's true." Meg waved in Judy's direction and Rick noticed the look between the two women, a silent warning spoken from Judy's eyes to Meg's.

"Women like to dance," Meg told him as she turned and walked away.

Good to know.

After dinner, when the music started, Judy and Mike hit the dance floor with a little drama and flourish. At one point Zach jumped in and gave up Karen to dance with his sister. The photographers were having a field day with the four of them. It helped that Karen and Michael smiled and danced as if they hadn't once been married and were now happily divorced and living different lives. Rick knew the truth about their temporary marriage, but not many others in the room did.

Rick waited for the right moment, and when the music slowed and the couples paired up, he cut in and wrapped his arm around Judy's waist before she could see him coming. Before she could tell him no.

"Hey, babe," he whispered next to her ear. She stiffened, briefly, then relaxed in his arms and moved along with the music.

She was silent for about thirty seconds, then she managed, "You didn't call."

Instead of answering, Rick swung her around, led her into a spin out, and back in, getting more than one flash of a camera. Only when he had her back cheek to cheek . . . or in their case, he had to bend down to talk in her ear, he said, "I told you I wouldn't call."

She opened her mouth to say something but he spun her again, robbing her of a slow dance and making this one much more active. Talking under their breath on the dance floor wasn't what he wanted, not where she might get the opportunity to blow him off just as easily as a phone conversation. It wasn't as if he would call her out with an audience watching. However, he would make sure anyone in the room who might be watching her knew of his attraction.

Rick wound his hand around her waist and pulled her even tighter, leading her, and used the music to weave heat onto her cheeks. She was smiling, almost as if she couldn't help it.

"Where did you learn to dance?"

The question was innocent enough, but he blinked, nearly missed a step. "It wasn't the military."

The hand resting on his chest pushed back and she moved her gaze to his. "Well . . . you're good."

Happy she didn't quiz him more, he moved her around, giving her ability to follow his lead a solid test. "You're not bad yourself, Utah."

The music started to wind down, both of them with it.

"About that lack of a phone call . . ."

"I'll call next time."

Some of the couples around them broke off the dance floor.

"I don't know if—"

Rick didn't like where that was going and he cut her off with a finger to her lips. He replaced it briefly with his kiss. Chaste, simple, and full of promise.

The earpiece buzzed, ending their dance-floor kiss. "Rick, we need you out back."

He pulled away, happy to see Judy's lips grinning. "Have to get back to work, Utah. We'll talk later." He kissed her forehead and left her standing on the dance floor.

Chapter Eight

Meg nudged Karen's elbow and brought her attention to the kissing taking place on the dance floor. "Check it out."

Karen glanced over her shoulder and let out a soft whistle. "I knew that was coming."

"Judy's really crazed over him."

Neither of them stopped staring while the kiss ended and Rick said something in Judy's ear.

"Crazy good or crazy bad?"

"A little of both."

Rick left Judy staring after him, and when she swiveled toward the two of them, both Karen and Meg turned their attention to the wineglasses in their hands. They couldn't have been more obvious.

"Is he a good guy? I mean, he seems like he is."

Karen brought her drink to her lips and talked over the rim. "I've never seen anything that raises any alarms. He's been Neil's right hand for over two years."

"Does he date a lot?"

"I've never seen him with anyone. I'm sure he's been out, but not with anyone he's brought around us."

Zach slid up alongside his wife, placed a hand on her shoulder. "Was that Rick kissing my baby sister on the dance floor?"

Karen leaned into her husband with a giggle. "There is not one other man in this place that can be mistaken for Rick except Neil, and we both know how happy Neil and Gwen are."

Zach's eyes narrowed toward the door Rick had used to escape the room. "Hmm."

Meg glanced over and saw Mike talking with Judy. Both Mike and Zach had the same expression on their faces.

Zach started for the door and Karen caught his arm. "What are you doing?"

"Nothing," he said a little quickly.

"Don't do anything stupid. Judy's a grown woman."

Zach kissed the side of Karen's head before walking away.

Meg watched with appreciation. "As an only child, I've never had a brother or sister worry about the guys I've dated."

"Me either," Karen said. "It's nice to see."

Mike met Zach at the door and they both walked side by side to confront Rick.

"Should we warn him?"

Karen shook her head. "No, but I sure do want to watch."

Meg liked her spirit. "You watch. I'll catch up with Judy."

Rick circled to where two guests were getting a little heated about whose name was last on the list before the auction table closed. Security stood to the side and watched while one of the auctioneers attempted to resolve the situation as quietly as possible. Unfortunately, the men weren't having anything to do with the woman's negotiations.

"I have to go with the last name on the list, Mr. Phifer. Perhaps we can contact the organization that donated this item and have another one offered."

Mr. Phifer wasn't happy with the possibility of not leaving with the auction item. He glared at the taller man standing on the other side of the volunteer. "And if they don't?"

"We can only try."

"If you really want something here, you need to stand over it," the taller man snarled over the voices around him.

Rick had no idea what the men were fighting over, but it couldn't be so important that two grown men should have it out at a charity event to obtain it.

Mr. Phifer pushed in, almost sandwiching the volunteer.

Rick made his presence known with one step. Between them, Rick circled around with a smile. "Gentlemen? Have you forgotten why you're here?"

Accusing fingers were pointing; both men started voicing their argument. It soon became apparent that they'd both been drinking and neither was listening.

Rick turned and reached for the clipboard in the volunteer's hand. He offered a more genuine smile to the fiftysomething lady and glanced at the last name and the amount on the bottom of the sheet. "You're Mr. Connors?" he asked the tall man.

"I am."

"Your last bid was for two thousand five hundred."

"That's right."

"And you're Mr. Phifer?"

Phifer wiggled his pudgy finger over the entry prior to Connors. "That's my bid, which was done right as the time limit for this table was up."

Rick glanced up to see Zach and Michael walking toward him. They stopped short to watch.

"Well, since there seems to be some discussion about timing, let's do the diplomatic thing and make this a live auction. The bid's at twenty-five hundred, Phifer, will you offer more?"

Phifer narrowed his eyes. "Twenty-six."

Rick swiveled his head to Connors.

"Three thousand."

Rick turned to Phifer.

"This is crap. My bid was the last one and on time."

Connors crossed his arms over his chest with a shit-eating grin on his face. The lookie-loo crowd around them had grown silent.

Rick had no idea who these men were, or how connected they might be to Karen and Zach, but he was getting a serious headache.

"If it's too steep for you, back off," Connors said.

Phifer attempted to push around Rick.

Rick pushed the clipboard into Phifer's chest, the smile on his face dropped. "I wouldn't even try."

Michael took that moment and lifted his voice above the mumbling. "Six thousand."

The crowd gasped and all eyes swiveled to the celebrity.

Then, as if it was a game, Zach added, "Seven thousand."

"Eight."

When it reached ten grand, Zach patted Michael on the back. "All yours, brother."

Connors and Phifer glared at each other but then seemed to notice the scene they'd both made. When the two men moved in opposite directions, neither of them winning, the crowd dispersed.

"Man, Zach, you need to screen your guests better."

Zach shrugged.

The volunteer thanked Rick and moved to the next table.

Rick turned to find the focus of both men on him, their expressions unreadable. Then he remembered the small public display of affection with Judy.

"What can I do for you, boys?" The coming conversation was inevitable. One better off done and under the table.

"Just a chat," Michael said as he led them away from the mass of bodies in the auction tent.

Zach started first. "So, Judy?"

Just the mention of her name brought a smile to Rick's face.

When he didn't say anything, Michael added, "Our baby sister."

"A sister, yes, a baby, no." Nothing about Judy was infantile.

Both men glared at that.

"Should we be worried about you?" Zach asked.

Rick would have been offended if he didn't know that these men were only trying to protect their sibling. "I don't think it's me you need to worry about." He turned to Michael. "Do you want to enlighten Zach about the conversation you had with Judy as you were leaving to come here?"

Michael narrowed his eyes, then realized what Rick was talking about. "Alliance."

"Right. I don't think any of us want to see Judy signing up . . . am I right?"

Zach glanced beyond the two of them toward the house. "She wouldn't."

"I don't know, Zach," Michael said. "She was talking about it."

Zach clutched his fists. "No. Just no."

Rick let out a sigh.

"Judy's sensitive, Rick. Messing with her just to keep her from Alliance will backfire," Michael told him.

He shook his head. "Who said that's what I was doing?" Exploring the possibilities wasn't messing with someone, was it? He questioned his own intentions for about ten seconds. The chase was exciting, the sizzle worth the run. Besides, he'd waited nearly a year to pursue his little pixie.

"Don't hurt her," Zach warned.

"It's hard to hurt her when she won't agree to go out on a date."

Michael laughed. "You're kissing her and not dating her?"

Zach shook his head, tossed his hands in the air. "I don't want the details."

The three of them started back toward the house when Michael asked, "So what did I win at the auction?"

Rick, realizing he still held the clipboard, looked at the auction description and burst out laughing. "Looks like you and four of your youngest friends are going on a studio tour at Nickelodeon."

———

Judy purposely wore what she called her power suit. It wasn't a suit, but a black pencil skirt complete with black boots and a red blazer. If anyone at Benson & Miller was going to notice her, she needed to start forcing some eyes her way. She showed up thirty minutes early Monday morning and finished the mail detail before the receptionist answered the first call.

As expected, Mr. Archer had a pile of papers, mainly crap from his desk that needed to be sorted and filed or given back to him in some kind of order before noon. She could have finished the job in two hours, but took her time looking over the designs, the contracts for future projects.

Two of the projects were remodels of office buildings, nothing too grand, and nothing that required anything other than a facelift on the interior. The third project was nothing more than a bid with a few sketches on a blank piece of paper. A performing arts center was going up in Santa Barbara, and Benson & Miller were apparently in the running for the contract. The size of the proposed site would house the square footage needed for an eight-thousand-seat hall. The conservative bid wouldn't lend itself to much in the way of details. She pored over the estimates, the details of what the committee in Santa Barbara wanted, and started to sketch. The mission-style buildings in the area helped the overall design in her head take shape. The morning flew by, and when she glanced at the clock it was eleven thirty. She made a dash to the copy room, made her own portfolio of the project to take home, and then gathered up all the files to return to Mr. Archer's office.

With her hands full, the phone on her desk rang. It never rang. "Judy Gardner," she answered.

"Uhm, Judy?"

It was the receptionist, Nancy, and she sounded winded.

"I'm running to Archer's office, Nancy, what's up?"

"Y-you have a visitor. Uhm . . . can you . . ."

Judy rolled her eyes. There was only one person who generated that kind of frazzled female.

Get noticed, he'd said. *It's easy*, he'd said.

"Tell him to come on back."

"But it's—"

"Yeah, I know."

She met Mike in the main hall just feet from Mr. Archer's office.

Eager faces poked out from cubicles, and more than one executive stepped from an office as word of Michael Wolfe's presence made it through the office like a California wildfire during a Santa Ana wind event.

"Hey, sis." His Hollywood smile had her shaking her head even harder. "Am I too early for lunch?"

Judy shifted her load to her other hand. "I didn't know we had a date."

"Didn't I mention it? Oh, let me help with that." Mike took the papers from her. "Where do you want these?"

She offered a coy smile, glanced at the manager of landscape design, who poked her head from her office, and then lowered her voice so only Mike could hear her. "I should be mad at you."

"I wouldn't be doing my job as your big brother if I didn't bug you in some way. Now where do you want these?"

Twisting on her foot, she moved around the corner into Mr.

Archer's office. "You can set those here," she said, pointing to the top of the cabinet.

Mr. Archer sat behind his desk, his jaw halfway to the garage floor of the building. "Sorry to bring a stranger into your office, Mr. Archer, but my brother is early for our lunch date and our mom never let us girls carry anything if one of our brothers were around."

"Uhm, it's . . . ah, OK."

Maybe her brother wasn't the only one in the family with the talent for acting. "Oh, I'm sorry, you haven't met yet, have you? Where are my manners? Mr. Archer, this is my brother, Michael."

Mike raised an eyebrow, knowing damn well she never called him Michael. Only Hollywood called him that. Mike stepped forward and offered his hand. "A pleasure. Judy's told me a lot about you."

"Has she?"

Nothing good.

"She has. Truth is I'm not in town very often and wanted to sneak up on her a little early today to see where she works. Hope that's OK."

"It's fine."

"Good, good. Nice place you have here."

Judy nudged his arm. "I need to file these before we can leave. If you want to wait—"

"You can do that when you get back." Mr. Archer's eager eyes kept swinging back and forth between her and Mike.

"It won't take a minute." Mr. Archer always reprimanded her on anything that wasn't done exactly when he wanted it.

"You came in early, seems only right that you have a few extra minutes for lunch."

Wow, he actually noticed.

"All right then. Let me grab my purse," she told Mike.

He followed her out. "Nice to meet you, Mr. Archer."

"Call me Steve."

Good God . . . who knew the man would be so thrown back by a movie star? *Call me Steve. Please.*

Judy snagged her purse from her desk drawer and placed the strap on her shoulder. "There's a café on the corner."

"Lead the way."

She slid the chair under her desk with a grin.

"Oh, for you." Mike pulled a magazine out of his back pocket and tossed it on her desk. "Looks like we made the front page."

Sure enough, a shot of the two of them dancing at the fundraiser graced the cover of the gossip magazine. The glimmer of her gold dress almost matched the smile on Mike's face. "I'll read it on my coffee break. C'mon, if we make it to the café even five minutes before noon we can grab a table in the back. Maybe then we can eat in peace."

Mike looped his arm over her shoulders and walked with her out of the office.

Every eye in the place followed them out.

Only when they were in the elevator did Judy start laughing. Mike joined her but then kept a straight face when the elevator stopped and let on other passengers.

One man stared while the woman who stepped in nearly fell over. Mike caught her elbow to keep from having the woman fall into him. "Oh, my . . . are you? You are!"

Mike just smiled, completely comfortable in the chaos his mere presence created. "You OK?" he asked the woman as she steadied herself before the elevator started its descent.

"I am. Wow, that's embarrassing. Sorry."

"It's OK." He winked at the poor flustered woman and turned his attention to Judy. "So, Judy, my manager Tony is coming by tomorrow to pick up my car. Wants to impress his date so I told him he could borrow it."

"The Ferrari?"

"Yeah. Didn't want you to worry that someone had stolen it."

The elevator met the lobby floor and they all left the small space. Mike's arm fell on her shoulders again and he bumped her butt with his.

"You really are making sure everyone sees you, aren't you?"

"No. I'm making sure everyone sees you with me. It will be up to you to ride this."

Mike slid his sunglasses over his eyes the minute they met the outdoors. The café was only a block away and they managed to snag a table in the back.

"I should have known you'd show up today," Judy said once they managed to get the waiter to stop staring and start writing down their order.

Mike leaned back, stretched his long legs out. "I'm flying out tonight and wanted to make sure we had some time alone."

A woman from an adjacent table kept turning around to stare.

"When will you be back?"

"Production isn't wrapping up for a month and a half, but I'm flying in for a few days the first week in September."

The waiter brought them their drinks, smiled, and walked away.

"You weren't kidding when you said you're never home."

"I wasn't. I'm happy you and Meg are keeping my place occupied."

Judy giggled. "It's a hardship. Such a hassle after a two-bedroom apartment with one toilet and a shower without a tub."

"I don't want you in a hurry to move out."

"It's hard to be in a hurry when I'm not making my own living yet." She'd gotten over the fact that her brother was supporting her and it was Meg's income putting food on the table. She'd stretched her living expense money during her last semester in college to help carry her for the first few months in LA. But that was quickly dwindling.

"I talked to Mom and Dad."

"Oh? Is everything all right?"

"Fine. They told me they don't know how you're paying for gas."

"I saved."

Mike looked over the rim of his sunglasses, which he kept on even though they were inside. "Judy."

"I'm OK, Mike."

"You might be . . . right now."

"Really, I'm fine." She hadn't yet felt the poverty that would descend upon her before the holidays. Hard to feel poor when she lived in Beverly Hills and danced with the rich and famous.

He reached into his sports jacket and pulled out an envelope, slid it across the table to her.

She didn't have to look inside to know its contents.

"Mike, no." She moved it back.

"Judy, yes. I assured Mom and Dad you were fine. And after our little conversation the other day about Alliance, I know you might be feeling the pressure."

"It's normal pressure, Mike. Every college graduate needs to find their feet and get a job."

"Which you'll do. You're working for free to gain experience. It's like you're not out of school yet. Consider this a student loan."

She knew arguing wasn't going to get her anywhere. And why fight it anyway? She didn't have to spend the money. Giving it to her would give her brother and her parents some peace of mind. "Loaning money to family is a bad investment."

"A graduation gift."

"You gave me a party."

"I gave my gardener's daughter a party when she turned fifteen. I can give my sister more." He slid the envelope back her way. "Take it, Judy. Use it."

Pushing her pride aside, she took the thick envelope and tucked it in her purse. She leaned over and kissed her brother on the cheek. "Love you."

"Love you, too."

The waiter showed up with their food, and the conversation around money ended.

Forty-five minutes later Mike was walking her back to her office building. "Should I go back in with you?"

"Love ya, big brother, but the girls in the office are going to be hard to peel off as it is. Another Michael Wolfe dose might be too much for the water cooler to bear." She gave him a big hug. "Safe flight."

"I'll text when I land so you won't worry."

She liked that. Liked the fact that she knew what was going on in her brother's life. For too many years, he'd been absent. His temporary marriage to Karen seemed to have reminded him about his family, and Mike was working overtime to make up for some of the lost time. "Thanks again."

"Anytime."

People were still staring as Mike walked into the parking garage.

Judy made it back into the office before the majority of the staff returned from lunch. She took a moment to glance at the amount of money Mike thought was a graduation gift.

She stopped counting at ten thousand dollars, closed the envelope, and rested her head on her desk. *I don't have to spend it.*

It was nice, however, to know emergency money was close at hand. She opened the drawer to her desk and started to place her purse inside. A copy of the magazine Mike had given her was there. Someone must have seen the magazine and placed it in her desk . . . but when? It wasn't there when she left for lunch.

Not entirely comfortable with someone going into her space, Judy tucked the envelope with all the cash inside her boot, closed her purse in her desk, and made her way to the ladies' room.

Chapter Nine

Tuesday started with a little more buzz than normal. Seemed everyone needed a night to sleep on the activity of the day before.

Nancy greeted her with more than a wave. "You didn't tell me Michael Wolfe was your brother."

"I don't even know if you have a brother," Judy said with a laugh.

"I do, but he's no Michael Wolfe."

"He's probably just a brother who picked on you growing up and didn't drop the toilet seat."

"I guess. But wow."

Judy waved her off and found many of the same conversations following her throughout the day. On her desk were a couple more magazines her brother managed to find himself in. Most didn't even have her face on them . . . just Mike's. Looked like the staff had picked up on her celebrity brother and were running with it by leaving the magazines.

One of the junior architects found her in the mail room and picked up a stack of mail to help.

"It's José, right?"

"Yeah."

Judy shoved a large envelope in Ms. Miller's box in the top row.

José wasn't a lot older than she was, but he already had a ring on his finger and she knew he had a picture of his two-year-old son on his desk.

"Tell me, José, who did the mail before I came on board?"

He moved through his stack of mail faster than she did. "We have interns every six months."

"And do all of them have mail duty the entire time they're here?"

"Depends on the intern." He handed her an envelope that said *Design Manager* but was missing the name.

Judy placed it in Marlene's box.

José handed her another letter, this time to the marketing director.

Judy filed it only to find José handing her several pieces of mail, none of which had names, only departments. When he stopped handing her mail, she realized they'd gone through all of it.

"Thanks for your help," she told him. "Guess I'll see what Mr. Archer needs me to file today."

"Actually, you'll be spending most of today with me. You have everyone's name down and the departments they work in, now it's time to match the faces." José turned away and called over his shoulder. "Coming?"

She scrambled to catch up with him. "Wait, the mail thing was a test?"

"Not a test. A practical need. Everyone in the office will work with each other at one point in a project or another." He kept talking as he made his way down the hall to his tiny corner of the huge center office. "A good architect knows their team, knows who is responsible for every step of the design process, that way when you go to the boss and pitch your designs you have more than just your input on the table."

For the first time since she'd walked into Benson & Miller Designs someone was talking architecture with her. Her heart skipped and a real desire to greet the rest of her day made her smile.

They rounded the corner of José's office and Judy noticed an oppressive pile of papers.

José sat behind his desk and grabbed the stack. "I'm presenting this to the boss next Monday. It's a redesign of the Valley Street Mall. Not the most exciting project, but the bread and butter of Benson and Miller."

Judy understood that. A junior architect needed to show their worth with the smaller projects before any firm would advance them to the bigger projects team.

Before Judy could comment, someone poked his head into the office. "Sorry to interrupt."

"Oh, hey, Mitch."

The delivery boy glanced at Judy and then handed a box to José. José signed for the box and waved him off.

Alone again, Judy asked, "What do you want me to do?"

The rest of the morning was a journey meant for flats and not the three-inch heels on her feet. She matched a face with nearly everyone on José's small team to check facts, gather more materials from their offices, or ask questions. Once she felt familiar enough with the individuals, Judy made the phone do her footwork. By lunch, she had a pile of work she actually wanted to do. She considered working through the hour but wasn't given the opportunity to stay in the office. Seemed many of the female employees wanted her to join them for lunch. Judy wasn't naive enough to think they had a sudden need to know the new employee, but wanted the inside scoop on her brother.

Either way, by the time her lunch hour was up, she felt more welcome than the week before.

She sent Mike a quick text, telling him she owed him.

In return, he sent a winking emoticon.

The message center on her phone told her about a missed call.

Rick's voice made her smile.

"Hey, babe . . . told you I'd call. So, Saturday at five. Wear something nice."

She just stared at her phone. His presumptive pushy self might have ticked her off on a different day. Today she was riding the wave and decided to give him a little of his own medicine.

She texted Dan, Lucas, and Meg first. `Pool, Saturday night?`

Dan responded first. `Lucas and I are in. Seven?`

Meg was next. `Can't. Sam is sending me to New York. I love my job! Details later.`

"New York?" Judy whispered.

Judy responded. `Such the jet-setter. Fine, Lucas and Dan, meet you at the dive at seven.`

Then, since her texting fingers were hard at work, Judy sent a message to Rick. `Can't Saturday, I have plans.`

She hit *send* and then started on the next message. `Friday at the Getty. I'll meet you at the tram at seven thirty.` The Getty was public, urban, and in her element. All the details needed for a first date where she didn't trust herself to remain vertical.

With Rick, remaining vertical was a must.

Rick replied in seconds. `Friday. I'll pick you up at your brother's at seven for the Getty.`

Negotiation was good.

She did a little happy chair dance before stowing her phone and moving on with her day.

———

"You caved!" Meg called out the second Judy walked into the living room.

She tossed her purse and the folder with her pet project on the kitchen counter. "I did what?"

"Caved. Agreed to a date with Rick."

Judy pulled a bottle of cold water from the refrigerator, leaned against the counter, and twisted off the lid. "I thought you didn't see Rick very often."

"I don't." Meg sat on one of the overstuffed chairs in the great room, her feet dangling off the arm. "He showed up after lunch asking me about the Getty. Asked if I could *help a guy out* to impress you."

The man managed to place a smile on her face even when he wasn't around. "And what did you say?"

"I told him the Getty was boring as all hell. Only redeeming quality was the wine that all those artsy folks drink."

Judy rolled her eyes. How Meg was going to blend with the ultrarich was beyond her.

"And he said?"

"Nothing. I think he growled. I didn't know grown men growled . . . well, outside of a bedroom."

Great. Rick already thought an evening at the Getty was going to suck. Maybe an evening at a pool hall was a better match. Yet Judy knew she eventually wanted to date someone willing to try new things, learn about culture and design. They already knew they both had something in common shooting pool.

Instead of probing further, Judy asked, "So what's this about New York?"

Meg's legs flew off the side of the chair and she jumped to her feet. "I love my job. Have I told you that?"

"You have."

"Sam is sending me to New York . . . and not just sending me, she's sending me on their private plane. Did you know they had their own plane?"

"I think someone said that at some point." For the life of her she couldn't remember who or why the conversation had been brought up. Maybe something about Mike and Karen's pretend honeymoon . . .

"A private jet. I'm going to some women's seminar. Did you know that the governor's wife used to work for Sam . . . actually I think she still has some interest in Alliance."

Judy didn't interrupt Meg when she got on a roll like she was now.

"Eliza and Sam are like this." Meg crossed two fingers and waved them in the air. "Eliza is a keynote speaker at the event and she's going to mentor me in how to approach potential clients for Alliance. Can you fucking believe that?"

Meg's language would make a sailor blush when she was drinking heavily or overly excited.

"In this new world, yeah . . . I believe it."

"I never thought a business degree would land me a job like this. Great clothes, private planes, and trips to New York? How the hell did I score this?"

Judy always knew Meg would make the most of any position she took. She was more driven to succeed than anyone she knew. It was one of the things they had in common.

"When are you leaving?"

"Friday morning. I'll be sipping martinis in New York while you're yawning at the Getty."

"I like the Getty. I'm looking forward to the view of the city and the glow of the lights on the museum."

Meg made a show out of yawning.

Judy tossed the plastic top of the water bottle at her friend.

"If your date with Rick ends well, you'll be able to come back here without any interruption." Meg wiggled her eyebrows.

"I'm not sleeping with him."

Meg winced. "Good God, why not? The man is yummy with a capital Y!"

"I agreed to a date, Meg." She wasn't even sure why at this point. "Something tells me he wasn't going to let up until I did."

"That and the fact that his kiss kept you up late at night with carnal fantasies."

Judy wished she had something else to toss at her friend. "Why do I ever tell you anything?"

"Because I'm your best friend. If there was some hottie after me as much as Rick is after you, you sure as hell would know all my thoughts on the man."

It was Judy's turn to growl. "One date and he'll stop calling me *babe*."

"You like the *babe*. You grin every time you say it."

"I do not." Judy forced her smile into a firm line.

Meg cocked her head to the side and waited until Judy's smile appeared again.

"Sometimes I really hate you."

"No you don't. You love me like I'm one of the Gardner clan. I expect a full report Saturday morning."

"A good friend would accept my phone call in the middle of the night."

Meg sat back in the chair and reached for the remote control for the big screen in Mike's living room. "I'm just hoping you'll be too busy to call in the middle of the night to bother with me."

"I'm not sleeping with him, Meg."

The TV sprang to life, the volume set way too high. "Yeah, yeah . . . I expect a call in the morning, where you'll say, 'Meg, I wasn't *planning* on sleeping with him.'"

Judy finished her bottle of water and lobbed the plastic across the room, only to land at Meg's feet. "Bitch."

Chapter Ten

Rick had to admit, he'd not spent this much attention on the details of a date since he dated Sally Richfield, the lead cheerleader in high school and the second girl he'd ever slept with. He learned then that it didn't take a lot to sway a teenage girl, but he didn't know that going in and planned every detail of the date from the kind of flowers Sally liked to her choice of entrée. In the end, Rick had her in bed, where she returned for over a month before her steady boyfriend swayed her back.

No, Rick hadn't worked as hard to date a girl since Sally. Judy was entirely different. She wasn't playing hard to get because of a desire to attract an ex. She wasn't saying no because she wasn't interested. No, Judy was skittish because she was attracted and for some reason that eluded him, afraid to let herself go. Maybe after a night at the Getty, Rick would know the reason why.

A special event was taking place on the summer evening, some kind of Greek festival complete with special food and picnics on the grounds where guests could enjoy the sunset. He was fairly certain Judy had no idea about the event or she would have known how difficult it was to obtain tickets for the evening. Rick knew people . . . and those powerful people always had tickets to events as snooty as the one at the Getty on Friday night.

Rick knew nothing about art. He could take an AK apart blind-folded, but telling the difference between a Monet and a Rembrandt . . . not his gig. He wasn't going to embarrass himself by pretending knowledge. Instead, he'd ask Judy. Let her educate him.

The phone on his desk rang, catching him off guard.

"Rick," he answered.

"Hey, Smiley." Neil used his old nickname from the service.

"What's up?"

"Have you clicked into Michael's today?"

Clicked into Michael's meant the video and audio feeds. And since this was one of the days he wasn't exclusive to monitoring, he hadn't. He'd been busy researching the Getty and attempting to acquire the necessary tickets.

"No." Rick walked with his cordless phone to the office space with the monitors. "Is there a problem?"

"Not sure. I've seen a car parked outside the gates a couple of times. Might be the paparazzi. He seems to have something he's pointing at the gate when one of the girls leaves."

The video feed outside Michael's gate didn't host any cars when Rick turned on the monitor.

"Do you have a recording?"

"I do. I've sent it over. It's probably nothing. My guess is just some hopeful attempting to make a buck when Michael was in town. Odd that he didn't clue in that the actor left a few days ago."

Rick clicked into the feeds Neil sent him. Sure enough, a car sat outside the gate and took pictures of Meg and Judy leaving. He didn't seem to wait long before he moved along, only to show up another time to do the same thing again.

"Are there any clear shots of this guy's face?"

"None."

"Hmm. Think we should alert Judy and Meg?"

Neil snorted . . . or let loose some sort of noise that resembled a snort. "Need an excuse to stop by?"

"No. In fact, I'll be there tomorrow night to pick Judy up."

Neil fell silent, then he asked, "Personal bodyguard?"

"No. Just personal."

Neil laughed, encouraged him to watch the feeds, then hung up.

———

A lot of the staff left the office early on Friday. Taking advantage of the lack of eyes, Judy stretched the plans she'd been drawing up on a drafter's table and spent some time attacking the details of her idea for the performing arts center.

At five, the office cleared out completely. Judy kicked off her heels and tuned in her radio station from her phone. Traffic right at five always sucked, so staying an extra half an hour would actually grant her a less stressful drive home. Going into her date with Rick stress-free would be a plus. Rick picking her up would give her a few more minutes to get ready.

She was singing along, off-key, to one of her favorite songs and mapping out details of an acoustic ceiling that would have to house several catwalks and rows of lighting, when she heard someone clearing their throat behind her.

A little startled, she swiveled to find Debra Miller, as in the *Miller* of Benson & Miller, standing behind her with a smile on her face. "I sure hope you draw better than you sing," she said with a tiny lift of her eyebrows.

Judy scrambled with the control of her cell phone to turn down the volume. Heat met her cheeks. "Oh, sorry . . . I didn't think anyone else was still here." How embarrassing. She'd barely waved at Debra Miller in passing, knew who she was but had not yet needed to actually talk to the woman. She was in her midforties, dressed as a successful businesswoman should be, and slender enough to attract men half her age if she wanted to. Her dark hair shaped the side of her face. Artful, tasteful, and not overly done, her makeup looked as if she'd just applied it.

Debra Miller offered a short laugh and glanced over Judy's shoulder to the design on the light table. "I think I'm the last to leave, except for you. What are you working on?"

Judy actually scrambled in front of the desk, blocking Debra's view. "It's, ah . . . just . . ."

Debra looked around her, her lips stopped smiling. "The Santa Barbara Performing Arts Center?"

Oh, God. She wasn't supposed to be working on this. In fact, no one knew she even had the specs for the place. Was she overstepping her limitations as an intern?

"I'm just playing. It's nothing I've been asked to do, Mrs. Miller."

"It's Ms.," she corrected while she moved to Judy's side and stared at the design. If it was anyone other than Debra Miller, Judy would have shoved in and kept her from viewing an unfinished design.

"Oh, sorry. Ms." Flustered, Judy started to fidget.

"Don't be. The Mr. to my Mrs. was an asshole."

Judy let out a nervous laugh.

"What's this?" She pointed to a pop-out design for the sound barriers that often hung over the main auditorium in performing art centers.

"Acoustic panels that drop from the ceiling."

Ms. Miller pointed to the main drawing where the ceiling didn't show the panels, but instead held the vaulted expanse seen in any of the California missions up and down the state. "Why aren't they here?"

"They're portable."

Judy lifted the drawing to show one below that demonstrated their use. "My brother—"

"Michael Wolfe? The man who drew production to a halt on Monday?"

"Uhm, yeah. Sorry about that. He's not in town very often."

"It's OK, Judy. I'm just sorry I wasn't here to meet him."

Phew. Why was her heart beating so fast?

"So, your brother . . ."

"Right." The room felt ten degrees warmer. "Mike always complains about auditoriums that are meant for live theater hosting concerts, or concert halls that attempt live theater not having the right acoustics."

"What do you mean?"

Judy pointed to the stage. "During a concert a band will have stacks of speakers amplifying the performers. Yeah, a good sound guy can work with what the auditorium has to offer, but most are used to big empty spaces without the aid of vaulted ceilings and acoustic panels of any kind. There are a couple of outdoor concert venues in Santa Barbara, but not many indoor ones. I'd think that any performing arts center that houses five to eight thousand people would be ideal for concerts." Excited about her design, Judy forgot to be nervous and she kept rattling. "A performing arts center should always keep in mind the perfect balance for stage performers. Yeah, they wear a mic now, but most stage actors understand about projecting their voice and if an auditorium can hold in the sound of a single voice on stage . . . nothing captures the attention of an audience more. It's magical."

Judy flipped back to the top drawing.

"Having the panels there when they're needed, and gone when they're not . . . I think it might make this the best choice for all kinds of entertainment. The panels themselves can be redressed to set the mood. Lighting can be used for effect."

Ms. Miller flipped through her design a second time. "How long have you been working on this?"

"About a week. Mainly at home . . . for kicks."

"For kicks?"

"Sure. Helps keep up some of the skills I learned in school that haven't been put to use yet. It's exciting. Isn't it?"

Ms. Miller stared at Judy for a long minute. "I'm trying to remember if I was ever in love with design as much as you appear to be."

"I do love it. I think an artist might feel the same way when they place a brush to a canvas." She looked down at the design. "Even if the end result isn't beautiful for anyone but the artist, the journey is worth the effort."

Ms. Miller offered a half smile. "Well, Judy who is drawing up an entire project just for kicks. I want to see this design when you're done."

The air stood still. "Y-you do?"

"I do. I'm not going to lead you on. I think some of the elementary design ideas are just that, juvenile. Your insight on the building, however, is thought-provoking and worthy of a second look."

"It is?"

Ms. Miller gave her a full smile now. "It is."

"Wow. Thanks."

"Don't thank me yet, Judy. This has to continue to be a side project for you. It wouldn't bode well to give an intern something like this when I've had junior architects working for me for half a dozen years that never get off the strip malls."

Judy gave an enthusiastic nod. "Got it. Thanks." She extended her hand to shake her boss's.

Ms. Miller left her standing with a slack jaw and giddy excitement swimming up her spine.

Judy turned toward her stack of papers and did a full-on happy dance. She turned in a full circle and her eyes fell on the clock. Six twenty. "Oh, shit!"

She rolled up her plans, shoved them into the tube used to transport the large drawings, and scrambled to leave the deserted building. Halfway to the elevators, she realized she didn't have her purse. She ran back to get it.

The parking lot was practically empty. The low ceilings and dark lighting never bothered her when she walked to her car during the day. Abandoned, it felt isolated.

Judy reached into her purse and removed her cell phone to check the time. She was so late. Rick would just have to wait.

What sounded like a coin hitting the concrete floor behind her had her jumping at the noise. Two cars, several yards apart, sat at the far side of the lot, closer to the elevator. She knew she was probably just being paranoid, but the feeling of eyes on her made her walk backward for several steps before she turned around.

The hard body of a man stopped her. Before she could look up, he had an arm around her throat and was pulling her into the deep shadows of the parking lot. The tube holding the plans dropped to the floor and rolled away.

Terror stunned her, kept her from all cohesive thought.

She struggled against him and opened her mouth to scream. Meaty fingers clamped over her mouth.

"Shut up, bitch!"

This isn't happening. Oh, God.

"You're not so tough now, are you?" She felt his breath, smelled something minty.

Processing the man's words added confusion to the horror when the man pinned her body against his and the wall of the garage. He slid something over her head, giving her a chance to yell.

His hand clasped over her mouth again as he pulled her away from the wall far enough to slam her against it. The back of her head hit hard enough to see stars in the darkness of the cloth that kept her from seeing her attacker.

He was going to kill her. She felt it deep inside.

Something sharp scratched her arm, leaving hot pain in its wake.

"It would be so easy . . . so fuckin' easy." It took his hand crawling up her thigh to make her fight with every ounce of strength she owned.

It took both of his hands now to control hers. Using her feet, she kicked, most of the time landing against the air.

She landed on her purse when they fell to the floor. Her one hand still clenched her cell phone. Why she managed to hold on to it, she didn't know.

Her knee landed a shot and her attacker slammed her head a second time. A warm trickle of blood started to flow down her neck. Nausea rolled up her throat.

"Not much of a fighter, are you?"

She shook her head, attempted to yell behind his hand that clamped over her mouth.

The man holding her shifted and tears started to roll down her cheeks. The only thing she could see was the dim light of the garage through the cloth. His shadow loomed over her. *Please God. No.*

"Next time," her attacker said against her ear right as something hit the side of her head, and the world went dark.

I'm being stood up.

Rick paced the inside of Michael's house, more than a little irritated that the clock on the wall told him Judy wasn't there. He didn't see her as the kind of woman to play this kind of game. A phone call, a text . . . anything was better than this.

A little itch in the back of his throat told him his Judy wasn't that kind of woman. She was honest with him when she didn't want to go out, and wouldn't hesitate to tell him to his face that she changed her mind.

He was about to give up and take the walk of shame back home when his cell phone buzzed in his pocket.

Judy's name filled the screen.

He hesitated, wondering what her excuse would be . . . or would she just tell him no again?

He pressed *answer* and lifted the phone to his ear. He forced a smile and said, "Hey, babe."

At first, there was nothing. Then every cell in his body turned ice cold. "Rick?" Her voice was soft, scared. Judy sucked in a cry. "Rick?"

The skin on his arm stood on alert. "Judy? What is it? Where are you?"

"Rick?" She was crying full-on now.

"Judy?" He wanted to crawl through the phone. "Honey, what . . ."

"Let me help you," he heard the voice of a woman and the shuffle of the phone. "Rick Evans?"

"This is . . . what's wrong? What happened?"

The sound of a siren added to the alarm inside his head. Rick ran to the front door and jumped into Michael's Ferrari, which was already waiting for his date.

"Mr. Evans, Judy is on her way to the ER at UCLA. She asks that you meet her there."

With a direction, Rick sped from the estate, the cell phone to his ear. "Is she OK?" What kind of stupid question was that? *Of course she's not OK.* "What happened? Car accident?"

"No. I'll let her explain. I'll tell the doctors to expect you."

The call disconnected, giving Rick two hands to drive bat-shit crazy all the way to UCLA.

Chapter Eleven

Sometimes it took defining moments in your life to explain where clichés came from. The term "the longest fifteen minutes of my life" never had a real meaning until Rick was pacing an emergency room lobby waiting for Judy to return from a CAT scan. Damn it if no one would even tell him what she needed a CAT scan of. No one would talk to him at all. Yes, Judy Gardner was there, yes, he was OK to see her when she returned, but, no, they weren't at liberty to tell him anything else.

His only savior of sanity was the knowledge that she wasn't rushed to surgery and that she was at least in a condition to tell the staff that she wanted to see him.

"Mr. Evans?"

He shot from his small corner of the lobby, rubbed a hand down his chin, and said, "That's me. I'm Rick Evans."

The nurse nodded toward the doors she stood behind and Rick proceeded to follow her into the bustling belly of the ER. She led him a few steps into the department and found a quiet corner before she stopped. "I'm Kim," she introduced herself.

Frustrated that he wasn't being led straight to Judy's bedside, he shuffled his feet. "Where's Judy?"

"Down the hall." She nodded in the opposite direction.

Rick turned away from the nurse only to stop with her stern warning. "Mr. Evans! I need a word with you first."

Rick hesitated, knowing on some deep level he didn't want to hear what the nurse had to say.

"She's banged up pretty bad."

"What happened?"

Kim looked at the plain tile floor, which had seen more grief than either of them ever would in their lifetime. "She was attacked."

Rick held his breath, his nose flared, and his fists were poised at his side ready for battle. "Attacked?"

"I'll let her explain, but she wanted you to have some idea as to why she's here. She's upset, of course. We're waiting for the CAT scan results and the doctor is going to need to stitch her up."

Rick only half listened. Someone attacked her. Who? Why? How?

"Tell me the police have someone in custody."

"I don't think so. I don't even think they have a description yet."

Rick met Kim's eyes. "Take me to her."

The short span of hall was a maze of people and medical staff going about their day. At the end of the maze sat a single door. Two uniformed officers were talking with the medical staff. Rick noticed them eyeing him as he walked through the door.

One look. It took one look to understand what might drive a man to murder.

His innocent small-town spitfire lay on top of a three-inch mattress on a gurney with IV lines and monitors. Dried blood ran down the side of her face, bruising already evident at her temple. Gauze covered one arm and around her head. Finger marks bruised her cheek. Her eyes were closed when he walked in so he moved slowly in her direction.

Kim caught his arm and cleared her throat.

The noise brought Judy to attention. "Rick's here," Kim said.

Judy couldn't open all of her right eye.

"Hey, Utah."

Two soft words and she was instantly in tears and reaching for him.

He moved to her side, fumbled with the side rail of the gurney, and pulled her gently into his arms. "Shh. I'm here. You're OK."

"I didn't see him." She clutched his back as if he was a life raft and she was sinking into an abyss.

"Shh." He rocked her, slowly, and wished to hell that he could take away her pain.

"I stayed late. The parking lot was empty."

Rick didn't like the image her words knifed into him.

Her words grew soft. "I was almost at my car when I heard him. I thought he was going to kill me. Oh, God, Rick, I've never been so scared."

Rick knew he was a big man, knew he needed to hold his muscles at bay while he held her and learned about the man responsible for her condition.

"Do you know who it was?"

"No. I never saw him." She moved away from him long enough to look in his eyes. "I never saw him. When I woke up he was gone."

"When you woke up?"

Her story was fragmented, her eyes unfocused. "He left me in the garage. One of the employees in the building found me."

Rick clasped both her hands. "Have you called Zach and Karen?"

She shook her head, her eyes swelling with new tears.

"You don't want them finding out about this from the media."

Judy cried in his arms for ten more minutes before she let him go long enough to leave the room for the phone call to her family.

Rick spoke with Karen first, encouraged her to drive, knowing that Zach would probably get them both in an accident en route.

Lord knew Rick nearly lost it on several turns on the way to the ER. His next call was to Neil. With no humor in his voice, something even Neil seldom heard, Rick offered only the facts he knew. Made the demands any Marine would.

"Judy was attacked in the parking garage of her employer."

"No."

"Yes. We're in the ER at UCLA. The local authorities are here but she's not ready to talk to them. Someone found her unconscious in the garage."

"Shit, is she OK?"

"We're waiting for radiology. I've not spoken to the doctors. He beat the crap out of her, Neil. She's a mess. I want a team on that garage. I don't want the local police to screw this up. Judy doesn't know who did this, didn't see the guy. I'll get you more details when I know them."

"I'm on it." Then Neil hung up.

Rick's calculating brain made its share of deductions and surged forward to unwanted conclusions. "Kim?" he called out for the nurse taking care of Judy before she walked back behind the closed door.

"I called Judy's brother and his wife. They're on their way. A colleague of mine, Neil MacBain, might show up as well."

"I'll tell the receptionist to let us know when they're here."

He stopped her before she could turn away. "One more thing."

"Yes?"

The need to know just how broken Judy was crawled up his skin. "Do we . . ." The words wouldn't come from his lips. "Was she?"

Kim's eyebrows rose. "Was she raped?"

Nausea filled his throat. "Yes."

"There's no evidence. She was knocked out at some point so we've done a preliminary exam. The doctors try hard to avoid rape exams if possible because they can be very hard on the patient when they aren't needed."

Some relief filled his soul.

"Would it make a difference if she had been?" Kim asked.

"For me?"

Kim nodded.

"No. I need to be sensitive for her."

The nurse seemed to approve of his answer with a single nod. "Treat her with kid gloves anyway. We really don't know what happened when she wasn't conscious."

Rick nodded and took a few deep breaths before he entered Judy's room a second time.

Rick sat by her bedside holding her hand when the doctor made his way into her room. "Looks like your scan of your head was negative," he told her.

"That's a good thing?"

"It is. But we want to keep you overnight for observation. Sometimes swelling isn't evident on the first film. We'll want to repeat it in the morning since you blacked out for such a long time."

Judy glanced at Rick, who offered a nod.

"OK."

The doctor smiled. "Good. The police are waiting to come in and talk to you."

Her heart skipped, knowing she was going to have to tell them everything she remembered. Rick's hand squeezed hers. "I'll stay here if you want me to."

"Please." She wasn't sure why she thought of calling Rick before her brother. Maybe it was because Rick was closer . . . or he was expecting her. Or maybe she just felt safe with him by her side.

"I'm going to have them come in now. They'll want to take pictures before I stitch you up."

She attempted to sit higher in the bed and winced with the pain traveling from her head to her arms.

"Let me," Rick said as he gently took hold of her waist and pushed her up. With him close, she felt tears in her eyes again.

She hated the weakness inside her and longed for the laughter and banter of where the two of them had been just a couple of days before.

"Thank you for coming," she whispered.

Rick looked at her as if she were crazy, leaned forward, and placed his lips to her forehead. "You don't have to thank me, Judy."

"Meg's not home and I didn't think about Zach and Karen until after—"

"You can always count on me."

A reply sat on her lips when two uniformed officers stepped into the room, one male, one female.

The various weapons and radios hanging from their belts made a sound with every step.

"Miss Gardner?" The woman questioned.

Judy nodded.

"We know this is a hard time but we need to get a statement from you to move forward with the investigation."

"I understand."

"I'm Officer Greenwood and this is my partner, Officer Spear."

Spear glanced at Rick.

Rick stood and offered his hand. "I'm Rick Evans," he told them. "A friend."

That was fair, Judy told herself.

"I'm also responsible for security at her current residence and head a security team that shadows her brother when he's in town."

Both police officers sent questioning looks to each other.

"My brother is Michael Wolfe."

"The actor?"

Judy nodded. "He's out of the country right now."

Greenwood wrote something down on the pad of paper she removed from a pocket. "We'll have to step up security at the crime scene."

"I already have a team en route," Rick told them.

"Private security doesn't hold jurisdiction."

Rick waved Spear off. "Let's not worry about that now. I'm sure Judy wants to get this over with."

Greenwood pulled up a chair and removed a recording device from her pocket. Rick fiddled with his cell phone and set it on the table. "Mr. Evans?"

Instead of addressing the police officer, Rick looked directly at Judy. "Do you mind if I record this?"

"Of course not."

Rick tilted his head toward Officer Greenwood.

"Fine. Start at the beginning, Judy. Anything, no matter how small or seemingly insignificant, can be the detail that helps us get this person."

Her palms started to sweat and it took her nearly a minute to begin.

"I stayed at the office late." She explained her position at Benson & Miller Designs and how she'd gotten caught up talking with Ms. Miller about a project. "I was so excited about the opportunity to work on something of importance I lost track of time. When I looked it was after six."

"Do you remember the exact time?"

"Six fifteen, six twenty. Rick and I had a seven o'clock date." She offered him a half smile and was relieved to see a small lift of his lips . . . something she hadn't seen since he walked in the room. "I was going to have to rush and even speeding I would have been late."

"So you were walking to your car at six twenty?"

"No. I gathered my things and realized I didn't have my purse so I ran back to the office. It was closer to six thirty. The garage was nearly empty." She closed her eyes and saw the cavernous structure in her mind. "I took my cell phone out to check the time and I heard something behind me. I turned around and didn't see anything. I was trying to keep calm, but felt someone watching me." She shivered and Rick reached for her hand again.

Judy stared at the legs beneath the hospital-issue blanket and plowed through what she remembered.

"He grabbed me around my neck, used his full arm." She lifted hers to demonstrate.

"A choke hold?"

"Yeah. I never saw his face. I was stunned, didn't even respond at first. When I screamed he covered my mouth and pulled me toward the wall." She winced and heard the crack all over again when she told them about slamming into the wall and having her face covered.

"I remember falling on my purse. He fell on top of me." Judy blinked a few times, tried to remove the feeling of his hands on her. "I fought him, but he was so much stronger and he kept slamming my head. The next thing I knew, someone was calling out to me and I heard the sounds of sirens."

Rick clasped his fingers with hers. She held them like a lifeline. If he'd been there, none of this would have happened.

"Did he say anything?" Officer Spear asked.

"Uhm, yeah. He called me a bitch. Said something about how easy it would be . . ."

"How easy it would be to do what?"

"I don't know. I was confused by his words."

"Was he a big man?" Greenwood asked.

Judy closed her eyes, let herself remember. "Taller than me. His fingers were thick."

"Thick?"

"Meaty. Almost soft."

"Fat?" Spear asked.

"I guess. I only felt them when he covered my mouth."

"Any accent?"

"No . . . wait, no. I don't think so."

"You didn't see the color of his skin?"

Judy was disgusted with her lack of knowledge on the man who attacked her. "He covered my head with something. I only saw shadows through the cloth."

"According to the witness who found you, your head was covered in a pillowcase."

Judy nodded. "That would make sense. It was big enough to slip over my head easily."

"Can you think of anything else?"

Judy swallowed.

"Judy, you were found unconscious after seven. Whoever did this was long gone. By your account you were in the garage at six thirty."

"Yes."

"How much time passed during this attack?"

"I don't know. A few minutes, maybe less before he knocked me out."

"So you were unconscious in the garage for twenty minutes, more or less?"

Plenty of time for the man to kill her if he wanted to.

"I guess."

Greenwood raised her eyebrow to her partner.

"One more thing, Miss Gardner," Spear said when his partner stood.

"Yes?"

"Do you have any idea who would do this to you? An enemy? An old boyfriend?"

The question shouldn't have shocked her, but it did. "I've only been in town for a month. All I've done is work. I don't have any enemies."

"Everyone has enemies," Spear countered.

Judy squeezed Rick's hand. "I can't imagine anyone we know doing this."

Officer Greenwood removed a card and handed it to Judy. "If you remember anything, call me."

"I will."

Rick lifted her hand to his lips and kissed her fingertips. "I have a question," he said, stopping the police from leaving the room.

Why his words felt so much softer, less threatening than the police, Judy couldn't say. "Yeah?"

"Do you know where your purse is?"

"I-I don't know. I managed to hold on to my phone during the attack. I'm not sure why. Did the paramedics bring it with me?"

Rick looked around the room. A bag with her ruined clothing sat in a heap inside a patient belonging bag. He stood and brought it over to her.

She looked inside, noticed the blood-soaked clothing. Her purse wasn't among her possessions.

Judy looked at the officers. "Do you know if they found my purse in the garage?"

"A tube with blueprints was found a few feet away, but no one has said anything about your purse."

Judy shrugged. "I didn't have a lot of money in it anyway."

The nurse stepped back in the room, paused at the door. "Are you about done? The doctor wants to clean her up."

"We are. I'll go get the camera."

"Your brother and sister-in-law are in the lobby."

"I don't want Zach to see me like this. He'll freak."

"It's OK, Judy, we'll keep him out until you're ready," Kim said.

"I'll go tell them you're all right," Rick said.

He stepped out of the room and Officer Spear followed him.

Officer Greenwood stepped closer to the bed and lowered her voice. "Now that your boyfriend is gone, I have one more question."

"OK?"

"Judy, there is no evidence to prove this man left the moment you lost consciousness. You were at his mercy for a long time and completely oblivious of his actions. I know the initial exam didn't show evidence of a sexual assault. Are you sure he didn't . . ."

Judy started to shake. "I don't think so. My whole body hurts."

"But you're not sure."

Judy looked at the nurse, her gaze met that of sympathy.

Kim sat beside the bed. "A rape exam consists of a pelvic exam, much like a pap only with more swabs, hair samples. Anything that could capture DNA. If you want your boyfriend—"

"We just started dating. We haven't . . ."

"Fine. We can keep him out. This is your decision, Judy. If not knowing if this man sexually assaulted you is going to keep you up at night, then it might be better to take a closer look. If you've been sexually active in the past couple of days it might be difficult to tell."

"I haven't had sex in nearly a year."

Kim sighed. "Then it will be easier to determine if something did happen while you were knocked out. It's up to you."

Officer Greenwood offered a different kind of advice. "DNA evidence is what puts most of these predators behind bars."

Judy's skin crawled. The thought of anyone spreading her open, scraping for answers, left her cold. But how could she move forward with the ugly question in her own head? The memory of the man's hand on her thigh reminded her of the fear of him doing exactly what these women were worried about.

"My sister-in-law, Karen, is in the lobby. Can you ask her to come back during the exam?"

"Of course. I'll tell the doctor of your decision."

Alone in the room, Judy realized that her tears had completely dried up.

Chapter Twelve

He took it back . . . the first fifteen minutes in the lobby held nothing on the last forty-five. Rick had barely made it into the crowded waiting room to talk with Zach and Karen before the nurse followed him out to retrieve Karen. In hushed tones, Kim told them Judy agreed to a sexual assault exam because of the time she had been unconscious.

By the time Neil arrived in the ER, Zach and Rick were doing their best caged-animal impressions. They finally moved to the outside where they couldn't scare the small children.

"I don't think the media has wind of this yet," Neil told them. "The garage is swarming with police. Once word got to them about whose sister Judy was, the team doubled."

"Are there any cameras in the garage?"

"Only by the exit and the elevators."

"Will we be able to view the tapes?"

Neil stood taller. "Remember Dean Brown? He worked on Eliza's case." Dean was a detective and connected to Gwen, Eliza, and Samantha. If strings could be pulled, he'd be the one to do it. "Dean's working with the locals. Being a pseudo-father to the first lady of the state had its advantages. We should have something to look at in the next few hours."

Zach reached for his phone. "I should call Mike and my parents."

"Hey."

They all turned around and found Karen, ghost white and stoic, standing in the automatic doors of the emergency room lobby.

Rick approached her first.

Karen shook her head. "She wasn't. He didn't."

Rick held on to the wall beside him to stay standing. *Thank God.*

Zach slid a hand around his wife's waist to hold her up. "Can we go in?"

"Yeah, but just for a few minutes. The stitches took longer than the doctor thought they would. This bastard carved into her arm."

Rick remembered the bandage on her arm, but assumed it was scrapes from the garage floor.

"What?"

Karen turned her wrist up and made an X over the underside of her arm. "Could be a letter or just slash marks. One cut rather deep and it started to bleed a lot when the doctor started cleaning it."

Rick turned to Neil. "I want this bastard."

Neil clasped his shoulder. "We'll get him."

It was a promise, one Rick would hold his friend to.

———

Nightmares plagued her sleep. Memories, images, and the feeling of a stranger's hands on her body threatened to rob her sanity. The first time she woke, Karen was at her side, the next her mother was there holding back her hair when the food they'd given her the night before emptied into a basin.

Much later, the pasty film in her mouth had her lips sticking together when she uttered the word *water.* Somewhere in the night, she'd been transferred into a larger room with more monitors and more IVs going into her.

Meg scrambled to her feet when Judy woke.

"Hey . . . here." Her best friend looked like she'd slept in a chair. Meg offered her a pale orange cup with a straw. "Just a sip."

It only took a sip to make her stomach reject the fluid. The passing of time was evident, yet she didn't remember any of it.

"You're not in New York."

Meg tilted her head. "You know who I am?"

Judy's swollen right eye made her wince when she smiled. "Of course. That's a stupid question."

"You didn't yesterday. Oh, Judy. We've been so worried."

"What? I remember leaving the ER, then I fell asleep."

Meg held one of Judy's hands in both of hers. "You fell asleep and didn't want to wake up. They did a second CAT scan and found a little swelling." She patted the side of her head. "The doctors brought you up here and said we just needed to wait."

"Up here?" She looked around the room.

"ICU."

That explained the amount of medical equipment, the glass doors. "Is my mom here? I remember her being here."

"She is. Everyone is." Meg choked up. "I called your cell on Saturday. When Rick answered, I was all laughing . . . happy that you two hooked up. Then he told me what happened. God, Judy. I'm so sorry."

Though her friend cried, Judy couldn't feel the tears. She knew if she started to shed them, she'd never stop. "I'm OK, Meg."

Meg swiped at the tears under her eyes, a pathetic smile followed. "I told the nurse I'd let her know when you woke."

Judy stopped her before she left the room. "Meg. What day is it?"

"Monday. Almost four in the afternoon."

The bastard took more than twenty minutes. He took two days of my life.

A slow, steady stream of people visited her once the nurse managed a few tasks. Her parents were first, both had swollen eyes and heaps of remorse. She assured them she was going to be fine. Her dad never wanted her to go to LA, wanted her home in nowhere, Utah, where she could find the right man, settle down, and raise a few kids. She couldn't offer her dad anything other than a repeated statement of, "I'm fine." The lie came to her lips freely.

When Mike walked in the door, she met him with a frown. "What? Aren't you supposed to be making all the women happy in another country?"

Mike offered a smile, even though his eyes told her he didn't feel it. "You're the only woman I'm thinking about right now."

She accepted his hug. "I'm OK, Mike."

"Really? Yesterday you were doing an *Exorcist* remake. I'd have made a YouTube video if I needed the money." His eyes were smiling a little now.

When Judy laughed, her skin stretched over the swelling on her face. "It hurts to laugh. Stop."

"I was born to entertain, sis. Can't help it."

She took a deep breath and let it out slowly. "I needed that."

"What, the snarky *Exorcist* comment? I'm serious. You kept telling me to put the toilet seat down. Scared the crap out of me. To which the toilet seat was down."

She laughed and pain rattled her entire body. "Stop."

"How are you feeling?"

The lie was there. "I'm fine. Only hurts when I laugh."

Zach and Karen made their way in with her younger sister, Hannah, at their heels. There were equal parts happiness to see her awake and to find her comprehending their words and concern.

At some point, the doctor made an appearance and asked that everyone leave. Her lack of appetite told him she still wasn't ready to leave the observation of the ICU. She might be making sense but they wanted to keep her another night at a higher intensity of care until they saw a clear CAT scan and a return of her desire to eat.

Karen and Meg returned to the room after the doctor left. "You don't need to stay," she told them.

Meg snuggled into her chair and flipped on the TV. "I told Rick I was going to be here until he returned."

"And I'm Meg's ride," Karen offered.

"Where is Rick?"

Karen and Meg exchanged glances. "He and Neil are investigating the guy who did this to you."

No one had even mentioned the assault since she woke. It was as if an act of God had placed her in the hospital.

"Do they have anyone yet?"

Karen shook her head. "No. The videos didn't show anything."

"Videos of what?"

"The garage had some surveillance videos. Not a lot, but some. The man who found you didn't see anyone running away," Meg said.

"They'll find him," Karen told her. "Gwen told me they've mobilized a small task force. They'll find him."

She couldn't think about any of that right now. Her body hurt too much, her head was ready to explode with every brain cell used on the man who did this to her.

"I assume someone told my boss where I am."

"Are you kidding? The police have talked with just about everyone in your building who might have been there Friday night," Meg told her.

"No one was in the office when I left."

"Well, the police closed the parking lot all weekend and have questioned everyone from the security guards in the lobby to your boss."

"I'm not complaining," Judy said, "but I'd imagine women are abused in a city this size every day. Why are they working so hard on this for me?"

Karen twisted the blinds to curb the direct light of the setting sun. "There is the Neil and Rick factor."

"What factor is that?"

"Marines. Those two aren't going to rest until the man who did this is behind bars."

Even in pain, Judy felt her insides warm to know Rick cared enough to work hard to find the man behind her pain.

"Then there is the Eliza factor."

"I hardly know Eliza." They'd met a couple of times. Yeah, it was impressive to meet the governor and his wife. To know that Karen and Eliza were good friends was a nice perk.

"But I *do* know Eliza. She and Carter take it personally when someone in their circle is hurt."

"I'm not in their circle."

Karen offered a small smile. "You are, hon. Sometimes family isn't about the people you're born to, but those who care enough about you to support you . . . or pull a few favors to help right a wrong for someone you know. What happened to you was beyond wrong. Getting this dirtbag off the street is a public safety concern for everyone. The fact that the governor has a direct line to you makes this a priority."

"Don't question it," Meg told her. "You just need to get better so we can both move back into Michael's house."

"Wait . . . you're not there? Where are you staying?"

Meg bit her bottom lip. "Oh, well . . . either with Karen and Zach or at the Tarzana house. Everyone thought it was best."

"Why?"

"They never found your purse. We changed the key codes and locks, but we thought it was best that no one was there alone until after this guy is caught. There are two extra rooms at the Tarzana house."

"Not that you need to think about that," Karen said. "You'll stay with us when they let you out of here."

"That's crazy. The commute to work would take hours."

Karen and Meg just stared at her.

"What?"

"You're thinking about work?"

She wiggled up in the bed and frowned. "Well, maybe not today."

Karen waved her off. "No need to think about that now."

Meg changed the subject. Told her that Lucas and Dan stopped by the night before only to be stopped in the lobby. The media had gotten wind of the assault. Now that Mike roamed the halls of the hospital, they were camped out to gather a statement or two.

———

Rick was exhausted. The sleep he managed in the past three days rivaled that of some of his missions overseas. It didn't stop him from turning over the active investigation for a few hours to sleep in an uncomfortable chair by Judy's bedside, a task he only relinquished to Judy's mom for a few hours on the second night.

Word had come via Zach that Judy was awake and making sense. Rick had seen his share of enlisted men with their bells rung to know about concussions. The swelling was minimal, so he knew it was only a matter of time for Judy to come back to them. Not that he was ever more than an hour away at any time.

The investigation was an exercise in frustration. They had little to go on. No eyewitnesses and not one camera that captured even a shadow.

As Rick parked in the now-familiar lot, he shoved his keys in his pocket and looked around. Even the hospital lot had cameras. It helped that there was a hefty fee for parking, which often gave the driver a false sense of security. But in the case of the hospital lot, there was actual uniformed security riding around in golf carts. Not armed security, but at least someone with a uniform and an ability to call for help.

Rick parked on the third level, the lower two were filled with doctor parking and spaces reserved for special guests. Most of the upper levels cleared out after five. It was nearly seven and the lot was quiet. Much like when Rick roamed the lot where Judy had been attacked, he looked for the cameras and made a point of walking down the stairwell where no cameras were found. Just like that in the garage at Benson & Miller's.

At some point the day before, one of the investigators from the local police suggested this was a random act or even a simple purse snatching.

Both Neil and Rick caught wind of the conversation and dismissed it. Whoever did this cased the parking lot, knew how to get in and out without detection, and targeted Judy. They roughed her up, but didn't kill her.

Why?

That was the sixty-four-thousand-dollar question.

Why?

The nurse buzzed him in to the ICU, where he walked by the long bank of desks that housed the staff.

Before walking in the room, he noticed Judy sleeping in the bed with Karen and Meg watching the TV quietly. He waved them out to talk to them without waking the patient.

"How's she doing?"

"Better," Karen offered. "She's not even stuttering today."

"She eating yet?" he asked.

"Not much. The doctor thinks by tomorrow her appetite should come back."

"Good. That's good. I'll be here all night. You should both go home and sleep."

Karen rested a hand on his arm. "You need to sleep sometime, too."

"I will. That chair in there folds out."

Meg huffed out a breath. "Hardly enough to fit me. You're a tad bigger."

Rick looked down on Judy's petite friend and winked. "I'll be fine."

The girls were too tired to argue.

He slowly moved into the room, sat beside Judy, and just stared at her. The bruising on her face was turning purple and the edges were yellow. Thankfully, the fingerprints of the man who'd held her down were no longer visible.

There was one less IV bag hanging from her bed, but the monitor kept constant surveillance on her vital signs.

She would heal. The body was good that way, but her head . . . that might take a little longer to feel right in the world. He knew from experience the many things that could fuck with your head and make the world an unsafe place.

He couldn't imagine how a woman as small and innocent as Judy was going to cope with the aftermath of the past few days.

Rick kicked back in the reclining chair and gently placed his hand under hers. She moved on the bed but didn't wake. There wasn't a concern he'd be told to leave. The staff had been told from the moment Judy was admitted that if it wasn't Rick or Judy's family at her bedside it would be the local police. The doctors agreed a familiar face was better for the patient.

Rick closed his eyes and willed his own personal demons away. At another time in his life, he sat beside someone he loved and held her hand.

But that was a long time ago, and better off buried.

Chapter Thirteen

Leaving the ICU and the hospital should have resulted in a little less attention as everyone's lives returned to normal. This wasn't the case in Judy's life. She didn't balk at staying at Zach and Karen's house. It made sense in light of her recovery. Her muscles had grown incredibly lax while lying in the hospital bed. It didn't help that she'd not managed much of an exercise routine since moving to Beverly Hills. Besides, Meg spent a lot of time at the Tarzana house, which would leave Judy alone. Being alone felt a little too much like the stupid girl going into the basement on a stormy night after the power went out. She couldn't help but wonder if walking into any parking garage wasn't going to give her the same uncomfortable feeling.

The fishbowl of the hospital didn't compare to having her family hovering over her. Her father, who never took a lot of time away from his hardware store in Hilton, Utah, was going on nearly a week in California. Her mother hadn't stopped fussing over her, making homemade soup and big roast dinners for everyone. Even Mike stuck around until Judy finally convinced Karen to call her brother's personal assistant to push the man back to work.

Rick always made his way to Zach's house before she retired, but there was a place setting for him at the table tonight in case he came earlier.

Exactly one week from the attack, during a large family meal, Judy found herself picking at the pot roast her mother had been cooking for the better part of the day. Her eyes settled on the bandage covering her right arm while the conversation around the table spoke of everything from the weather to the gossip in Hollywood and Hilton.

He carved into me. Marked me so even after I healed I'd always remember. Why?

She dropped the fork on her plate and picked at the bandage. Tape pulled at the hair on her arms, but she tugged on it anyway. She had avoided looking at the mess on her arm. The sutures were coming out the next day. She knew she'd no longer need the gauze to hide what the man had done to her.

"What are you doing?" she heard someone ask. Instead of responding, she fisted the gauze and ran her thumb over the coarse bits of synthetic string that held her skin together.

Slash marks. Spaced-out slash marks traveled down a narrow margin of her arm. She knew how close they were to arterial veins because of the trouble the doctor had in stitching her up.

"Judy?"

It would be easy . . . so fuckin' easy.

She picked at a bit of gauze stuck to a suture, grew frustrated with its desire to hold on.

"Judy?"

She picked harder. *This should come off easy. So easy.*

"Judy!"

"What?" she said much too loud to an entirely quiet room. Rick knelt beside her, placed a napkin over her bleeding arm.

Everyone stared at her.

Karen's eyes were wet with unshed tears, Zach and her father shifted their gazes from her eyes to her arm. Her mom and Hannah let the tears flow, and Meg's tight jaw showed nothing but anger. Even Devon and Dina were looking at her as if she'd grown horns.

So many eyes. There was blood under the fingernails of her left hand. Her arm burned under Rick's hand and she realized she'd done more than pick at a piece of lint.

When she started to shake, Rick placed his arm around her and helped her to her feet. "C'mon, Utah. Let's get you cleaned up."

Her head spun the moment she stood and her legs lost their ability to hold her.

Rick swept her up and walked her out of the dining room as if he was taking the morning paper off the front step on the way to the mailbox.

He took the stairs in silence, kicked open the door to her room, and walked straight to the adjoining bathroom. Once the water flowed to a temperature Rick approved of, he removed the napkin from her arm and placed the mess under the flow.

"Did I do that?" A good inch of what should have been healed skin now bled, turning the water pink.

"Yeah," Rick told her.

The supplies she'd been using to dress the wound sat on the end of the counter. Using one hand Rick pulled the box over, found what he wanted, and covered her skin with a tight dressing.

"What happened?" she asked him as if he'd have the answers.

He released a long sigh and kept wrapping her arm. "You lost it back there."

"I did?"

"Yeah. It happens." He used his teeth to remove a section of tape. Once the bandage was secure, he stood tall with her arm clasped in his firm grip. "What were you thinking about?"

She blinked. No one else wanted to talk about what happened. They skimmed the issue, redirected the conversation, stopped talking when she walked in a room . . . not Rick.

"Why? Why this? Why did he carve deep enough into my skin only to leave me alive?"

Rick's Adam's apple bobbed before he managed an answer. "Maybe he heard something and was scared off before he could do more."

Judy shook her head. "No. *It would be so easy. So fuckin' easy.* He could have killed me, knew he had the advantage." She met Rick's green eyes and knew he'd already come to the same conclusion. "You already know that."

"I don't *know* anything, Judy."

She slammed her free hand against his chest, taking him by surprise. "Don't lie to me."

He lifted his chin. "Fine. He could have killed you. Abused you more than he did."

Good, he wasn't lying, the same deductive thought met his eyes like when they'd first met and they were trying desperately to find Becky, who'd been abducted by her abusive parents.

"Instead he marked me. Made sure I'd always have a physical scar of his attack."

"Which makes it personal."

"I don't know anyone that hateful."

"Someone at your office. Someone who might have known about the project you were working on?"

Judy squeezed her eyes shut. "Ms. Miller spoke to me only minutes before the attack. No one knew about it."

Rick brought her bandaged arm to her lap and gently held on to her while they spoke. "Hustle any pool since you've been in town?"

"That's absurd. I don't hustle. I play and Meg is always right there to tell anyone that I'm good. Other than you, I've only ever played for twenty bucks at a time."

"Someone from Seattle?"

"I've thought about that. I know it sounds lily-white but I don't make enemies. I didn't steal anyone's boyfriend or rat on anyone for cheating. Meg and I were loners most of our senior year. We'd go out, play pool, do a little partying, but there weren't any casualties along the way."

"You think this was random?"

She shook her head before she uttered any words.

"Me either."

Her head hurt. Judy hated how much her head hurt the past week. "I should eat something." Her entire dinner was sitting on a plate surrounded by her family.

"Do you want to go back downstairs?"

"No. Please, I can't take one more sympathetic look, one more tear."

Rick lifted one side of his lips in a half smile. "I'll go get us both something to eat. So long as it's OK that I'm exempt from the masses."

She was much steadier on her feet when he led her into her room and tucked a few pillows behind her on the bed.

Rick returned less than ten minutes later with a tray filled with food for the both of them. He didn't let anyone else in the room even though he struggled with the laden tray, nearly spilling it on the floor more than once.

"This smells amazing."

"My mom's a good cook. Lots of practice when the town you live in doesn't have that many restaurants."

Rick placed the food in the center of the bed, lay at the foot, and kicked off his shoes.

Judy tucked her feet under her, sat Indian style, and picked up a fork. Her stomach growled with happiness with the first bite. "I've missed this."

He hummed around his food with appreciation.

She pulled up another forkful. "They want me to go back to Utah."

Rick's fork hesitated before he took a bite. "Is that what you want?"

"No. I know it's going to be hard. The thought of walking back in that garage makes me physically sick. Going back to Utah now would be hiding. And who's to say if this man is somehow after me that he wouldn't follow me there?"

Rick swallowed, chased his food with a drink of water. "That's a long way to travel for a criminal to seek a victim."

She kept eating, trying hard to remove her name as the victim in their conversation. "And lightning doesn't strike in the same place twice."

"You're a strong woman, babe. I knew that the first time we met."

There was an actual smile on her face. "We're back to the *babe* thing?"

"Yeah, well . . . I put off the Getty for a little while. We still haven't been on a date."

"Dinner in bed doesn't count?" She motioned toward the half-eaten food.

He shook his head. "Nor does breakfast in the hospital." He shoveled in more food, swallowed quickly, and loaded his fork again. "A date requires a shower, dinner with wine or at the very least an adult beverage, and shoes." He leaned over and tickled her bare toes.

She laughed, really laughed for the first time in over a week. Rick seemed just as pleased with the sound coming from her lips as she did.

They finished their meal in quiet conversation about almost nothing. When Judy had enough, Rick polished off her plate. He set the tray aside and leaned against the bedpost facing her.

"I need everyone to go home," she said with a heavy sigh.

"Me?"

She smiled, laid a hand on his lower leg as if to prove he was not part of the *everyone*.

"Not you. My parents, Hannah. Zach needs to get back to work. Karen hasn't even been to the Boys and Girls Club since last week. Thank goodness Mike listened and left. Now if I can just get everyone else to follow his lead. It's like everyone put their lives on hold."

"Family does that."

"I know. And I appreciate it but it feels like everyone is staring at me, waiting for me to break."

Rick ran his thumb over her instep with gentle strokes. "Kinda like you did tonight at dinner?"

"Is that what I did?"

"It is. Being alone when it happens again might require more than a bandage."

She knew enough about post-traumatic stress syndrome to understand she wasn't exempt from harboring unhealthy emotions. It had only been a week and the truth was she wasn't sleeping well. Seemed she wasn't often hungry . . . well, except when Rick was close by.

"I don't want to be alone." She shivered. "I just don't want to be the quicksand that keeps everyone from their lives."

He picked up her other foot, rubbed it. "I'm happy to hear you don't want to be alone."

The foot rub nearly made her miss his next words.

"When you're ready to go back to work, either myself or someone from our team will drive you and pick you up. One of us will be at Michael's home twenty-four/seven."

Twenty-four/seven? "What?" She opened her eyes, blinked a few times.

"Until this guy is caught, you won't be completely alone."

"I told you I was tired of the fishbowl."

"There won't be a fishbowl. The security detail is to keep you safe, not make you home-cooked meals."

"But—"

"Look me in the eye and tell me you believe with all your soul this man isn't coming back. He took your purse, didn't kill you when he could have, went through some serious effort to go in and out of that garage to corner you alone. Look me in the eye, Judy, and tell me he won't be back."

His words scared her. Primarily because he was right.

She leaned against the bed again, and pulled his foot closer to rub. She wasn't sure why he was working so hard to protect her. He didn't owe her. Hell, they weren't technically even dating. A few stolen kisses and some seriously heavy flirting summed up their relationship. Still, there wouldn't be any complaints from her lips.

"When I do go back to the office . . . that first day . . . can you be the one who takes me?"

The dimples on his face managed to grin even if his lips didn't. "I wouldn't have it any other way."

Chapter Fourteen

Rick shook himself awake a few hours later, realizing that he'd fallen asleep with Judy's feet in his lap. She was sound asleep as well. He eased off the bed and tucked the blankets around her. Chances were she'd wake in the middle of the night, uncomfortable with the amount of clothing she had on, but there was no way in hell he was going to take the liberty of undressing her. Maybe at a different time in their life, that would be acceptable. Not today . . . and not in light of everything she'd been through.

After dimming the lights, he made a quiet exit with his shoes dangling from his fingertips.

Down the hall, he noticed the flickering of a television set and poked his head inside.

Sawyer, Judy's father, and Zach were both propped on easy chairs watching the late news. Seemed everyone else had gone to bed.

"Hey." Rick made himself known with a simple greeting.

Sawyer sat up, his face a mask of worry.

Rick tossed his shoes to the floor and sat on the sofa between the two of them.

"How is she?" Zach asked first.

"Sleeping." But that wasn't the real question. "Your sister is a strong woman, Zach."

"Didn't seem strong tonight at dinner," Sawyer scoffed.

"No. She didn't. Those things are to be expected, Mr. Gardner. She'll get through this, not let it beat her down."

"She should come home with us. It's safer in Hilton."

Rick might not be a father, but he understood the need to keep Judy safe.

"If she hides in Utah now it could cripple her forever. The world isn't any more unsafe today than it was yesterday or will be tomorrow. The sooner she joins the world again, the stronger she'll be."

Sawyer glared at him. "I can't watch over her from home if she's not there."

"Are you suggesting you'll stick to your daughter's side every hour of every day? My guess is the days of you doing that passed a long time ago." Rick was too tired to get in a pissing match of right and wrong with Judy's dad, but the stubborn man wasn't listening to reason.

"This wouldn't happen in Utah."

"C'mon, Utah has problems, too, Dad," Zach told him. "Judy has us here." Rick was happy to see Zach nod in his direction to be included with the "us."

"I hate this, Zach. Didn't want her here to begin with."

"We all hate this. We all want her safe."

Rick sat forward and met Sawyer's eyes. "Judy will have round-the-clock protection, not only with a physical bodyguard taking her to and from work, but weekends and evenings. Michael already approved more audio and video monitoring of his home. We will find who did this to her, and she will be protected while we search for him. I want this bastard more than you can possibly know, Mr. Gardner. I'll keep your daughter safe."

Sawyer pointed a finger in his direction. "I'm keeping you to your word."

Judy's father grumbled as he lifted his tired frame from the chair and retired for the night.

Zach and Rick sat in silence for a several minutes, the newscast flashed images of all the awful things happening in the greater Los Angeles area. The media had grown tired of the criminal activity around one of Hollywood's elite, which suited Rick just fine. The picture of Michael and Judy dancing was the primary shot the media managed to use over and over. The same feed of the parking garage filled with police and caution tape was a constant reminder when Rick turned on the TV.

"Maybe she should go home for a while," Zach said.

The skin on Rick's arms chilled. "I have more resources here to protect her."

"No one is after her in Utah."

It was time to bring Zach closer to a truth realized by the authorities. "This man is after her. He targeted her and there's no guarantee he wouldn't follow her to Utah or anywhere else to hurt her again."

"Are you sure?"

Almost 100 percent. "In the service, going with your gut often saved your life."

"So keeping her here is going with your gut?"

Didn't sound like Zach agreed. "Judy wants nothing to do with going home. In fact, she wants everyone visiting to return to their lives. She's going back to Michael's on Monday, where I will have someone shadowing her every moment she's not at her desk at work."

"And if this dirtbag works with her?"

Rick had thought of that, too. He and Neil had already placed a temporary worker at the office building who would watch her there as well. Between the undercover spying and the monitoring of everyone surrounding Judy, they should know if there was any unusual attention given. "She's covered there as well. Just not an obvious shadow."

Zach sighed. "I guess that's all we can do. I don't think any of us are going to rest easy until this guy is caught."

Rest easy. Hell, the only restful sleep he'd had was the past two hours at Judy's side. The mention of sleep had him covering a yawn.

"You can crash here," Zach offered.

Being close to her, even a few bedrooms away, would give him some peace for a few hours. He knew he needed to reboot his brain. The only things waiting at home were blank monitors and an empty house. "I think I'll take you up on that offer."

Zach pushed off the chair, turned off the TV. "C'mon. The advantage of having a house this size is accommodating a large family."

"We wouldn't be doing our job if we didn't question you, Mr. Evans." Detective Raskin had taken over the investigation from the reporting officers. He and his partner, Detective Perozo, sat on opposite ends of the table. From the defensive pose of Perozo, he was playing bad cop, where Raskin kept a smile on his face.

"Damn right it's your job," Rick told him. "Should have questioned me within twenty-four hours."

The detectives glanced at each other then back at him.

Rick knew the delay had more to do with his personal circle of friends and diplomacy. But in his opinion, those things shouldn't ever take precedence over some protocols. Questioning a boyfriend, or in the case of him and Judy, a romantic interest, should have been a major priority.

Rick let them lead the questions. They started with the usual suspects, when had he met Judy, what was the nature of their relationship. Where was he when Judy was attacked and was he with anyone?

"I arrived at Mr. Wolfe's Beverly Hills home at ten minutes before seven. Our date was set for seven."

"Where were you prior to that time?"

"Experiencing the joys of traffic. Before that, I was at my residence in Tarzana. My home and that of Mr. Wolfe have twenty-four-hour video surveillance which will show me leaving and arriving."

Detective Perozo leaned forward. "But at six thirty you weren't captured on any videotapes."

"None that our team monitors. I gave myself forty minutes to get to Judy's. I left my house at six twenty, give or take a few minutes."

"What do you drive?" Detective Raskin asked.

"A Ducati."

"A motorcycle?"

"Yes."

"So you can weave in and out of traffic but you left forty minutes early for your date on a route that should have only taken you what . . . twenty minutes, less even?"

"I picked up flowers."

"Where?"

After Rick told them, they both grew silent.

He knew what was coming, even before the next words were uttered.

Perozo pulled a chair from the table, turned it around, and straddled it. "So you leave your house at six twenty. It's possible with a Ducati to make some good time and arrive close to Beverly Hills, or say Westwood by six thirty."

Rick's fist clutched in his lap. He hadn't mapped out his own timeline and realized now how bad it might look. "Looking in the wrong direction will only delay you finding the right man."

"You said yourself we wouldn't be doing our job if we didn't look at every possibility."

They asked questions for the next half hour, which Rick answered, but with as minimal information as he could offer.

With the police station behind him, his firearm secured to his side where it belonged, Rick dialed Neil's number.

"I need you to pull up all the surveillance tapes of the Tarzana house and Michael's on the night of the attack."

"Wanna tell me why?"

Rick straddled his bike and kicked the stand up. "Because I just became their number-one suspect. I'll meet you at your place in fifteen."

An hour later Rick would have been pulling his hair out if it wasn't already military short.

Neil sat quietly and studied the tapes. "There's no way they can pin this on you." He backed up the Tarzana feed, watched as Rick walked through the house and set the alarm. The next time they witnessed Rick was driving into the Beverly Hills estate. He removed a single rose from the back pocket of the bike. It was banged up from the drive, but it was there. The time stamp said 6:52.

"We're looking at this knowing I didn't do it. They are looking at this thinking I did. I leave my home at six twenty, haul ass to Westwood, manage to ditch the bike somewhere nearby and wait for Judy to leave her work."

Neil stopped him. "How do you know she's at work? Did you call her?"

He grew hopeful, then the hope faded. "I tapped her car."

"You did?"

"Shortly after she moved in. She thought the security was a joke."

Neil kept staring at him.

"You telling me Gwen's car isn't tapped?"

Neil broke off eye contact.

"Exactly." He went on. "So I know she's at work. A court order will find the tap, and removing it now or denying it makes me look guilty."

"And you know about cameras in parking lots. Have you been to her work?"

"I drove by it once before she moved here. Never went in and didn't go in the garage."

"But a lawyer will twist that."

Lawyers sucked that way. "They'll assume I know the garage, know her routine."

"Her routine changed that night. She stayed late, got caught up talking to her boss. How would you know that?"

True. "I wouldn't. I left my home to get to hers for date night." For the first time since he left the station he started to breathe again.

"We do specialize in surveillance. Military background . . . they'll assume and look for some way that you'd know she was still in the office or see what she was doing."

"They won't find anything."

"But they'll look."

"OK. What's my motive? I like this girl. She finally agreed to go on a date with me. Why would I attack her twenty minutes before?"

Neil shrugged. "You're upset she wasn't preening for you? Upset she didn't take the date serious enough to get home early? Your manhood wasn't strong enough to endure all the rejection and you're twisted up now that you are going on a date."

Rick rolled his eyes. "Lame."

"Each potential motive will have to be proven wrong. And that will keep them from arresting you."

He ran a hand down his face as if wiping it would erase all this bullshit.

"They will also conclude that because of the nature of your current employment and your taping of Judy's initial questioning, and our involvement from the beginning, that you're making sure you cover your tracks."

"Jesus, Mac, you're not helping."

"Oh, am I supposed to be helping, Smiley? I thought I was supposed to think logically. You want sugarcoating, go to the candy store." The use of their old names back in active service sobered him.

"All that aside, driving to Westwood in ten minutes on the 405, even with a motorcycle, would take quite a daredevil act. The route through Beverly Hills isn't exactly a swift entrance and exit."

"I bought the flowers."

"Most flower shops aren't magnets for crime. Chances are there won't be any cameras and even if there are, the likelihood any footage was kept would be slim after a week. Best we can hope is for an eyewitness that can ID you."

"That can ID me and give a time I was in the shop."

"Exactly."

No matter what angle he looked at, he didn't look good.

"We're doing exactly what the cops are doing. We're focused on me and not on who did this."

Neil nodded. "If we don't focus on you, clear your involvement, they will never look for anyone else."

Chapter Fifteen

Rick and Neil arrived at Zach's house together, both wore stoic masks, and neither of them volunteered anything before Rick whisked her out the door.

The offshore winds kept Judy's hair blowing in every direction. The way Rick kept glancing at her as they separated from everyone in Zach's house made her nervous.

"How's your day been?" he asked, which he'd already managed to ask when he walked in the house.

When she didn't answer, he finally met her eyes.

"You've already asked that. Something's happened."

They reached the bench overlooking the sea and he encouraged her to sit. Sitting before talking was never a good sign.

"Did you find out something about him?"

He shook his head with a heavy sigh. "No."

It wasn't often Rick didn't have a smile close to the surface.

She reached for his hand, and for the first time since the attack tried to cheer someone else up. "How bad can it possibly be?"

His beautiful green eyes kept hold of hers. "The police questioned me today."

It took a moment to process his words. "You?"

"Normal procedure, actually. They should have brought me in before now."

"Why you? I don't understand."

He squeezed her hand in his. "It's normal to obtain alibis from husbands, boyfriends, guys that you're dating."

She'd seen enough crime fiction television to understand that.

"And since you didn't see this guy, they need to check the whereabouts of all the men in your life."

Judy didn't like it, but she understood it. "I get it, I guess. I don't have many men in my life so the list isn't that long." Rick still wasn't smiling. Being questioned really bothered him. "If you knew they were going to question you, why are you so upset?"

His gaze moved to the waves below them. "The night of the attack I left my place to pick you up at six twenty, picked up flowers on the way, and pulled into your drive at ten to the hour."

Judy swiped at her hair blowing in the wind. "Outside of the part where I never got the flowers, I don't see the problem."

He didn't even laugh at the flower joke. "I drove my motorcycle. The police believe I could have made it to your office in ten minutes, give or take . . . then back to your brother's house . . . after."

She blinked, too stunned to speak.

"Neil and I are positive they are working hard right now to prove I could have attacked you."

"That's absurd." Rick, *her Rick*, who had been her protector from the moment she arrived in LA, was not the villain here. "They're wasting their time."

"I know that. You know that. But they don't."

Judy released his hand and jumped to her feet. "Well I'll tell them."

She turned toward the house, determined to get one of the detectives on the phone. Rick reached out and held her arm. "Tell them what, Judy?"

"That it wasn't you." She didn't even try to tame her hair. It blew in the wind like her temper.

He stood at her side and placed both hands on her shoulders, trying to calm her.

"They won't listen to you."

"I'll make them listen. I was the only one there. I know it wasn't you. If they focus on you they won't look for the real asshole who did this." Frustration made her tremble. That and anger toward the police, who were supposed to be smart enough not to go after the wrong guy. Rick was the wrong guy.

Rick lifted his chin in challenge. "Tell me how well you know Rick."

"What?"

"I'm the detective. Tell me how well you know Rick."

Oh, she got it now. He wanted to role play. Fine! She could do that. "I met Rick last year when he helped a poor, innocent girl escape her abusive parents."

"You've been dating Rick since last year?" His questions came fast.

"No. I finished college and we met up when I moved here."

"He works for your brother?"

"Yes. As a security specialist and sometimes bodyguard." She puffed out her chest, happy she knew all the answers to these questions and none of them made Rick look bad.

"How long have you been dating?"

She knew he was trying to corner her with that question. Instead of being vague, she took the opportunity to derail him a little. "We've been flirting around dating more than dating. Our first technical date was set for the night of the attack."

"Why didn't you date earlier?"

She narrowed her eyes. "Trying to pry answers from my lips, Rick?"

"As much as I want the answer to that question for my own reasons, I know the detectives are going to ask. You don't have to answer me."

Judy's chin pushed out to meet his attitude. She didn't have anything to hide, and in light of everything they'd been going through, playing a game wasn't necessary. "Well, *Detective*, if you really need to know . . . I grew up in a small town where it seemed every girl there went to college, met a guy, and then never did another thing in her life other than have babies and go to PTA meetings. I want more in my life, so I picked plan B. I fell in love with design on my first trip to LA during one of my brother's premiers. I want a career. Something that will define me more than a married last name."

Her confession sank in slowly. She saw it meet Rick's brain and shake hands.

"Rick triggers something inside me that makes me feel like he'd derail my plan." Her confession continued to roll. "Agreeing to a date felt like putting the pieces into place to make plan A move forward without permission." Maybe her brush with death the week before gave her confidence, or maybe she realized, after said brush, how important it was to have someone in her life to share the good *and* the bad.

They stood in silence for a few seconds. Any questions Rick may have had were certainly flowing out to sea now. The wind whipped her hair around her face but she just met his green-eyed gaze and set her jaw.

One of his hands traveled up her arm and cupped her face. He stepped into her personal space and took ownership of her lips. The kiss was desperate and so damn raw, tears ran down her cheek when she closed her eyes and sucked in the essence of the man delivering it.

She might as well sign up for PTA president now. Maybe she could design a carnival booth for the elementary school fundraiser.

He kept kissing her, chaste kisses that tingled everywhere but she knew weren't meant for complete surrender.

When Rick finally let her go, he ran a gentle finger under the bruised eye. His eyes weren't completely dry and that warmed her more than any kiss could.

He leaned his forehead against hers and closed his eyes. The pain in his face ran over her when he started in again. "Did Rick know any of this before the attack?"

"No."

They stood at the edge of the sea cliff, holding each other and continuing with the ridiculous questions. Each time Rick spoke his voice was more detached. Less him. "So he might have thought you were just leading him on?"

"Is that what you think?"

He shook his head. "It's what they'll think."

"If I was leading him on I wouldn't have agreed to a date."

"Maybe Rick doesn't know this . . . maybe Rick is a sociopathic womanizer that doesn't like the word *no*. Maybe he has relationship issues of his own and he's scared of dating you . . . of rejection."

"That's so stupid. I don't know a more confident man than you. You can bottle it up and sell it and make a fortune."

Rick smiled for the first time in their conversation. "Thanks for the confidence, Utah. But the detectives are going to come up with their own answers to these questions and work them into their theories."

She didn't like the thought of this . . . any of this.

"I know where you live, what you drive. I had the ability to know you were still at work and if I drove like a man on a death wish I could have made it to your work in the time that you were being attacked."

The tips of her fingernails dug into his thick arms with every word. Deep inside she knew he wasn't capable of hurting her. How could anyone think differently?

She started to speak and he covered her lips with a finger.

"I could have made it in and out and been in Beverly Hills for the cameras that I know are there."

"They can't do this."

"They can. And unless we find another direction for them to look, they will."

Judy wrapped her arms around him, absorbed his heat, his strength. Why had she pulled away from this man . . . ever?

They walked back to the house, his arms sat on her shoulders as he attempted to shelter her from the strong winds blowing off the ocean.

So many emotions swam inside Rick on that short walk he felt like a pot of stew filled with tons of beef and the perfect amount of vegetables to add color and spice to the blend. He knew that with time what he and Judy had going could be the most amazing thing they'd ever tasted . . . ever experienced.

She hadn't wanted to date him, not because of anything he did . . . but because of her fear of losing herself in the process. Did she not know that her drive, her spunk was what drew him to her in the first place?

Rick stopped her two feet before the front door and stepped in front of her. Words tumbled out of his mouth as if they'd just finished the conversation in his thoughts. "I'd never keep you from your dreams, Judy."

There was no hesitation in her response. "A week ago someone tried to steal my entire life. Dating you isn't nearly as scary. We'll get through this."

He reached over and pulled her against him as they walked in the house. "We have to try a real date. So far our track record sucks."

Laughter met his ears when he opened the doors.

Worried gazes met them when they walked in the living room.

Neil looked at him while everyone else stared at Judy.

Neither Rick nor Neil had wanted anyone in the family, mainly Judy, to learn about the detectives' conclusions before the two of them expressed them. Rick had the easy part. He spoke to Judy . . . Neil had to take on the entire family.

"You OK?" Meg asked first . . . the question directed at Judy.

Judy tilted her chin higher. "I'm fine. Ready to go home." She looked at her parents. "To the home I made here in California, and get on with my life."

Sawyer took a step forward. Janice caught his arm. It had to be hard for a father to let his child make her own decisions.

Rick stood back and let this play out.

"Dad . . . Mom . . . I love you. I know you want me safe but so does everyone here. Moving back to Utah means this guy won. Yeah, he didn't kill me, but he would have killed my dreams, my life. I can't give him that power. I belong here and I'm not going to let this stop me."

Rick squeezed her shoulder in silent support.

Janice stepped forward and hugged her daughter. "You always have a place with us."

"I know that, Mom."

Sawyer made eye contact with Rick. "You need to keep my girl safe."

Rick drew in a breath, pushed out his chest. "I will."

While Judy said good-bye to her family, Rick shook Neil's hand and pulled Zach aside. "We're ready for round-the-clock supervision," Neil told Zach. "In light of the new situation we'll have more patrols at the house even if Rick is there."

"Nobody thinks you did this." Zach's confidence made him stand taller.

"The surveillance isn't to clear my name, but to watch for whoever might think no one's eyes are out there. In order to catch this scumbag, you need to think like him. If he thinks all the protection is on the inside, he might roam the outside."

Zach forced air from pursed lips. "See . . . this is why I like construction and not all this conspiracy shit. My mind doesn't even go there."

"By-product of the military, I'm afraid," Neil said.

Rick extended his hand, shook Zach's. "I'll keep her safe for as long as I can."

Zach stopped shaking his hand, his grin faded.

"The police will pick me up. It's only a matter of time."

"You're serious."

"Even if it's for a long interrogation. I'll be picked up unless this guy strikes again in a short amount of time."

Zach closed his eyes and shook his head. "I never understood *innocent until proven guilty* until last year with Karen. Seemed every report on the news gave a clear explanation of a crime and the guilty party was a given. Only it's not that way and the guilty are free to do whatever the hell they want."

"If and when I'm taken in, Judy will be the weakest. She'll need everyone. This guy preys on weakness or he wouldn't have attacked her when he did. He didn't kill her because the chase, the thrill . . ." Rick swallowed the nausea building in his throat. "The thrill of hurting her gave him more pleasure and he'll want to do it again."

Neil patted Rick on the back. "The problem is this guy might hit her one too many times and end his pleasure."

Zach grew white. "Maybe we should keep her under house arrest."

"Is your sister going to go for that?"

Zach glanced across the room. All of them followed his eyes only to see Judy lift her gaze to them with a shrug.

"No. Judy won't let this guy have that kind of power."

Chapter Sixteen

The building might have been in the exact same place and hadn't been modified by paint or construction in the short amount of time she'd been away. But it *was* different.

Judy stared out the window of the passenger side of her car.

Rick pulled the car up to the curb and cut the engine.

"We'll take this one step at a time."

Her answer was a nod.

"Today is walking through the door, getting through the stares and questions. I'll be on your floor before five to take you home."

"I can meet you down here."

"Humor me."

Fine. Humoring Rick until she found her sea legs again was OK by her.

"Let's do this," she said as she pushed from the car with her purse in her hand.

He walked around the front of the car and placed a hand on the small of her back. "Ready?"

She'd brushed her hair around the section that was removed to stitch her up and knew that scar was hidden. Long sleeves were useful to hide her arm and the carving the butcher left with her. A little foundation, a lot of concealer, and it didn't look as if she'd had too many nights without sleep.

They walked together inside the building. Already the air conditioning was working overtime to keep the heat outside.

The lobby consisted of a security desk with a guard that stood behind it watching everyone as they walked in. He'd offer a good morning and addressed many people by name. There wasn't a checkpoint that only employees of the building could walk past, and she and Rick sailed by the security guard without any words.

She didn't notice the stares until they stood by the elevators waiting for the lift.

"Is that her?" someone whispered behind them.

Rick must have heard the question, too. His hand kneaded her lower back and he inched closer.

Inside the elevator was worse. Besides her and Rick there were seven more people crammed in. All except one person kept glancing her way.

The slow, steady climb, with several stops along the way, took way too long.

Rick led her from the elevator and onto the floor that belonged to Benson & Miller Designs.

Nancy popped her head up from the reception desk and opened her mouth like a guppy. She swiped the headset from her head and walked around the desk. "Oh my God . . ."

Rick stood back as the woman wrapped her arms around Judy as if they were the best of friends.

"We heard . . . we all heard." Nancy stood back. "Are you all right?"

"I'm better now, thanks."

"My ex loved using his fists. I know it's not the same, but if you ever need to talk."

"Thanks, Nancy."

Nancy slid her eyes to Rick for the first time. "Wow . . . boyfriend or bodyguard?"

He glanced at Judy and started to answer.

"A little of both," she answered for him.

Those dimples made an appearance and he winked.

"Do you have a brother?" Nancy asked.

Judy felt laughter in her gut.

"Just me," Rick answered.

Nancy fanned herself and turned her back so only Judy could see her face. *He's hot*, she mouthed.

Judy walked into her office, giggling.

Her cubicle hadn't changed much in her absence. It was tidier than she left it and in the corner sat the tube holding the plans she'd been taking home the night of the attack. Her gaze caught the tube and held.

"This is your desk?" Rick asked.

"Yeah."

The tube hit the ground first. Over her staccato breaths, she heard it rolling away.

"Babe?"

Shut up, bitch.

"Judy?"

His breath was on her ear, blowing against her hair. "You're not so tough now, are you?"

She squeezed her eyes shut and when she opened them, Rick was there, leaning over to force her to see him.

"You back?" he asked.

She nodded. "I remembered something."

"What?"

"He said, *You're not so tough now, are you?* I remember being confused. His words didn't match what he was doing."

"*You're not so tough?* Are you sure that's what he said?"

"Positive."

"Do you remember anything else?"

Something else was there, tickling her head and scratching at her memory. Then it was gone.

"That's it."

Mr. Archer walked by her cubicle and stopped. "Judy?"

It was strange hearing her real name from the man's lips. "Mr. Archer. Hi."

"It's good to see you back."

"Thanks."

The man actually smiled. "If you need anything . . . or need to leave, just let someone know."

"That's generous of you, Mr. Archer, but I'll be OK."

Mr. Archer looked at Rick then back to her. "Well, if it changes. I know José is backing up so you can pick up with him. We have someone new in the mail room, so don't bother there."

"Sounds good."

Rick stood and offered a hand. "Rick Evans."

"Oh, sorry."

"Steve Archer." They shook hands.

"Mind if I took a look around, Steve?"

"Not at all. The police already did. I don't think they found anything in here."

Rick leaned back on his heels. "I won't take long."

Mr. Archer walked away, leaving the two of them alone.

"You won't blend walking around the office."

"I don't want to blend. I want everyone in this place to know my face." He leaned forward and brushed his lips to hers. "I want everyone to know I'm your boyfriend." He kissed her again. "I want them to know they will be messing with me if they mess with you."

She stopped his next kiss. "Territorial much?"

"Very."

He kissed her again and someone cleared their throat.

Judy jumped back.

Debra Miller stood by the cubicle wall. "Is this a kissing booth and where do I buy tickets?"

"Ms. Miller." Judy felt her cheeks warm as Ms. Miller's smile grew wider.

"So good to see you back, Judy."

"Thanks." Judy glanced at Rick, who leaned against her desk as if he belonged there. "And sorry. Rick just wanted to make sure I made it here safely."

"That's understandable."

Judy made introductions.

"So a bodyguard and a boyfriend? Isn't that a conflict of interest?"

"Not to us."

Ms. Miller didn't question further. "Security has been escorting all the women to and from the garage during off hours and most of us leave in groups. We've all been on edge."

Judy hadn't thought of that. She wanted to tell her boss that the attack felt personal, that she didn't think anyone else needed to worry. Instead, she kept that to herself in case she was wrong. She'd hate to have something happen to someone and be the reason they weren't watching their backs.

"Rick wants to look around the office. We cleared it with Mr. Archer, but are you OK with that?"

"Be my guest. Why don't you show him around?"

"A quick tour, and I'll get to work."

"Great. I'm looking forward to that project we talked about."

When Ms. Miller walked away, Judy felt much better about being back.

———

Meg glanced up from the computer screen and pushed away from the desk. "I think a temporary move of the business is necessary," she told her boss, who directed her son to the backyard and balanced her not-quite-two-year-old daughter, Delanie, on her hip.

Samantha shifted Delanie to her other hip. "I was hoping you wouldn't say that."

She clicked a few links and brought up the database. "If Rick and Neil are right, and the police manage a search warrant, all this information would make it into their hands." It wasn't that Alliance itself had anything to hide. The clients that used Alliance, on the other hand, had plenty to worry about going public. "The move will be temporary. Once Rick clears his name in this we can move everything back."

"You're right. I know you're right but it feels crazy to have Alliance anywhere but here. We've considered an office location more than once but it didn't feel safe."

"So skip a storefront. The phones all forward to the mobile. Keep the number here. Since I'm your main girl on the computer, I'll take this baby home and set up an office. It will be better for all of us for a while."

Delanie rejected her mother's arms and Samantha placed her on the floor and shadowed her while they talked.

"The more people coming in and out of Michael's home right now the better. The security is stepped up there." Meg continued to plead her case.

"Fine. I can't say I'm in love with the idea, but I know you're right."

Eddie ran in from the backyard, a handful of flowers with plenty of dirt-covered roots dangling from his fingertips. "Look what I found for you."

Meg laughed at the trail of dirt the boy brought into the house.

Samantha knelt down, scooped her flowers into her hands, and hugged her son. "Thank you so much. They're lovely."

"Daddy says boys give girls flowers."

"They do."

Eddie's big eyes took in Meg's presence and he turned around and ran back outside.

Samantha put into motion a team of movers to come to the house and, with Meg's direction, remove the files and everything Alliance, and move it to Beverly Hills.

With a handful of dirt-filled flowers, Meg waved good-bye to her boss and waited for the additional help.

It was after noon when Rick made his way into the house. He stopped at the office door and frowned. "What's going on?"

Meg continued to pack a box and seal it with packing tape. "What are the chances of this place being searched?"

Rick dropped his keys and cell on the top of the desk with a sigh and helped her pack.

———

"Hey, babe?" Rick said when Judy walked into the foyer of her work at the end of the day. In his hand were three pink roses.

"You didn't have to." But she had to admit she was happy he did.

"I told you I was picking you up."

She sniffed the flowers and smiled. "The flowers, you didn't have to."

"Doesn't that make them more special?" He handed them to her and removed the tube from her hand.

"Thanks."

He turned to Nancy, who was packing up her things. "Are you walking out?" he asked.

"I-I'm in the garage. Just waiting on the group I walk out with."

The office buzzed about the attack in hushed tones all day. Judy knew her presence would get people talking, but for the most part, no one treated her differently.

Like when he'd dropped her off, he parked in front of the building in what was usually reserved for loading and unloading. The security guard outside the building waved and smiled at Rick as he walked by.

"I take it you made some new friends."

He opened her door and tucked the tube in the backseat. "I'd rather not be responsible for your car getting towed."

Rick pulled into the mass exodus of traffic and drove in the opposite direction of home.

"How was your day?"

He looked over the rim of his sunglasses. "I'm much more interested in yours."

She reflected on it as she watched the cars around them. "Good. It was nice to get back to work, do stupid meaningless crap most of the day that kept my mind away from . . . well, away."

"You went to lunch with someone from the office like I suggested?"

"Nancy. She wanted to know all about you."

He lent a smile but didn't comment.

"Where are we going?"

He inched through the street traffic at a crawl. "It's not the Getty. Just a dinner date to celebrate you getting back to work."

"You used to ask and now you're just going for it, eh?"

She really did love his smile. "Yep, that's about it."

Cozy and tucked back from the main road, Carino's tempted her taste buds the moment she stepped from the car. "I love Italian."

"Much as I want you to think I'm a genius, I asked Meg. She said you and pasta were like this." He lifted his hand and crossed two fingers.

They walked hand in hand into the restaurant, where the aroma seeped into her pores.

The hostess seated them immediately when Rick told her his name. There was already wine at the table. "Wow. Impressive."

"That's me, Mr. Impressive."

While she settled behind the table, Rick poured the wine and lifted his glass. "To saying good-bye to the word *babe*."

Judy held her glass but didn't clink his. "To first dates."

She wasn't a huge wine drinker, but the red was light enough to tempt her into another taste shortly after the first. "I don't know what impressed me more, the fact that you asked Meg what I liked, or that you confessed asking her for the information."

"It's useful having your girlfriend's roommate working within shouting distance. It will be strange without her there."

Judy opened the menu. "Where is she going?"

"She and Samantha moved the office today."

"Why?"

The waiter arrived to tell them the specials before disappearing. Rick's lack of answering the question made her think he'd forgotten it. "Why did they move?"

He took a sip and looked inside the glass. "This isn't half bad."

Now she knew he was avoiding. "Rick!"

He toyed with his glass. "The nature of Alliance is all about privacy. They're a little concerned about the police searching the house."

Oh . . . oh. "You're really worried they'll try and pin this on you."

"I'm not worried. Not about me."

That made one of them.

He reached for her hand and squeezed it. "Let's talk about something pleasant. Something we can actually control."

"There has to be a way we can control this."

"If you figure it out, you need to let me know. Now, tell me about the project you brought home with you."

Thankful for the distraction, she launched into her design ideas and really loved how Rick listened and asked questions. "I know Ms. Miller won't pick my design, but to think something grabbed her attention enough to ask me to work on it is huge."

"Don't doubt yourself, Utah. Zach and Michael have both told me how talented you are. Who knows where this will take you."

She pushed her plate aside, surprised at how much she'd managed to eat. Rick eyed her leftovers and she pushed the plate closer to him. That man really packed it away and yet didn't have an ounce of fat on him. "Where do you put it?"

He lifted an eyebrow. "It's the workout."

She knew he must dedicate some serious hours to keeping himself in shape, but she'd not seen him actually do anything but drive her around and come to her rescue. "What's your routine?"

"My workout?"

The wine gave her a nice little buzz, which beat the headache that seemed to plague her daily since the attack. "Yeah."

"A little cardio, a little weights, a lot of laps through the boot camp track at the park."

"Boot camp track? What's that?"

"I'm sure it's not called that. There's a hill course by the house with stops every quarter mile with different activities. Pull-ups, push-ups, stuff like that."

Her gaze ran down his thick shoulders and a nice hum of appreciation of how he filled out his shirt spread heat throughout her body. Peeking out of one of his sleeves looked like a graphic inked into his skin. Unable to stop herself, she reached over and lifted his short sleeve to see a tattoo wrapped around his biceps. "From your military days?"

He glanced at his arm. "This one is."

"You have more than one?" She never wanted a tattoo of her own but was always intrigued about the draw for those who had them.

"A couple."

The desire to lift his shirt to see them herself was strong. "Not going to tell me where and what?"

He shoveled more food in, swallowed. "If you want to see me naked, Utah, all you have to do is ask."

She gave his shoulder a playful slap.

"I'm serious," he told her.

"I'm sure you are." Behind his laughing eyes was a thin layer of heat that if blown on, would probably blossom into a ball of fire. "Can I join you on your workout? Meg and I used to do an organized workout in Seattle that was called Boot Camp. There are programs here, but they're so expensive."

"Are you up to working out again?" His gaze softened.

Her bruises were gone, all the soreness of the attack nothing more than a nightmare. "I'm ready."

"You can join me on one condition."

"Oh, I'm given conditions now am I? OK, Mr. Negotiator . . . what's my condition?"

"You bring Meg and let me teach you both some self-defensive moves."

His request took her back a notch and removed some of her smile.

"I want you safe and I can't be at your side every second of every day." It was more than that. He was worried about when and if the police were going to pin the crimes of another man on him. Yeah, Judy had met Russell and Dennis, both "colleagues" and both watching her anytime Rick wasn't. But Rick was invested.

"I think that's a great idea."

"I work out early."

She narrowed her gaze. "Trying to talk me out of it?"

"I'm like a drill sergeant."

"Hello, Mr. Marine . . . I'd expect nothing less. If I get to call *you* my boyfriend, I can't go getting all soft."

His dimples put fire in her belly.

Suddenly the restaurant was entirely too busy and home felt too far away.

Chapter Seventeen

The conversation back to Beverly Hills was as platonic as it came, though Rick had a hard time concentrating on anything other than the image of Judy in skintight workout shorts and a skimpy shirt. The date had been everything he wanted. Easy conversation, no secrets, heat, and promise. It killed him not knowing when the world was going to crash down. Killed him not to know how much time they'd have before the detectives either took him away or placed doubt into Judy's mind.

There didn't seem to be any doubt now. Not in the tiny glances she offered when she didn't think he watched her. Not in the way she fanned her skin in a car that was cooled to sixty-seven degrees. Not in the disappointed sigh when she mentioned Meg being home.

A gentleman would thank her with a kiss for the perfect date and promise to call.

Only Rick never thought he was soft enough to be labeled a gentleman. He carried her design plans into the house and set the alarm behind them.

"How was the pasta?"

"I'm stuffed," Judy told her friend while Meg turned down the volume on the TV.

"What? No leftovers? You must have been hungry."

Judy nodded his way. "Leftovers aren't possible with this one."

Meg laughed. "That doesn't surprise me."

The girls chatted briefly about her first day back and Rick took the opportunity to do a sweep of the house.

With everything clear, he glanced at the clock on Michael's side of the house. In two hours, Dennis would begin his shift of watching the house. Even if Rick stayed on the inside, the new rules were clear. If Rick left the house at nine, the night patrol would come inside the gates and keep watch from the inside. If Rick stayed . . . which he sincerely hoped he would, even if it was across the hall, then the night team would watch from afar. At least for now.

He clicked off the light and moved into the main living area of the huge home. With Rick's presence, Meg abruptly ended her conversation with Judy and jumped from the couch. "Wow . . . would you look at the time."

Judy growled at her friend and Rick hid a smile. It was early . . . really early.

"I'm in the middle of a good book?"

"Meg!"

"Whatever! You two kids have fun." She grabbed not one, but two beers from the refrigerator, and moved down the hall to her bedroom. Just when it appeared Judy was about to regain her composure, Meg yelled, "The walls in this house are really thick."

"Margaret Catherine!"

Meg laughed until Rick heard a door shut.

"Margaret Catherine? Really?"

Judy hid her face behind her hand, her pink cheeks a testimony to her embarrassment. "Sorry about that."

"The only roommates I ever had were in the Marines. I think Meg would make a good Marine."

"Fit right in, would she?"

"Probably." Rick removed the space between them and ran the backs of his fingers across her cheek. "Did you ask her to leave?"

She studied the buttons on his shirt. "I-I . . . yes."

He didn't even try to hide his grin. "It's the ink, isn't it?"

"You've figured me out," she said with a giggle.

He cupped the back of her head, careful with the tender parts left over from the abuse she'd gone through. When she met his eyes, his smiled slipped into something more serious. "Not worried about plan A any longer?"

The gold flecks in her brown eyes seemed to glow in the dim light of the room. "Most guys would freak if a woman they hadn't even started dating told them what I told you. But you're still here."

"Well, we're *now* officially dating, and plan A doesn't scare me at all." He wasn't even sure why.

"Would you tell me if it did?"

"I see no reason we can't be completely honest with each other, do you?"

She placed her hand on his chest and lifted her lips closer to his. "Honesty is a good thing."

He molded his body to hers and offered a grin. "What do you want to do with the rest of the evening, Judy?"

She sucked in a deep breath, for courage, or maybe she was finding the oxygen in the air thinner than normal like it was for him. "I want to see you . . . all of you," she said.

He hardened with her words and tightened his grip on her neck. "You sure?" he whispered.

Her answer was a timid kiss and Rick responded with a hunger he didn't recognize. Her lips passed over his like a feather of an angel tempting everything inside of him, and he threatened to engulf her like a devil staking his claim.

He cautioned himself and eased his grip but held her closer. Her tongue matched his, searching and tasting. A hint of the wine they drank flavored her scent.

Judy lifted her knee and slipped off her shoes. He had a good foot on her and had to lean over to keep their lips together. Rick's palm met the small of her back and moved lower.

Her moan of approval shot through him, threatening his ability to go slow.

He lifted her hips and her legs wound around him. The maze of shoes and living room furniture didn't deter him as he carried her down the hall to her bedroom. The low pounding of the bass from Meg's TV met his ears. Once closed in the room, that bass reduced to a soft drum. *Thick walls.*

He kicked the door closed behind them and crossed to the massive bed in the middle of the room. Without effort, he pushed Judy into the soft mattress and almost lost it when she lifted her hips to touch more of him. She squeezed his ass and tugged at his shirt, all the while attempting to suffocate him with her lips.

Their kiss broke, both of them gasping.

Plump with his kiss, her lips were as round as her eyes when she spoke. "I don't see that ink yet, babe."

She could call him *babe* forever and it wouldn't grow old. He swiped his shirt from his shoulders and tossed it off the bed.

Judy sat up, ran her fingers over the symbol on his right shoulder, and placed her lips in their wake. "You're so thick," she told him.

He took advantage of her sitting up to pull her shirt over her head. Her pale breasts peeked from under a light gray bra and it was his turn to kiss what he wanted to taste. His tongue dipped under her bra. "You're perfect."

Tiny rosebud nipples met his tongue when he made her bra follow her shirt. "I could play with these all night."

She giggled. "The rest of me would be jealous."

"We could try . . . an evening of tasting," he muttered as he used his teeth on her nipple and felt her nails dig into his back.

"Or not."

She raked her nails down over his ass and he pushed closer to her.

"Or not," he repeated her words. He'd never make a whole night of foreplay, not with Judy.

Rick pulled her hips farther up on the bed and centered them both. He memorized her curves with his slow fingers as they traced the lines of her exposed skin. "You were sitting in that police station," he said, reminding her of the first day they'd met. "So out of place and trying hard not to look at me." He leaned over her, kissed a trail between her breasts.

"You just stared at me. So bold."

He lifted her as if she weighed nothing and rolled her over onto her stomach.

"I wanted you then."

The zipper on her skirt started from her spine and went down the cheeks of her firm butt. He inched it down, placed his lips on the swell of her hips. The rail-thin frames of many of the women out there did nothing for him. Her full curves made his mouth water. Judy unwound something inside him he didn't even recognize.

Her skirt met her shirt and Rick took his time rolling his hands down her hips, over her small panties, and down her creamy thighs. As much as Rick wanted to take advantage of this position, he didn't want to risk scaring her. He rolled her on her side and stretched out beside her. There wasn't any hesitation when her leg lifted to wrap around his hip. "You were cocky and bold and hot. Seeing you again at graduation . . . I knew we'd end up here."

He kissed her again, broke when she reached for the zipper to his pants. "This is a great place."

Judy didn't leave his boxers with him. "Steroid-free zone!" she said, tracing his hip and touching. Her touch wasn't timid or chaste, it was bold, leaving him pushing into her. He reached for her then, slid his hands under her panties and spread her open. The desire to rip her clothing, rid her of any barrier, needed to be tamed. She kicked them free and came back for a kiss. Both of them free of any clothing, she moved her kiss to the ink on his chest, her tongue lapping the edges, branding the feel of her deep inside him.

He knew, somehow, she'd be just like this, fire and passion without any worries of the world around them.

Judy rolled on top of him, barely giving him time to reach for his wallet.

"Wait," he told her, pulled his pants from the floor and removed a condom from his wallet. He fumbled with the plastic, twice, and she removed it from his fingers with a laugh.

"Out of practice, hon?"

He stopped her pursuit in opening the small package with his hand covering hers. She met his gaze and looked deeper. "I met you," he told her. "There's been no one since."

She blinked several times, took in the information, and kissed him. "Oh, Rick. I never stopped thinking about you. I couldn't date, couldn't sleep."

Narcissistic as it was, he loved the sound of that.

Together they slid the condom over him, her hands slid lower, cupping him.

Once protected, she moved over him, took him. Her wet sheath was so tight and so needy she was milking him before he could catch his breath.

"Slow down, babe," he whispered.

"I can't. You feel so right."

He slowed her down by sheer force, though it wasn't easy.

He'd been with enough women to know her first orgasm was close. He kept his own wave back and let her take whatever she needed. He kissed her, held her, and welcomed her moan when she shattered on the inside. Only when she collapsed on him did he tuck her under him to show her his idea of making love.

He slowed down, found her spots, showed her his before backing up his cocky smile and leaving her limp. When his own release gripped him, he called her name and claimed her.

Judy was his.

Now.

Forever.

———

Rick's arms erased the pain of the world around her. Judy's body buzzed and her mind was numb with a post-orgasmic daze. With her head resting on his chest, she ran her hand over his pec, traced a thick vein that ran down the length of his arm. "I know it's completely shallow of me," she told him, "but you have the most amazing body."

His hand caressed her hip. "You're the one who's sexy hot."

She wasn't going to be one of those women who told her guy she should lose weight. Those words always seemed to need a follow-up of a man telling her how wrong she was. Truth was, she wasn't unhappy in her skin. Rick seemed to enjoy her . . . thoroughly.

The ink on his arm circled his biceps with decorative black and red Xs. "So what's the story behind this one?"

He lifted his arm, flexed his biceps. *Damn he's hot.* "Marines plus alcohol. Everyone on our team left with something."

"Do you miss the service?"

He sighed, the hum in his chest tickled her ear. "Sometimes. But I won't go back."

"Did it end badly?"

"It did." He leaned to his side and she saw a white scar across his flank. "Our last mission," he explained. "I was one of the lucky ones. Mac and I made it out alive."

"Mac?"

"Neil. We called him Mac."

"What did they call you?"

"Smiley."

She laughed, loved the feeling inside her. "I've heard Neil call you that. Fitting. It's easy to tell when you're serious. Those dimples go away."

"My grandmother still pinches my cheeks when she sees me."

"Gotta love family. My aunt Belle is convinced my sister Rena conceived her son before she was married. Never lets anyone forget about it."

"Was it a shotgun wedding?"

"I don't know gestational periods in humans to be eleven months. Not that it would matter. Rena and Joe are very happy." She lifted her head and kissed the tattoo on his shoulder. "What about this one?" On close inspection, it looked like a bleeding star. It was beautiful in a strange kind of way.

His silence made her look into his eyes. The lack of dimples made her pause.

"That one's for Roxy."

"A woman?" Now she was sorry she asked.

"My sister."

Oh. Judy wasn't expecting that. "I take it you're close."

"We were. She died when she was seventeen."

"Oh, Rick. I'm sorry I asked."

He kissed the top of her head and encouraged her to lie back on his chest by stroking her hair.

"It was a long time ago."

She was about to ask if he wanted to tell her about it when he started in with the story.

"Roxy had a big fight with her high school boyfriend and when he left all pissed off he took a curve too fast. Stupid kid. He didn't survive and Roxy blamed herself."

She closed her eyes with the image of a teenager dead, another one broken. "It wasn't her fault."

"Hard for a young kid to accept. She fell into a depression that left her hospitalized. I used to spend time just sitting with her, talking to her about life . . . anything to make her smile. I thought she was coming out of it toward the end of her junior year. We took dance lessons together and I took her to prom." He grew quiet again.

"What happened?"

He sucked in a deep breath.

"You don't have to tell me."

"It's OK. She a . . . she slit her wrists, and when that didn't seem to do anything she took a handful of sleeping pills in a bathtub."

"Oh, Rick . . . did you find her?"

He shook his head. "No. My mother has to live with that memory."

Judy looked at him now, saw the shadow of his sister's death in his eyes. "How awful."

"I joined the Marines the day after her funeral."

"It must have been hard on you . . . your parents."

"I worked my grief out in boot camp and spent every day try-ing to stay alive . . . make a difference. Now when I think of her I remember the good times, her laugh. This star reminds me to keep going . . . no matter how hard life might be."

She kissed the star again. "And you've been playing hero for the world ever since."

"Ah, Utah," he said, cupping her face and drawing her closer. "I don't mind playing hero for you. The world at large can go bite themselves." His kiss was tender, just like the way he made love.

She drew away and sucked in his beautiful eyes. "The world needs more heroes."

"The people close to the hero keep him fueled . . . that person for me is you."

Judy knew his words took a chunk of her heart and handed it to him with a big red bow. "I like being your fuel."

He tucked a strand of her hair behind her ear. "You're not scared anymore?"

Only two things scared her at this point . . . the threat of the police taking Rick away, and her attacker returning. "Not of you . . . not of this." She shifted a finger to both their chests.

He made love to her again, slowly, with soft words and occasional laughter. Dreams of laughter and lazy beach days helped her sleep the entire night.

———

"It's four thirty, woman! The day's half over."

A hand slapped her naked ass, crashing all her dreams. "What the?"

Rick climbed over her, fully clothed in shorts and a tight T-shirt, and kissed her briefly. "My workouts are early, babe. We gotta go, get sweaty, and get you back here showered and dressed before work."

Judy glared through slitted eyelids. "It's dark outside."

"It won't be when we start running. C'mon. I'll wake Meg."

"Wait! I didn't even tell her about the workout yet."

"Saw her last night in the kitchen when I went for water. Told her to be ready bright and early."

Judy nodded toward the dark window. "It's not so bright, buddy."

Rick pulled the warm blankets back, leaving her cold and bare to his stare.

She squealed.

He licked his lips. "Tempting . . . so tempting." He slapped her butt instead.

Right as the sun started to make an appearance Rick had her and Meg running up a long trail and back down as a warm-up. On the second lap they stopped at a station where Rick had them doing push-ups. Every time she dropped, he was there to push her to do five more. All the while, he'd switch between one-handed push-ups, or one-leg push-ups . . . anything to make it harder on himself. Meg cussed like a sailor halfway through the circuit and swore revenge. "I need coffee for this shit."

"Coffee is your reward, Margaret Catherine," Rick teased. "Now get your chin over that bar."

Meg glared at Judy. "You just had to tell him my full name, didn't you?"

Judy struggled to pull her body weight up with her arms and didn't have the energy to snark on her friend. Rick grasped her hips and helped her with her last three chin-ups. She dropped to the ground and struggled for a breath. "You're killing me."

Rick grabbed the bar sailed through twenty-five reps.

"Five more, Utah."

She managed three, and two with help.

"You just want to play with her ass," Meg teased while she controlled her breathing during her break.

"It's a nice ass," Rick said. He started running up the hill to the next station.

When they finished, they picked a patch of grass to stretch.

"Half an hour and I'm beat!" Meg fell on the grass, her arms stretched beside her.

"We'll start on the self-defense stuff tomorrow. Give your muscles a chance to wake up."

Judy leaned over her legs. "My muscles are awake and cursing you."

Rick winked.

"It feels good though," Meg said. "And so much cheaper than those classes we did in Seattle."

"Think of all the money we'll save feeling this beat-up."

They finished their stretches and made their way back to the car. A few more cars were parked close by than when they arrived. At the far end of the lot sat a car with a man wearing a suit leaning against the door with his arms crossed over his chest.

Judy peered closer. She elbowed Rick, who had opened the passenger door for her and Meg. "He looks familiar."

Rick followed her gaze. His smile fell. "Detective Raskin."

She paused. "Why is he here?"

The detective slid into the unmarked car, turned over the engine, and waited.

"Watching me."

She didn't like it, not one bit. "This isn't right."

"He's doing his job, Judy."

"No he's not. He's working to nail the wrong guy." She wanted to scream.

Rick ushered her into the car. They drove in silence until Meg interrupted their thoughts. "How about we work on some self-defense stuff in the evenings . . . starting tonight."

Rick glanced in the rearview mirror. "You think you'll both be up for that so soon?"

Judy watched her friend and knew she had more to say.

"I'm ready . . . what about you, Judy?"

The uncertainty of Rick's long-lasting freedom was the reason for the rush.

"I'll be ready," Judy said.

Rick picked up her hand, kissed the back of it.

Chapter Eighteen

"Russell couldn't find anyone at the flower shop who remembered you."

This was not the information Rick wanted Neil to tell him. "I'm assuming the police already have this information."

"We can assume. And the flower shop records over their surveillance footage every third day."

Rick slammed his hand on the desk in Neil's control room. "Damn it."

"They won't nail you for this," Neil assured him.

"The hassle of being arrested, the vulnerability of Judy when they do . . . the fact they aren't looking for this guy . . . that's what's pissing me off." Rick pointed toward the monitor outside his home several miles away. The camera in front of the house was pointed toward the street. Parked on the opposite side was a government-issue surveillance sedan about as inconspicuous as a heart attack. "Everywhere I look, I see these guys. I'm trying to teach Judy to trust her instincts when someone is watching her, only there's always eyes on her . . . or me if I'm with her."

Neil leaned back in his chair, rubbed the stubble on his chin. "How are things going with you two? Dennis says you've been staying over every night for the last week."

Rick smiled into the memory of her trying to distract him from their morning workout. A sexual bribe, but a bribe nonetheless. "I care for her, Neil. The thought of being locked up and not getting to her makes me ill."

"You won't be locked up for long. We have a lawyer on standby. If they pick you up, keep your mouth shut and call me."

Rick gave him a mock salute.

Neil clicked into the monitors and brought up the Beverly Hills home. "Tomorrow is three weeks."

"Yeah. Hard to believe it's only been that long."

"Our guy's been quiet."

Rick ran a hand through his short hair. "He was quiet before."

"But this was personal, and when it's personal the perp doesn't just disappear. I've been thinking about what you said she remembered. *Not so tough now.*"

"That's bugging me. If we were in Seattle, I'd want to know all the places she played pool, who she beat. She is tough with a pool cue."

"You two might want to visit the pool hall she and Meg visited when they first got here."

"Already ahead of you. I had Meg talk with their new friends to meet us there tomorrow night."

"Good. I've searched her social media history. She hasn't been on much since the incident, but before that she updated at least once a day."

"You mean Facebook?"

"Yeah." Neil pulled up her profile and scrolled down the page. Two of the articles about the attack were tagged and placed on her page by her friends. It looked like Meg had gone on her own profile to assure everyone she was recovering. "I'm going through her friends, seeing if anything rings an alarm. About half the people on this thing don't have their privacy setting set up, giving me access to just about everything. It's crazy how people think they're safe on this stuff."

"Find anything interesting?"

Neil scrolled down. A picture of Judy at her graduation and hugging Michael had dozens of comments.

"Most of it is meaningless to me. People asking questions, stuff about school . . . new friends following her from her work. I can't help but feel there's a clue in here somewhere."

"Any disgruntled pool players?"

"There's a couple of 'meet you at Bergie's tonight' comments. Nothing else. She has over two hundred friends on here. I wonder if she knows each one personally, or if some of them share a common interest that brought them together."

"I can ask her."

"Do that. See if we can access this complete account so we can do a little digging around." Neil turned off the monitor.

"It's been too quiet."

"Might have something to do with the tight security. Judy hasn't been alone since this happened."

"I'm not going to open her up just to attract this guy."

Neil looked wounded. "I wouldn't think so. But if he's in need of making a statement, he might go after someone close to her. Or figure a way to approach her at work."

"Meg has been on alert. She's a quick study with the self-defense moves. At work, Judy is always with someone." He looked at the time and cautioned himself for Judy's pickup time.

If something happened to Meg, Judy would be devastated. "We should have more eyes on Meg."

"We're stretched a little thin. Dennis has an old friend I'm checking out now to help us out," Neil said. "Good thing Michael is out of the country."

Rick couldn't imagine trying to watch the movie star and his sister. "Still think we need eyes on Judy's best friend."

Neil reached for the phone on his desk. "Dennis? Yeah . . . I need you at the Wolfe residence."

Rick nodded with agreement.

"No, Meg. Rick is on Judy."

The monitor on the Beverly Hills property switched automatically, tracing movement. "Gardeners come on Thursdays," Neil told him. "And yes, we've already screened them."

"I'm out of here. Gotta go pick up my girl."

"Be safe out there," Neil said.

Rick patted his sidearm. "I'm always safe."

———

Judy's palms were moist with anticipation. Today was the day . . . the day she walked back in that garage, got in a car just like every other employee, and drove home. Well, Rick would do the driving. The results would be the same.

"You ready for this?" Rick asked as they stood outside the elevator doors in the foyer of Benson & Miller.

"No. But I can't avoid this forever. The sooner I get it done, the better."

He held her hand and called the elevator. Inside were several people from the building, most of them chatting with each other and completely oblivious of her discomfort. Rick pressed P-3, the very level where the attack had taken place, and stood back.

They inched toward the garage and Judy forced slow, deep breaths into her lungs as if she were Meg and her lungs were closing in.

The doors to P-3 opened and Rick encouraged her first step out the double doors. The others in the elevator stepped around them when she and Rick didn't move fast enough for their taste. Judy noticed the nameless employees walking in separate directions from each other. "How soon everyone forgets."

Rick narrowed his brow.

Judy nodded toward the lone woman walking to her car.

"Human nature. People never think something will happen to them until it does. Truth is, you've walked into a parking garage all your life and never thought twice about it. Now you'll think about it every time."

Judy's gaze moved to find her car. The garage was still busy, even for a Friday night when many employees left early.

Rick directed her away from the elevator and kept a hand on the small of her back. With him at her side, the space didn't suffocate her . . . until she rounded the corner and her eyes drifted to the dark corner her attacker took advantage of.

"Oh, God."

"I'm right here. Deep breath."

She sucked in one and then another. "I'm OK."

The elevator far behind them dinged and the sound of voices traveled in their direction. Rick continued to walk toward her car. She avoided looking at the corner and hurried into the car.

Rick closed her door and walked around to the driver's seat. Once inside, she pressed the door lock, closing them inside.

Only when he pulled out of the parking lot did he ask how she was doing.

As the building slowly disappeared in the rearview mirror, her heartbeat slowed to normal. "It wasn't that bad."

"You're such a bad liar."

She wiped her palms on her skirt. "OK, it sucked."

"It sucked, but each time it will get better."

He leaned over and opened the glove compartment. Inside was what looked like a cell phone. On closer inspection, it looked like a child's toy meant to look like a cell phone.

"What's this?"

"It's a stun gun meant to look like a cell phone." They'd talked about carrying a stun gun when they practiced self-defense. "I have one for Meg, too."

She opened the box and removed the device.

"You put the strap on your wrist and hold it."

Judy placed the strap next to her bracelet and put her thumb over the button on the side.

"It makes a lot of—"

She pressed the button and the car filled with an electrical buzz that made her jump. From the fake cell phone, an arc of electricity moved between the two points at the top.

"Noise," Rick finished with a laugh. "You press that against an attacker and he'll be down. I guarantee it."

"What if he takes it and uses it against me?"

They stopped at a light and Rick grabbed the device from her hand. The wristband stayed on her arm. He pressed the button and nothing happened. "The current is cut off when that pin is disconnected."

The light turned green and she connected the device again and pressed the button. Sure enough, it worked perfectly. "Clever."

"And effective. Remember to place it on your wrist when you leave work, or are alone working out . . . anytime, really."

She tucked it in her purse and left it there. She wouldn't need it any time soon. Not with Rick at her side.

———

Lucas and Dan met the three of them at Penthouse Pool. "This place is a dive!"

"Completely," Meg said with a huge smile. "It's part of its charm."

Rick didn't see charm . . . he saw a dirty bar with equally sketchy patrons.

"Cheap beer," Lucas added.

"Cheap pool," Dan said.

"Cheap people who don't want to part with twenty bucks lost in a game?" Rick asked.

Judy shrugged. "I think you're looking under the wrong table-cloth, babe. I played one person who gave up after what, one game, Meg?"

"Yeah, I think it was only one."

"What about the guy who hit on you when Meg told him you were lesbians?" Lucas asked.

Rick looked at his little pixie with surprise and admiration.

"It's a great excuse," she told him. "And again . . . I don't think so. He didn't look back."

"Let's grab a table, play a couple rounds, and see if anything comes back to you." The beer was cheap, but to be safe, Rick stayed away from the tap and grabbed a round of bottles for their little party.

Dan and Judy played a game while Rick sat watching beside Meg and Lucas. While they chatted, Rick studied the bar. The five of them stood out for their sobriety. It was early and there were already men sloshy drunk and leaning against the bar for support.

"It looks like she's bouncing back," Lucas said.

"She is," Meg said with a sigh. "But . . ."

"But what?" Rick asked.

"She's not back completely. I can't even put my finger on why I feel that way. She bitched about work all the time, before. Now there's almost nothing."

"Work is getting better."

"Yeah. I know." Meg glanced at Judy taking down a striped ball. "It's little things. She's not spending any time online decompressing with those stupid games she plays. She stares off sometimes."

Rick took a swig from his beer. "She plays games on her computer?"

"On her tablet, mainly. She was obsessed with this war game and now she doesn't play it at all. It's stupid, I know . . . but it was her favorite procrastination pastime."

Lucas nudged Meg and looked toward Rick. "Maybe she has a new favorite procrastination pastime."

"I guess that's true. She hasn't had a lot of alone time since all this happened."

Meg didn't sound convinced. If anyone really knew Judy, it would be her best friend.

Something at the front door distracted his attention away from Meg.

Wearing suits, and not even trying to blend in, walked Detective Raskin and Detective Perozo. *Damn it.* He'd been waiting for the shoe to fall, and it looked as if it was about to.

"Is that . . . ?"

"Yeah."

Raskin noticed them and started walking their way.

Rick wasn't sure if the room grew quiet, or his own anxiety had him hearing his heart beating in his ear. "Hey, Utah?"

Judy lifted her gaze and followed his stare. The small smile she'd managed since they walked in the room disappeared. She tossed the cue on the table and moved to his side.

"You don't think—"

"I do. Call Neil," he told her.

"What's going on?" Dan asked.

Rick looked at the other men. "Stay with the girls until Neil or someone on his team relieves you."

"Where are you going?" Lucas asked.

Raskin stopped in front of them. Judy slid her arm around Rick's shoulders.

"Hello, Judy." Raskin addressed her first.

"Detective."

"Mr. Evans."

"Detective."

No one said a word. The music on the jukebox filled the room; the attention of everyone in the bar was on them.

"We have a few more questions for you, Mr. Evans."

A few questions . . . right!

"I can come in the morning and answer them."

Raskin actually laughed. "We'd like you to answer them now." He nodded toward the door.

Well, I had to try.

Judy sat on his lap and glared at the detective. "You're looking in the wrong direction." Her voice hitched higher.

"Mr. Evans, let's do this quietly, shall we?"

"He didn't do any—"

Rick cut Judy off. "Stay in control, babe." He kissed her cheek. "Call Neil and stay with the team."

"What the hell is going on?" Lucas asked.

Rick helped Judy to her feet and stood. He placed his hand on his front pocket and Raskin turned to the side and bared his gun.

Rick stopped, placed his hands in the air. "Keys to the car so Judy can get home."

"I'll help you with that."

Before the detective approached, he lifted his hands higher. "I'm carrying two. Right side and left leg."

He didn't stop the detective from removing his firearms and the keys to Judy's car.

Taking no chances, Raskin turned him around and slapped cuffs on him before he marched him outside.

"Holy shit!" Dan yelled. "What's going on?"

Dan and Lucas followed behind along with Judy and Meg.

A crowed gathered as Raskin frisked him before putting him in the back of the unmarked sedan.

Meg had her arm around Judy's shoulders. Instead of falling

apart, Judy looked like she wanted to hurt someone. *Stay in control. Stay alert.* He hoped his thoughts made it to her head with nothing more than his eyes.

"Am I under arrest or what?" Rick asked as they pulled away from the curb.

Raskin turned in his seat. "You have the right to remain silent . . ."

Well, that answered that!

———

Something inside her fractured when she watched the police put Rick in the back of a car in handcuffs. Rick made her feel safe, gave her the confidence to walk tall and dare anyone to touch her. He was one of the good guys . . . the guy your mom tells you about . . . the one you wait for.

As the car drove away, she was vaguely aware of her friends talking. She opened her purse, found her phone, and called Neil. While the phone rang she pocketed the stun gun Rick had given her only hours before.

"MacBain," Neil answered.

"It's Judy. They took Rick in."

There was no surprise in Neil's voice. "Where are you?"

She gave him her location and looked up and down the block. The small crowd from the bar was already moving back inside. "Meg and I are here with friends. I don't know where they are taking him, Neil. Do you have any idea?"

"I'll find out. Don't worry about Rick."

She blew out a frustrated sigh. "That's like asking you not to worry about Gwen. Listen, I'll head home and wait for you there."

Neil agreed only after she agreed to have the men in the car with them.

The drive home was quiet. Judy let Meg show Lucas and Dan

around the house while she turned on the outside lights and looked around like she'd seen Rick do more than once. Confident that no one was lurking in the shadows, she placed a call to Mike, asking him to call her back as soon as he could . . . day or night. Asking for his financial help for Rick was easier than asking for herself. She had no experience with bail and jail . . . but she'd learn.

"They really think Rick attacked you?" Dan asked when they were all waiting for Neil to show up.

"It wasn't him," she told them. "Not even close."

"Judy didn't actually see the guy. The only thing the police are going on is a lack of an alibi," Meg told them.

"They have to have more than that . . . don't they?"

Judy shrugged. "I don't know."

Neil arrived with Russell, and Dan and Lucas left with a promise to call in the morning.

Neil wasn't a hugger, which suited Judy at the moment. Sympathy might have flashed on the man's face, but he wasn't going to dwell on it. "Blake has a call in to his lawyers. We should have suits on the ground in a few hours. The problem is the weekend. We think the detectives purposely made the arrest tonight to spread out any arraignment, keep him away from you longer so they can approach you without him close by."

"Why do they need to approach me? I don't have anything else to say to them. And if they're going to try and use my words to prosecute the wrong guy, I'll just keep quiet."

"It's not that simple, Judy. This isn't a domestic violence issue, cut-and-dry . . . you can't drop the charges. The district attorney is who will file charges against Rick since they think he's responsible for the attack."

"He didn't do it!" She was yelling at the messenger and tossed her hands in the air to calm herself. "Sorry. I'm not mad at you."

"Be prepared for the police showing up to talk to you."

"Do I have to cooperate?"

"No. We have a separate lawyer on call for you, someone to advise and help direct questions. If the police show up, tell them you want counsel present. They have to respect that. It won't keep them from talking *at* you, however."

"I put a call in for Mike. I'm sure he'll post the bail money."

"I have that covered, Judy."

Her relief only lasted a minute. "Now what?"

Neil blinked . . . twice. "We wait."

"Great! We wait and the bastard that knocked me around is still out there and the man who has protected me is in jail. How is that fair?" She wanted to scream, wanted to hit something.

"Russell will stay here. I'm going to the station and meet up with the attorneys."

"Can't I come with you?"

"There's no point. Chances are the only one who will see Rick is the lawyer until he's released."

"And when will that be?"

"Best guess . . . Monday, if the judge grants bail."

"Why wouldn't the judge grant bail?"

"I don't have that answer." Neil didn't seem happy about his own information.

Neil left a few minutes later and Judy removed her laptop from her room and set it up on the table in the kitchen before brewing a pot of coffee.

"What are you doing?" Meg asked when she returned from her room wearing her pajamas.

"Crash course in law school. The evidence they have on Rick can't be any more than circumstantial. The question is how much can they assume before a judge thinks it's fact?"

It looked like Meg agreed with the idea of research when she returned with her own computer and poured a cup of coffee for herself. Hell, two newly retired college students knew their way around the Internet more than most.

Chapter Nineteen

Meg sat on the couch, her laptop on her thighs, one foot perched on the coffee table while she nibbled on popcorn. "According to this website, there's a good chance they will put you on the stand if Rick goes to trial. Even if you're a hostile witness."

"You think they'd do that?"

"I'm not the one to ask. I didn't think they'd actually arrest Rick."

Russell had taken up residence in one of the bedrooms, where he was hooking up surveillance equipment to show all the cameras around the property inside the house.

"I'll plead the Fifth."

Meg laughed. "You can't do that. Only Rick can. He's the one on trial."

"He's my boyfriend, there has to be something I can plead."

Meg clicked around the website she was on to see if there was something her friend could do to avoid giving testimony at any trial Rick might face. The word *spouse* had many links so she flipped through them. "Hmm . . ."

"What?"

"I didn't find anything for a girlfriend. But if you were Rick's wife, you wouldn't be forced to testify. The laws are clear on this point everywhere."

Judy moved from her perch at the table to sit beside Meg.

She scrolled the page to the beginning and pointed at the passage. "A spouse has testimonial privileges, the right to *not* testify. A spouse also has privileged communication where the conversations between spouses are confidential."

Judy leaned back and stared beyond the computer, thinking. "So if Rick and I were married, and I'm the only witness . . . I won't have to testify."

Meg wasn't sure she liked the deductive look in her friend's eyes. "Judy! You can't be serious."

Judy snapped her gaze to Meg. "My boyfriend is sitting in jail simply because he's in my life."

"But marriage?"

Judy pushed off the couch, now on a new mission. "If the Kardashians can marry for the sake of cameras and cash, I can get married to keep Rick out of jail. Besides, don't you arrange temporary marriages for a living now?"

"Well, yeah . . . eventually." She hadn't made a match yet, but she would. "What are you looking up now?"

"Marriage laws."

Meg narrowed her eyes. "Aren't you forgetting something?"

Judy barely glanced over her shoulder. "What?"

"Rick. What if he's not into this idea?"

Her BFF laughed. "He's grown attached to his freedom. My guess is he'll go for it."

"But he'll be married."

"To the woman he's been trying to date for an entire summer and who he's been messing the sheets with for the last week. Besides, we're not talking forever. We're talking until we find the ass who is behind all this. Once Rick's name is clear, we can get an annulment. You should know all about the dissolution of marriages in your line of work."

She did . . . but applying that to Judy didn't seem right. "I'll call Samantha in the morning and ask what she thinks."

"Perfect."

"Excuse me?" Russell poked his head into the room from the hall.

"Yeah?"

"Looks like we're having company."

The words left his lips and the buzzer for the gate told them of their late-night guests. On the monitor, red and blue lights glistened off the top of the black-and-white car in the drive.

Judy hit the button. "Yes?"

"Miss Gardner? It's Detective Perozo and Officer Greenwood. We'd like to talk to you."

They both looked at Russell. "Might as well let them in."

"Record them," Judy told him. "I don't want to miss anything they have to say."

Where Meg would be biting her nails, Judy answered the door with a strange smile.

Nice touch, Judy thought, watching Officer Greenwood walk into the room. It's like the police knew bringing in the guy who cuffed Rick would be a bad idea.

"What can I do for you, officers?"

"We just want to talk to you."

"I don't have anything more to say." Judy folded her arms over her chest.

"Mind if we sit, Judy?" Officer Greenwood's soft voice reminded her of her moments in the ER. She was a nice lady, even if she was currently working the wrong angle.

She moved to the table and lowered her laptop so they couldn't see what she was working on.

Detective Perozo looked over at Russell and Meg. "Mind if we talk to you alone?"

"Yes, actually I do. Russell is my temporary bodyguard since you deemed it necessary to remove my permanent one. Anything you have to say you can say in front of Meg."

The officers exchanged glances.

"Oh, and Russell, can you please call the attorney. Let them know I have guests."

"Absolutely." Russell glared as he removed his cell phone and punched in numbers.

"You don't need an attorney, Miss Gardner. You're not on trial."

Instead of saying anything, she smiled and nodded.

"We know you're confused as to why we brought Rick in."

She'd have the smile and nod thing down in no time at this rate.

"He had opportunity, knowledge of your every move, no alibi, and motive."

She kept her smile. "Motive, really? What might that be?" Asking questions wasn't the same as answering them.

"Did you know that Rick was allowed to retire early from the Marines?"

No, she didn't, but she kept her smile on her face and didn't answer the question.

"There was some question as to the mental health of the team he worked with. Reports from a paper in Colorado said he was responsible for a civilian's death less than two years ago."

She didn't know that. Not that it mattered. "He *is* in private security."

"Shot a man in the back in the forest."

Her eyes glanced to Russell.

He gave a curt nod.

"Why are you telling me this?"

"He's capable of hurting you."

"He didn't."

Officer Greenwood leaned forward. "Domestic abuse takes up four out of every ten cases of abuse. Did you know that?"

Judy bit her tongue to keep from responding.

"We know that Rick has been keeping tabs on you for months. Long before you moved to LA. Did you know that?"

Her tongue was going to bleed.

"My attacker sounded nothing like Rick."

"Voices can be disguised. There's no telling what the military trained Rick to do."

Judy went back to chewing her own tongue.

A buzzer from Russell's phone made noise.

Everyone glanced up, and he was now looking into his cell. "We have company," he said.

Detective Perozo jumped up.

Russell clicked on the main TV and flipped the feed coming from the gate cameras.

Outside the gate were several cars pulling along the narrow drive with men carrying cameras.

"What the?"

"Paparazzi. Police cars have a way of attracting attention," Meg said for all of them.

"Just when life was starting to get back to normal," Judy said. "Thanks ever so much."

"We're trying to keep you safe, Miss Gardner," Officer Greenwood said.

Holding her tongue wasn't going to happen. "No. You're trying to solve a case using the path of least resistance. Why don't you try a little harder and put the *right* guy in jail?"

"Do you know where Rick was yesterday after he dropped you off at work?"

The question stopped her smile. She didn't answer.

The buzzer from the gate sounded.

Russell answered.

"Looks like your counsel is here, Judy."

The police looked at each other and stood. "No need. We'll be in touch."

The Lexus passed the police car when the gate opened. Several flashes of light caught the entire exchange.

A woman stepped from the car, her jet-black hair slicked back in a long ponytail in the back, her dark clothing suitably fitting and stylish. "Was it something I said?"

Judy liked her instantly. "If I knew lawyers were cop repellant, I would have asked that you join us earlier."

The woman approached and extended a hand. "Kimberly March. I'm with the firm hired by Blake Harrison."

It took a minute to recognize the name. "Thank you for coming."

Kimberly watched the retreating car.

"C'mon inside. I suppose you're not needed now that they're gone."

"I'd like to know what they said."

Meg brewed another pot of coffee, this time decaf. "I'm starting to think this night is never going to end."

Judy hid a yawn and tried to smile. Russell left them to update Neil.

"I won't keep you up much longer."

"Can I call you Kimberly?"

"Please do. I've been brought up on the situation. The police feel they have the right guy, and everyone else knows they have the wrong guy."

"Yeah." The night was catching up with her, and Judy wanted to find something shiny to place on the cloud before she went to her lonely bed. For the first time in a week, her bed wouldn't house one amazingly warm body who made her feel protected and comfortable.

Meg sat beside them while Judy played the recording Russell had managed to capture of the conversation with the police.

"Sounds like you handled yourself well." In true lawyer form, Kimberly wrote a few things down on a large yellow pad while she talked. "Did anything they ask or say make you question Rick?"

Judy glanced at Meg, then the lawyer. "I don't know everything about his past, his years in the military. They wanted me to think he's not sane."

"Did you wonder?"

"No. Rick is one of the most levelheaded men I know. My famous brother is crazier than Rick."

Meg laughed beside her and spread her arms. "That's because he leaves this all the time to live out of a trailer on a set. Now that's crazy!"

Kimberly smiled. "Anything else?"

"Yeah." She paused. "Why do you think they asked me if I knew where Rick went after he dropped me off at work this morning?"

Meg pulled Judy's laptop closer and started clicking.

"Do you know where he was?" Kimberly asked.

"I had no idea where he was. I was at work."

Kimberly scribbled a note. "They were looking for his alibi."

"Why?"

Russell took that moment to walk in the room.

"There's more coffee. Decaf," Judy offered.

"I'm OK . . ." He ran a hand through his hair and seemed to wonder what he was supposed to do with it after that.

"What's up?"

"Neil . . . he a, told me . . ."

"What?" Judy's heart really couldn't take much more for one night.

"There's been another attack. Happened just after nine this morning. They found the woman just after five."

Judy swallowed . . . hard. "Found her?"

Russell had a difficult time keeping eye contact. "Back of a garage a few blocks away from your building. Dark hair, medium build . . . pillowcase over her head."

In an instant, the strong exterior dissolved and Judy remembered the terror inside the pillowcase, the horror of being at someone else's mercy.

So fucking easy. Her arm burned . . . *Next time.*

"Judy?"

She tossed up her hand. "Damn it."

"Is she alive?"

The answer was in Russell's eyes. No words needed.

Judy slowly shook her head.

"Are you OK?" Meg asked, placed a hand on her arm.

Judy didn't meant to shrug her friend off, but she did. "I'm fine."

Meg bounced away as if stung.

"Sorry." Judy instantly felt bad for pushing away. "I'm pissed. This guy is after me. I know it here." She placed a finger on her chest. "I know it. I don't know why, but he is. Now everyone's attention is on Rick and not finding this guy."

"A stranger's death isn't your fault."

"I know . . . I get that." Didn't stop her from blaming herself on a strange level. Not everyone had access to bodyguards and personal trainers. And she needed hers back. She needed Rick at her side.

"Kimberly . . . what I talk to you about is confidential, right?"

Kimberly smiled, her dark eyes lit with question. "Of course."

Judy looked at Russell. "Can you excuse us?"

Russell narrowed his gaze but left the room without incident.

Judy patted Meg's hand, her gaze still on Kimberly. "I need you to do something for me."

"OK?"

"You'll be able to talk to Rick's lawyer, right?"

"Joe Rodden is my colleague. We work in the same office."

"Great. I need a marriage license and I need Joe to propose to Rick on my behalf."

Kimberly blinked.

"I'm not forced to testify against my husband."

The lawyer's jaw dropped. She snapped it shut and started writing. "And if there is any eyewitness pointing a finger at Rick and this second attack?"

"There won't be. Rick is innocent and the police weren't sure of anything or they wouldn't have been here asking me questions. This bastard is after me. He wouldn't leave himself open to be caught until he has a second chance."

"How can you know this?" Kimberly asked.

Judy rubbed at the healing marks on her arm. "I just do."

Chapter Twenty

The plain white walls inside a prison cell did a wonderful job of giving those inside the opportunity to concentrate on their inner thoughts. Rick supposed if he were actually guilty of any crime, being alone with his thoughts would be painful. All Rick could think about was Judy. She was out there and he was in jail unable to get to her if something happened. He trusted Neil to watch over her, keep her safe, but no one was more invested in keeping her safe than him.

Rick met Joe Rodden in a secluded room the next morning. The lawyer dressed as a high-paid attorney should. His three-piece suit and impeccably groomed beard, peppered with a little gray, screamed confidence. They shook hands and settled behind the table.

"How is Judy?"

Joe lifted his eyebrow as he pulled a notebook from his briefcase. "She's fine. Neil asked me to relay that she's under twenty-four-hour personal protection."

He already knew that . . . but hearing it again helped him breathe easier.

"How are you holding up?"

"Beats the desert in the Middle East."

Joe tapped his pen and sat back. "Let's jump right in, shall we?"

"I want out of here."

"I'm sure you do. I'm going to make that happen as soon as we can get in front of a judge for an arraignment."

"Monday?"

"Unfortunately."

Two more nights.

"Do you understand the charges?" Joe asked.

"Yeah." Assault, attempted murder with special circumstances. Joe didn't miss a beat. "Did you do it?"

Rick met the man's eyes. "No!"

"I had to ask." He sat forward to get to work, but Rick couldn't tell if the attorney believed him or not. "So let's go over the timeline on the day of the attack."

Rick detailed out everything he remembered up to the point of walking into the hospital and finding Judy with the shit beat out of her. Joe asked about the military, his discharge. When he asked about Colorado and Mickey's death, Rick paused. "You'll have to ask the Marines about that. It's classified."

"I thought you said you've been out of active duty for seven years."

"I have. Two years ago, all that changed for a brief time. Once a Marine, always a Marine and all that."

"A man was killed."

"Yes."

"Shot in the back."

Rick laid a hand on his thigh, remembering the pain of recovery after Mickey nearly killed him. Saw Mickey's gun swaying toward Neil. He took the shot. "Not everything is as it seems."

"Everything you tell me is confidential."

"I'm more concerned with the long arm of the Marines than I am about confidentiality with an attorney. No offense, but I've known you for less than an hour. If the DA thinks they can use what happened in Colorado against me, they better be prepared for the USMC to shut that argument down."

"Before we go to trial, if we go to trial, the DA will disclose everything they plan on using against you. My job is to counter every argument and to do that I need the facts."

"If the DA brings up Colorado, I'll give you the name of my superiors on the inside."

"Fair enough."

A knock sounded on the door. "The police have more questions. I suggest we let them ask so that I can start working on your ticket out of here." Joe explained how he wanted Rick to wait for his approval before answering any questions. To keep his answers to as few words as possible.

Raskin and Perozo started with some of the same questions they had before. Where was he when . . . what time did he leave to pick Judy up for their date. Did he know that no one at the flower shop could identify him?

At one point Joe stopped the questions with one of his own. "It doesn't sound like you have enough probable cause for an arrest, gentlemen."

"Hold that thought, Counselor."

"How long have you had a tracking device on Judy's car?"

Rick glanced at his attorney. When he nodded, Rick answered. "Shortly after she moved here from Seattle."

"Why?"

"I take her security seriously. Michael Wolfe's fans have snuck on his property, tried to get close to those around him. As his sister living in his house, I thought it was best to keep close tabs on where she was."

Raskin didn't appear convinced. "Does Judy know about the tap?"

Rick held his answer.

Perozo tapped the side of the table with his toe.

"Not that I know of."

"Why keep it from her?"

"Don't answer that," Joe said.

Rick wasn't sure he could without sounding exactly like these guys wanted him to sound.

"You met Judy a year ago?"

"That's right."

"You've been keeping tabs on her ever since?"

"I'm head of her brother's security, it isn't uncommon of me to watch over all his family from time to time."

"But Judy lived in Seattle."

"So?"

Perozo tapped obsessively. "Michael has another younger sister, right?"

"Hannah," Rick told them.

"And where does Hannah go to school?"

"I have no idea."

"You knew where Judy went to school . . . knew where she lived."

Ahh, he saw where this was headed now. "It isn't a secret that Judy and I have an attraction. Yes, I'm head of her security, her brother's when he's in town. I kept track of where she lived so I could encourage her to move if she ended up in a bad neighborhood."

"Did she know you kept track of her?"

Rick glanced Joe.

"Don't answer that."

The detectives smirked at each other and it pissed Rick off.

"Let's speed up the clock a little. Where did you go after you dropped Judy off at work yesterday?"

"Don't answer that," Joe said before Rick could open his mouth.

"Why?" Rick couldn't be more confused about the question or his need to not answer it.

Joe shook his head.

"How many cameras are in this room right now?" Raskin asked before glancing around the stark room.

Rick looked around and then took a peek under the table. "Six."

"You're good," Perozo said.

"Keeping people safe is what I do."

The questions dried up and Joe requested a private room a second time.

Once alone, Rick asked, "Why did they ask me about yesterday?"

Joe brought out another stack of papers and proceeded to tap them on the desk. "Another young woman was attacked a few blocks away from Judy's building. Only she wasn't as lucky as Judy."

The hair on Rick's arms stood on end. "Why didn't you tell me this earlier?" *Another woman was attacked? And Judy is out there.*

"Because as of right now they aren't charging you with anything in regards to the second crime. Your reaction to their question wouldn't have been the same if you knew it was coming. You obviously had no idea what prompted the question."

"I don't give a crap about that. This girl, did she look like Judy? Work with architects?"

"I don't have those answers yet."

Rick rubbed both hands over his face, scratched the stubble he would normally shave away every morning. "I've got to get out of here. This guy is going to come back. I can't keep her safe if I'm in here."

"Relax, Rick."

"Relax? Have you ever had someone attack someone you cared about, Joe?"

Rick stood and started to pace.

"Listen, in regards to the assault case, it sounds like all they have is circumstantial evidence and Judy's testimony. If she started answering questions about not knowing you bugged her car or kept track of her when she lived in Seattle, it can be damning enough to move the trial forward. There shouldn't be any trouble getting the judge to grant bail, but chances are he'll tell you to stay away from Judy."

"That's not going to happen."

Joe shrugged. "Which might convince the judge to deny bail. Especially in light of the new attack."

"You have to be fucking kidding me." How the hell was this happening? He pushed both his hands against the wall and considered hitting his head to see if everything happening was just a nightmare and the jolt would wake him up.

"There is another route we can use to convince the judge that the DA doesn't have enough evidence to hold you."

Rick looked over his shoulder.

Joe took a deep breath and spread the papers out in front of him. "Spouses are not mandated to testify in any trial their husband or wife might be a defendant in. Right now Judy's pending testimony on the attack is the only real evidence the DA is going on."

Rick tilted his head. "Judy and I are dating, not married."

"I'm aware of that. A simple signature changes that, however." Joe tapped the paper in front of him with a ready pen. "If a judge understands there will never be testimony from your wife against you, he can't deny bail. Only your wife can ask for a restraining order and the court won't keep you away from each other."

The information was trickling into Rick's brain slowly. "What about the murder?"

"The police will question you on your whereabouts at the time of the murder and scramble to deny you have an alibi. A lack of an alibi isn't evidence that you committed the crime, or probable cause to hold you. They're going to have to work a whole lot harder to pin this on you without Judy's testimony. I'm not saying they won't try, but it won't be easy."

"I didn't attack Judy, and I didn't murder any woman."

"Clearing your name will be a lot easier out of here than in."

Rick took a step toward the table, glanced at the paper in front of Joe.

Certificate of Marriage.

Joe twisted it around to let him look at it.

His name was there next to Judy's. When his vision focused on Judy's signature, some of the anger inside him simply blew away.

"This was Judy's idea."

Rick glanced up from the paper. "Really?"

Joe smoothed down the hair on his chin and lifted one corner of his mouth. It was the only smile he'd seen on the man since they'd met. "Brilliant, really. I'd encourage her to study law if she hadn't just gotten her degree."

Rick sat and stared at the certificate, traced his finger over her signature.

"Kimberly, my colleague representing Judy, asked that I give you a message."

His pixie was willing to marry him just to keep him out of jail. He wasn't sure anyone ever displayed that kind of trust in him. "What message is that?"

"Judy asked that I mention Karen and Mike, and said you could work out concerns later. She said you'd understand."

He smiled. His smart, resourceful girl . . . "All I have to do is sign here and we're married?"

"Legally."

"She doesn't even have to be here?"

"Sad, but no. Lawyers have solicited signatures for legal marriages for hundreds of years. You sign this and you're married with all the laws that protect you with that union."

"And Judy . . ."

"She's half married already. Just needs you to seal the deal."

To think, less than a month ago he was happily pestering her to go out with him, and here he was adding his signature to a piece of paper making Judy his wife.

He traced his name after he added his signature. Too easy . . .

"Can you get a message to Neil?"

"Of course."

"Tell him to keep my wife safe."

"Dad is going to be pissed."

Judy stared at her brother and laughed. "What else is new? He can be pissed all he wants, it isn't going to change anything."

"But marriage?" Karen asked.

It was an intervention, only they were too late. Judy had the copy of the marriage certificate and Rick's signature was on it.

"This question from you, Karen?"

Karen glanced at Zach. "She has me there."

"Exactly."

Zach wasn't as easy. "There had to be another way."

"Maybe there was, but this was the easiest and fastest. Rick will be out tomorrow, and not worrying about him going back to jail will afford us time to find the real criminal."

"Since when are you part of the police department?" Zach asked.

"The police aren't looking for anyone, they think they have him. And I'm damn tired of having a chaperone every minute of every day." It was Sunday, and she'd been under a self-imposed house arrest with either Russell, Dennis, or Neil close by every hour since Rick had been taken away. "I can't live like this."

"How is it you're going to find this guy?"

Judy stared at her brother. "I'm not. He's going to find me."

"The hell!"

"Oh, don't go there. I'm not going to try to attract him. I'm not stupid. I just know he'll be back. Last night I remembered his last words before he knocked me out. 'Next time' . . . he said 'next time.' Only *next time* I won't be so alone or unprepared for him."

Zach rested a hand over hers. "Judy . . . you're a girl from a small town who plans on drawing for a living. You're not some super-woman who can take out anyone."

She patted Zach's hand. "I'm married to a Marine, Zach. And he *can* take out anyone."

———

His pixie wore red. The low-cut dress was skintight and stopped just above her knees. Rick managed a peek at the black hose she wore with two thin ropes up the back of each leg. To add to the allure, she topped her head with a hat that matched the dress. Damn he'd missed her. Her smile lit the room when their gazes met and held.

Judy sat among Neil, Gwen, Zach, Karen, and Meg. Every one of them dressed like royalty . . . well, except Neil, he just filled up his seat with bulk and attitude. He probably felt naked without his guns. Lord knew Rick did.

Since this was an arraignment and not a trial, Rick was forced to wear the blue jumpsuit every incarcerated man wore while inside.

Some media personnel had a presence in the back row of the courtroom. But they kept to themselves and wrote notes.

Everyone stood when the judge walked into the courtroom.

Rick was asked to stay standing and Joe stood along with him.

"How do you plead?" the judge asked as if it were a simple exercise.

"Not guilty."

The DA stood and started to ask the judge to consider holding him without bail when Joe stopped the prosecution. "Can we approach the bench, Your Honor?"

Rick turned and winked at Judy, who offered a little wave.

The attorneys stood at the bench, talking in heated tones.

"Married?" the DA said loud enough for everyone in the courtroom to hear.

There was more *not so hushed* talking, but catching every other word didn't do the argument justice.

Several seats in front of Judy and her entourage sat Detectives Raskin and Perozo. The confusion on their faces was priceless. *Idiots.*

The attorneys walked away from the bench, the DA tossing his papers on the desk while Joe wore a grin.

"Mr. Evans?" the judge said, looking Rick in the eye.

"Yes, Your Honor?" Rick stood.

"In light of the new situation, you're free to go without bail."

A sigh came from the back of the room.

"Mr. Perkinson?" the judge addressed the DA. "I'm setting the court date in two months. I suggest you not waste my time."

The DA glared at Joe and Rick. "Yes, Your Honor."

The judge smacked his gavel and called in the next case.

Rick shook Joe's hand and let the police guide him away so he could go through the process of getting his life back.

Chapter Twenty-One

The media attention spread from the courtroom and into the foyer. Outside the building, cameras were set up and ready for action.

"Can you believe this?" Meg asked, pointing to the chaos outside.

"Slow news day."

"I don't know about that. I overheard a reporter saying that Michael Wolfe's family's drama is more entertaining than his."

"They wouldn't even be watching me if not for Mike," Judy reminded her friend.

Gwen stood beside Karen and lifted her regal chin. "I wouldn't bet money on that. The camera loves you and the media has been known for making people famous just for being. Small-town girl roughed up in the big city . . . the police go after her bodyguard boyfriend. Small-town girl marries the bodyguard to protect him? The media will catch hold of that and ask for the movie rights. Cameras will be everywhere for quite some time."

Karen agreed with a nod. "I'm afraid Gwen's right."

Judy tilted her head far enough to shield her face from the cameras outside the building. "Having all these cameras on us might not be such a bad thing."

"How's that?" Meg asked.

"I'm sure I've read somewhere that criminals like to gloat . . . that they stand in the crowd and watch the attention from the outside for some kind of pleasure."

The four of them all took that moment to look out the windows in silence.

Neil walked up with Zach at his side. "Rick will be out in less than five minutes," Neil said.

When none of them responded to his comment, he followed their stare. "What?"

"Darling?" Gwen said. "What are the chances the man responsible for all of this is out in that crowd . . . watching?"

Now all six of them were staring.

Neil broke away first, tilted his head toward the mic in his ear, and started giving orders. Judy didn't hear them, but she could guess they were about her observation.

The media behind the cameras came to attention, and the buzz in the room changed.

Judy felt his stare, twisted slowly, and mimicked Rick's smile.

Hollywood movies held nothing on real-life reunions. Her heart tripped over itself with the sight of him . . . uncuffed and free. She pushed around her friends and ran as quickly as she could without breaking an ankle, into Rick's arms.

He was thick, warm, and perfect. He captured her lips and refused to let go. "We're married," he said, his lips still moving over hers.

She laughed, felt him laughing with her. "We are."

Judy felt her legs leave the ground and he spun around like a child with a new toy.

She held her hat on with one hand and clasped on to him with the other. Rick stopped spinning her long enough to kiss her again. On a sigh, she felt his tongue slide along hers for a brief promise of more. He pulled away and just took her in. When his eyes traveled to her hat, his smile offered a second set of dimples. "I knew you were ballsy, Utah . . . but hot damn."

"I felt rebellious."

"Love the red."

Red was quickly becoming her favorite color. He kept a protective hand on her waist and turned toward his friends.

After shaking hands and thanking everyone for being there, Neil coordinated their exit. Joe Rodden left first, drawing the media's attention and explaining that there would be no comment at this time. A press conference would be held at a later date.

Uniformed officers met them at the doors. Neil and Zach pushed through first, Gwen and Karen right behind them. Rick held on to her and Meg looped an arm through hers and walked tall beside her.

The media clamored for attention. "Mr. Evans? Rick? Is it true . . ." Microphones were shoved past the police, everyone looking for a sound bite. Judy kept hold of her husband and her friend and kept walking forward.

"Miss Gardner, is it true you're sleeping with the enemy?" Judy wasn't even sure which reporter asked the question, but she knew Rick heard it because his grip became harder, his pace faster.

The limo was in sight, the door to the back open, and Karen was slipping inside right behind Gwen. Someone gave her head a slight nudge as she climbed in the car. Neil was the last to get in, and the driver pulled away from the curb the moment the door shut.

"What a zoo," Karen stated for all of them.

Rick laced his fingers with Judy's.

Neil lifted his cell to his ear. "Collect as many shots as you can."

"What's that about?" Rick asked once Neil disconnected the call.

"The ladies pointed out something we might have overlooked."

"Oh, yeah . . . what's that?"

"This guy might be watching all this from close by. Blending in the crowd to catch a glimpse of Judy . . . of the circus he created."

Judy ignored the chill running up her arms. Rick released her fingers and pulled her closer.

"I have Russell and Dennis taking pictures. See if anyone sticks out."

"We can collect pictures off the Internet of the media coverage, see if there are any familiar faces," Meg suggested.

"Perhaps hold a press conference in a public place, observe the crowd?" This suggestion came from Gwen.

"No more press today, please," Judy pleaded.

"As much as you might hate their presence," Karen said, "the more you draw their attention the more likely this guy will keep his distance."

Rick agreed. "They'll act as virtual bodyguards. They'll watch us, and we'll be looking for who is watching them."

"Eventually the media will bore and move on," Karen reminded them.

"If they do, and we haven't found this guy yet, I'll call Mike." Zach winked at Judy. "If anyone can create some media attention, it's him."

They returned to the Beverly Hills home with nearly as much media outside the gates there as were outside the courthouse.

A catering truck sat in the drive, a few servers rushed around to unload food and bring it into the house.

"We're having a party?" Rick leaned over and asked Judy once they stepped out of the limo.

"Samantha's idea. Says appearances are more important now than ever. I don't get it, not really . . . but I'm not afraid to say I'm out of my element with everything that's been going on."

They held hands walking into the house. A deep sigh left Rick's lungs as he looked around the familiar walls.

"Neil brought over some of your things," Judy told him. "Everything is in my room if you wanted to go clean up." She removed her hat and shook out her dark hair.

"I do need a decent shower." His eyes ran down her frame. "But don't change," he said close to her ear so only she could hear.

A slow, sexy smile lit her face and he turned and walked down the hall.

The large walk-in closet housed many of his clothes, his shoes sat on the floor. Inside the bathroom, his toiletries sat beside Judy's as if they'd always been there. He should be freaking out . . . completely beside himself, but no. He was out of jail, thanks to his pixie and her quick thinking. And he was married. Yeah, it was a piece of paper with no guarantee it would ever be anything else, but for now he could go with the title of husband and enjoy the ride.

Rick opted for black slacks and a black silk shirt after his shower. Music spilled from the living room and mixed with the sound of familiar voices. He paused at the edge of the great room and leaned against the massive beam framing the space.

Judy was laughing at something her brother had said, a glass of wine in her hand.

He'd just spent three nights in jail with cold walls and inhospitable company . . . he should be thinking about how he was going to stay out of prison.

All he could think of was a different kind of confinement. The kind one voluntarily agreed to. The marriage kind.

For two nights he'd been married . . . sitting in a jail cell without a warm woman . . . but married. Knowing when he managed to get out he'd have a woman waiting for him filled him with something money couldn't buy. Someone was out there waiting for him . . . wanting him. He drew in a breath now, watching his wife without her knowing, and tried to remember that she married him to keep him out of jail and not for now and forever. Yet it was her suggestion . . . a solution to an immediate problem that plagued them both. Not many women would do that. Maybe if they were in their forties and had signed their name to a marriage certificate more than once, but not a twenty-four-year-old woman who grew up in a small town where marriage was the pinnacle of life.

Utah married him . . . signed her name long before he had.

He knew the moment she sensed him. Zach was talking and Karen stood beside him waving her hands, finishing her husband's sentences. Judy tilted her head to the side and then slowly leveled her gaze to his.

Zach spoke to the back of her head; at some point Karen nudged him and directed his attention across the room.

Judy glanced back at her brother for less than a second and then moved across the crowded room to him.

If being married meant owning this feeling his entire life, he was in. All-in. This he could get used to.

"Feel better?" Judy asked when she walked to his side.

He laughed. "Prison showers . . ."

She cocked her head. "You didn't drop the soap, did you?"

Laughter exploded from his lips, catching the attention of everyone around them. "I thought you were from a small town. What do you know about prison soap dropping?"

"Hey! I watch TV."

He pulled her close, dropped his lips to hers as if he had the right.

When the kiss went for longer than socially necessary, Meg shoved in. "Save it for later, kids. You have company."

Rick growled.

Judy broke their kiss and slid her arm around his waist.

Neil placed a beer in his hand and someone handed him a plate of food and drew him away from Judy's side.

"So why are we having a party?" he asked Blake and Neil, who sat with him on the living room sofa.

"According to my wife," Blake started, "appearances are important and letting the media know we expected you to get out of jail today by hosting a party is the perfect distraction."

Rick's head spun. "Parties for distraction?"

"It won't take long for the media to find out that you married while in jail. If it appears that you married only to get out of jail, there's no telling what can happen."

Rick shook his head. "It doesn't matter what anyone thinks. Judy and I married and public opinion doesn't hold court."

Blake waved his drink in Rick's direction. "Except if the media and public deem you innocent, it will be much harder for a trial of your peers to ever convict you. Therefore, a seemingly happy celebration between you and your new bride will go over well with the adoring viewers of the evening news and magazines. It's brilliant, really."

Rick had known Blake for a couple of years and seldom heard the British accent from his lips . . . tonight he did.

"The only way to really clear my name is to find the guy who attacked Judy." Rick looked at Neil. "Are we any closer to finding him?"

His friend shook his head. "I called Dean earlier." Dean was a friend in the police department. "All eyes were directed at Judy. If you were with her those eyes were on you as well."

"If Raskin and Perozo think I'm the bad guy, why wouldn't they have been watching me? How is it they didn't know I wasn't near the woman in the second attack?"

"Eliza," Blake answered.

"Excuse me?" Rick had met Eliza and Carter, the first lady and governor of the state of California, on many occasions, but their names weren't ones he expected to hear in this conversation.

"Eliza asked that if extra eyes were following this case, they be on Judy. She has a huge soft spot for the victims. Feels the attention needs to be on people like Judy and not on *not yet convicted* felons."

Neil picked up where Blake let off in the explanation. "The police department hardly has the funds to keep detectives on cases . . . making sure any extra help watched Judy and not you was an easy request."

"Easy for the governor's wife to request," Rick said.

"Only now we need to follow your path on the day the woman was murdered."

All this play-by-play of his life was a huge pain in the ass. "I grabbed a cup of coffee from the café outside Judy's office and left. I went home and caught up on some sleep."

Neil nudged his knee. "You don't have to tell us. We know you didn't have anything to do with the woman's murder."

Rick leaned back and closed his eyes. "Clearing my name . . . proving I'm innocent . . . When did this become my daily life?"

Blake glanced behind Rick, letting him know someone was standing there.

He tilted his head back. Judy's smile wasn't as big as it had been and Rick knew instantly that she heard him and took his complaint personally. "Hey."

She handed him the beer she'd obviously brought over for him and attempted a grin. "Thought you might like another one." He took it, but she didn't meet his eyes before turning and walking away.

"Excuse me," he told the guys.

Rick set the beer on the coffee table and moved to catch up with Judy as she headed out the back door.

She was several yards from the house before he caught up to her. "Hey, hold up."

She kept walking, an audible sniffle proved she was upset.

Stepping in front of her, he cut her off. "Judy," he said softly.

There were tears on her cheeks, each one a knife to his chest. "I'm sorry. I'm sorry this is happening to you."

"Hey! Don't." With one finger, he lifted her chin to bring her eyes to his. "This isn't your fault."

"You just spent three nights in jail because of me."

Rick shook his head but before he could say anything, she kept going.

"You get out of jail by getting married and you still have to prove you're innocent." She pulled her chin away from his hand and swiped a finger under her right eye, then her left.

He placed both hands on her arms before running them down to clasp her hands. "I spent three nights in jail because the police are blind to how much I care about you. Getting married to get out so I can be here . . . right here beside you, was brilliant." He squeezed her hands and bent his knees to meet her eyes. When he finally captured them, he slowly smiled, desperately trying to coax a grin from her. "I'm frustrated . . . but not with you. You're the only bright light in my day."

She blinked and shook her head.

"C'mere," he said as he pulled her to a two-person swing that sat on the edge of the yard. Holding one of her hands, he gave the swing a little push. "Remember when we met?"

She didn't say anything, just gave a half smile.

"I remember that day like it was yesterday. You tried so hard to hide the spark you obviously felt. You were so damn cute I couldn't get enough."

Her smile was a little more genuine now and he kept going. "When I came back to LA, Karen told me you went to college in Idaho."

"Why did she do that?"

"I don't know . . . a practical joke? You'll have to ask her some-time. Anyway, I had planned a trip to Idaho, thought maybe we could *accidentally* meet up. When I mentioned to Michael that I'd be in your neck of the woods, he corrected me. I scrambled and spied and found your address in Washington."

Her tears had dried up and she seemed genuinely intrigued.

"How come you didn't call?"

"I don't really know. I guess I knew you wanted to finish school and a distraction might actually work against me. When Michael told me you were applying for internships here, I just waited. Then I saw you hustling pool and that spark was just as strong as the first day."

"I don't hustle pool," she denied with a grin.

He released her hand only to put his arm over her shoulders and pull her closer.

"The denomination of the money earned doesn't define a hustle . . . knowing you can kick someone's ass in the game and betting makes it a hustle."

He sighed and when Judy's head hit his shoulder, he felt himself starting to relax. "Wanting to date me, hook up, isn't the same as going to jail and getting married for me."

He kissed the top of her head. "We definitely get a nomination for craziest dating dance ever . . . but in light of everything that's happened I wouldn't change it. So if I'm frustrated, or you're frustrated, we need to talk about it and not assume we're upset with each other. With the serious nature of everything going on, we need to be open and honest. Agreed?"

"Agreed."

This was good.

"Right now I'm really frustrated," he told her.

"Oh?"

"Yeah . . . we have a house full of people celebrating us and all I really want to do is unwrap that red dress and see the color of your panties."

Chapter Twenty-Two

Everyone had left and Meg disappeared into her room. Judy kicked off her shoes and wiggled out of her pantyhose, but left the dress on while Rick locked up the house. They'd come to an understanding in the garden. She was going to do her best to not blame herself for the craziness of their lives, and they were both going to keep their conversations open and honest.

When Rick didn't follow quickly behind her, she sat up on the bed and grabbed her tablet.

The game she'd played obsessively hadn't called out to her in weeks. She saw the icon and clicked into the game. Sure enough, there were many chat messages, all asking where she'd been. A few closer players, people she'd talked to off the game, asked her to send a private chat. All that could wait. She went through the routine of collecting money from her virtual buildings and restoring those that had been bombed by others. It was silly and mindless . . . and it felt strangely comforting to have a desire to pick it up.

Rick stepped into the room while she was vaulting the money she'd collected. While the dial spun, she glanced up and noticed him smiling at her.

"You're beautiful," he told her as he slid next to her on the big bed and looked at the game in her hand. "War games?"

She closed the tablet and tossed it aside. "Stupid, I know."

Yet he was grinning even bigger, his hand found her knee and started a slow ascent up her thigh.

She was pretty sure she purred.

"I think it's cute," he told her, his lips going straight for the V of her dress. Judy closed her eyes and slid lower in the bed.

"Cute? I'm a three-star general on that game. I kick serious ass . . ."

Rick's fingers were dancing up her thigh, sending shockwaves up her body. She arched into him.

"Tough as nails on the Internet, soft and supple in real life." He pushed the edge of her dress aside and exposed her breast.

His tongue ran over the tip, bringing it to attention and making her moan. She was warm, everywhere, instantly.

Rick started to move to the other side and paused . . . the hand on her thigh tightened.

When he didn't move, she opened her eyes to see him staring at the tablet.

"Don't stop now," she said, teasing.

He went from touching her, tasting her, to staring without an ounce of humor in his face. "Do you talk to people on that game?"

"What?" Her head wasn't following his thoughts.

He pulled away, his hands left her and reached for her tablet. "This. Do you talk to people on the game?"

"Yeah." She sat up, readjusted her dress so she wasn't hanging out of it. "We have chat rooms set up for wars . . . allies for battles. Enemies to conquer. All in fun."

He opened the device and glanced at the screen, which opened to the game since she hadn't shut it down before closing it. "Is it all in fun?"

"For me. Once in a while there will be a die-hard gamer that thinks everyone should dedicate their life to this . . . spend money to win wars. We weed those players out of our team once they start pitching a fit."

Rick's green eyes found hers and didn't let go.

Chills, and not the kind she wanted while in bed with Rick, made her shiver.

You're not so tough now, are you?

You're not much of a fighter, are you?

"Oh, God. You don't think . . ."

"Do you use your real name?"

"No . . . but . . ." But she knew many of the real names of those on her team. They'd been playing for over a year. She hadn't worked terribly hard to keep her name out of the game.

Rick tilted his head. "It's a lead, Judy. Our only one."

Without Rick's help, she changed into a pair of cotton pajama bottoms and a T-shirt and met him back in the kitchen, where he'd set up the tablet and her laptop. She freely admitted that her knees knocked a little as she made her way to Rick's side.

"What are we looking for?" she asked as she sat beside him.

"A link. A direct path to you from this game." He pushed her laptop over to her. "Log in to your Facebook account, Twitter . . . whatever you use."

She brought up the Internet while Rick brought a cup of coffee for her from the kitchen.

"Hey." Meg had on a long pink robe, her bare toes sticking out from under it. "I thought you'd be . . . well, I didn't think you'd be in here. What's going on?"

Judy exchanged glances with Rick.

"Rick thinks that maybe someone from the game I play online might be behind the attack."

"The war game?"

Judy nodded.

"It's a game." Meg's confusion was written in her eyes.

"A game where the top players spend serious cash to be in the top slots and get pissed if their team doesn't play with the same intensity." The more Judy considered the possibility that Rick was right, the worse she felt.

"But it's a game."

"I know, Meg. I feel the same way."

"It's also a sick world out there," Rick added.

Meg tucked into a chair. "I've heard of pedophiles using online games to find victims, but adults falling into the same trap?"

"Internet crime against adults isn't limited to monetary extortion." Rick pushed close to Judy and leaned over the tablet. "OK. Tell me how this game works."

While Judy explained the details of the game, Meg brought out her computer and looked up information about the game, the complaints, and the chat rooms.

The game wasn't complicated, and since there wasn't an active war going on there weren't a lot of people online chatting. Judy explained the chats and the way to have private chats. "There are very few women playing, so those of us who do have hooked up elsewhere."

"Where?"

Judy showed him her Facebook account and pointed out two women who knew her real persona. "My privacy settings are such that you have to be a friend to see all this."

There were pictures of her friends at college, a shot of her with Meg and Mike at graduation.

Rick started writing down names of her Facebook friends and a list of all those on her team in the game. "This is going to take some time." He looked over at the sofa and they both noticed that Meg had fallen asleep with her laptop on her knees.

"She's been a real trooper. The night you went to jail, we were up until after two, fact-checking marriage and testimony laws. Sometimes it doesn't feel like we've left school."

"You should go ahead and go to bed." He patted her hand.

She patted his back. "I don't think so, babe. I've been in a cold bed for three nights, and when I finally crash, you're going to be in there with me."

Judy woke Meg long enough to motivate her to bed and took her friend's place on the couch. She went through old messages on Facebook, searching for anything sketchy. She and Rick worked in a rhythm, she'd say a name, and he'd write it down or cross-reference it as a fellow student, a friend from Utah, or a friend of a friend or virtual stranger. Rick grew quiet while he was following people from her list around the Internet. Not sure what else to look for, she clicked into the topography of the Santa Barbara project until her eyelids gave up the fight and she fell asleep.

———

Rick took another look at the names of the women from Judy's game, his mind working backward. There were four of them, two were middle-aged housewives and the other two were both college students. Because he was on Judy's computer and acting as her, he was able to access everything on these ladies' accounts. Both girls had picked a picture off Judy's page of Judy and Michael. Rick was sure the draw wasn't Judy, but her famous brother these girls were all over. There were comments galore with plenty of *likes* from numerous friends. He started writing down names, clicking over to pages to see if any of them were unsecure. He was surprised at how many people put absolutely every piece of information about their lives on their pages. Phone numbers, addresses, where they partied every Friday night, who they had sex with and the when and where of it.

It boggled his mind.

Judy's page was conservative by nature. There was very little information about her day-to-day life with the exception of where she went to school and what she was studying. She hadn't even updated where she lived from Seattle to LA. Probably an oversight since she had posted a couple of pictures of the paparazzi pointing their cameras at her. There was something here . . . he felt it.

His eyes were crossing and he looked up to find Judy sound asleep. Her soft pink lips were parted slightly with the steady rise and fall of her chest.

What a resilient woman she turned out to be. His memory flashed to her beaten face from the ER and he flinched. He would find the man who touched her, and then the police would have cause to arrest him.

He powered down the computer and removed the tablet from Judy's lap. She twisted into a ball and rolled on her side. Instead of waking her, he scooped his hands under her and picked her up.

"Time for bed?" she mumbled as she snuggled closer.

"Shh."

She said something he didn't quite understand and he carried her to bed.

It took some time for his head to turn off. He lay there with Judy curled up beside him and simply cherished holding her.

When he'd returned to the States with Neil and what remained of their team, Rick wasn't sure he'd ever sleep an entire night through again. He learned quickly that he managed much better with a woman in his bed, but he still didn't turn off completely. Until Judy. Even thinking about her in the past year helped his brain find some form of hibernation at night. Now, as his eyes were drifting closed and the fresh scent of spring curled even closer, he realized what made Judy stand out from all the rest.

Judy wasn't some passing attraction, some easy fix for a lonely night . . . she was the real deal. The woman you took home to meet your parents, the woman you wanted to have your children.

Somewhere between Utah, Washington, and California, he'd fallen in love.

He held her even closer, kissed her sleeping head, and drifted off.

———

"I told them I'd come in for half a day and be back to work tomorrow. I've got to go," Judy argued while she towel-dried her hair and walked between the bathroom and the closet. "They've been really understanding but I can't keep disappearing. It's not like they have to keep me there."

She could tell by the scowl on Rick's face he wasn't happy with the thought of her going to work. "If it makes you any happier, we'll be taking the Ferrari." She knew how much he enjoyed driving Mike's car, and in light of the fact that Rick's constant need for an alibi was in question, everyone thought it was best he drive the flashiest car in Mike's garage. The Ferrari won.

Rick grumbled. "I don't like it."

"You're dropping me off after lunch and picking me up at five. I won't even leave the office."

His grumble now sounded like a growl.

"I can't hide." She walked back into the bathroom and talked through the door. "I'm no more or less safe than I was last week when you dropped me off and picked me up every day." Though she knew eventually she'd have to hike on her big-girl panties and make the trip solo. "Putting my head into my work will help clear it up . . . make it easier for me to consider who might be doing all this."

"You said you felt he was coming back for you." Rick had left his perch from the side of the bed and now stood in the doorway of the bathroom.

"I do. One of the many things I looked up while you were away was the mindset of a psychopath. It isn't often they actually give up the object of their obsession. This guy isn't going to corner me in a garage, or catch me taking the stairs at work." She brushed out her hair, put a handful of mousse into the locks. "Maybe we'll get lucky and some of the pictures you and Neil will be looking over this afternoon will point someone out."

"Maybe."

"If he's after me, he'll get frustrated not getting close and eventually screw up."

Rick's lips twisted to the side. "You've been watching crime TV again, haven't you?"

She applied a layer of mascara and pointed the tip of the brush at him through the mirror. "First, those shows aren't completely based on fiction, but no. Actually, Meg and I have been burning up the Internet. We've been professional students for the last four years. Everything you ever wanted to know about anything is on the Internet, all you have to do is know where to look."

Rick walked up behind her and slid both hands around her waist before nuzzling her wet hair. "I still don't want you to go."

"C'mon. Aren't you the one who said it would get easier every day?"

"That was before someone was murdered."

She didn't like that either. "I'm not going into the dark basement alone, Rick. I'm going to work. Lots of pencil-pushing geeks who draw for a living. I'll be fine."

"We just got married." He ran a hand down her arm and feathered his thumb over her ring finger. "You don't even have a ring."

She twisted around and offered a smile. "Then that's what you do today . . . go find me a ring." They hadn't yet consummated the marriage either, but she wasn't about to point that out or he'd never let her leave.

"Trying to get rid of me?"

She pushed him toward the bathroom door. "What was your first clue?"

The rest of her bathroom ritual went without complaint. Rick drove the Ferrari, keeping a constant eye on the road behind him.

The eyes on them had doubled since the last time they walked into the office. Most of the staff of Benson & Miller had yet to return from lunch, but there were a few people milling about the office when she walked in.

"See, safe and sound."

Rick conceded and dropped a kiss to her lips. "You need anything—"

"I'll call. Go."

He turned to leave, and she called out to him. "And cubic zirconia looks just as good as the real thing. No need to do anything crazy."

Chapter Twenty-Three

Judy dropped her purse in her desk and left the plans for the Santa Barbara project in the corner of her cubicle before working her way toward a cup of coffee. The lack of sleep the night before didn't have a chance of being made up by sleeping in.

By the time she made it back to her desk, the office was filling with employees.

"It's the lady in red," she heard José say with laughter in his voice.

"It's been a very crazy weekend."

"Tell me about it. Ever since you've been here, we've had nothing but excitement. Every day my wife asks me what's new."

She knew José wasn't referring to the actual attack, but the media, the famous brother . . . the parts she could smile and laugh at.

Nancy's voice sounded from down the hall. "You can't go down there."

Sure enough, a small flash mob of media was walking down the hall, past Judy's desk, and straight at her.

"This is ridiculous," she said.

"How did they get up here?"

Judy rolled her eyes and stood her ground. "They have their ways."

"Mrs. Evans?"

"Judy?"

She actually glanced behind her when she heard *Mrs. Evans* a second time. Then it dawned on her that they were talking to her.

She placed her hands on her hips and glared. "Brilliant. The best way to get me to say anything is to corner me at work."

Flashes of light came in all directions. All Judy could see was spots and a sea of opportunistic reporters and paparazzi.

"Is it true you married the prime suspect in the assault that happened to you?"

"No comment." She turned to José. "Don't we have security around here?"

"What about the rumors about your brother taking on a movie role about this case?"

Now she'd heard it all.

Along with more employees returning from lunch, security finally showed up and nudged everyone with a camera and an unfamiliar face out of the office.

Mr. Archer stood beside Nancy while the media walked by.

Judy held her breath for a moment, wondered if the reaction to the media was going to end her internship sooner than she'd planned. The constant chaos of her presence might be great watercooler fodder, but for the boss . . . not so much.

"Place a note in the lobby, Nancy," Mr. Archer said so everyone heard him. "Uninvited media presence will not be tolerated and trespassers will be prosecuted to the fullest extent of the law." He smiled toward Judy, turned on his heel. "Welcome back, Judy."

Her shoulders sank in a heavy sigh.

José patted her back. "Get settled. I need help on the Fullerton project."

Despite the crazy beginning of her day, Judy smiled on the way to her desk. She set the coffee down and sifted through a couple of the papers her colleagues had placed on her desk. She really did look good in the red dress, she decided.

She opened the top drawer to clear off her desk and froze.

There, sitting on top of drafting pencils and magazines, sat her driver's license. The one that had been in her purse her attacker made off with.

She lifted her hands off her desk as if it burned and nudged the drawer closed with her knee.

Forcing her lips into a smile, she cautiously stood and walked away.

After swallowing her first instinct, the one that told her to call the police, tell her employer what she'd found, she did neither.

Eyes followed her around the office. Only Judy now looked at everyone differently. Had someone in the office attacked her? If so, why? Or did the man responsible slip in the office over the weekend . . . with the media?

The Fullerton project received a fifth of her attention, but it didn't seem José noticed . . . or if he did, he didn't care. An hour in his office and Judy made an excuse to leave his desk. In the small kitchen, she found a box of sealable plastic sandwich bags, grabbed one, and returned to her desk. Using a tissue, she opened the top of her desk, carefully removed her driver's license, and placed it in the bag. *I really hope those crime shows on TV are right about collecting evidence.*

She removed her cell phone from her purse, snapped a quick picture of her license, and dropped the bag inside, where she could get it to Rick.

She attached the photo to a text message.

Found this in my desk. It was in my purse the night of the attack. Don't panic. Don't call.

She hit *send*.

Her phone buzzed within ten seconds.

I'm coming to get you.

No! Don't. Come a little early when it's time to pick

me up. Bring something to bug my office, small video, something. It's time we find this guy and stop running from him.

She glanced up, didn't notice anyone around her cubby. Her very stark space with very little room to hide anything. Her thumbs worked overtime with the next text. Send me flowers, a teddy bear...something. We need to hide what you bring somewhere.

When he didn't text back right away, she thought he'd blow off her idea and barge in the front door. When her phone buzzed, she read his message and smiled. Don't leave that office for any reason.

I won't.

And text me every hour.

She blew out a breath. Fine.

Her insides shook, but she plastered a smile on her face and acted like nothing had happened.

Nancy allowed the kid delivering the flowers into the back office. Heads turned when he found her in José's office. Yellow roses with white lilies.

Judy attempted to act surprised while she accepted the flowers. "Oh, wow."

Before the kid could run off, she told him she needed to get her purse for a tip. "All taken care of, Mrs. Evans."

The name kept pulling her back. The card simply said *Thank*. After arranging them on her desk, she sent a quick text to Rick. THANK?

He replied with a winking emoticon.

Not forty-five minutes later, the same kid arrived with a bouquet of sunflowers . . . big and beautiful. The card said *You*.

A small table in the corner of her cubby housed the sunflowers.

A dozen white roses arrived next, and José gave up having her in his office. Nancy walked with the delivery kid away from her office. Judy placed the card next to the other two. *Thank You For . . .* Safe to say Rick wasn't done.

It was hard to concentrate on work with her office looking like a florist exploded nearby. She was reminded of the time when Karen and Mike had fought and Mike had over a dozen flower deliveries sent to her childhood house in Utah. The difference was Mike was apologizing with gifts, where Rick was just following her suggestions. Still, the smile on her face was having a hard time going away, despite the reason for the flower deliveries.

Her phone buzzed at four o'clock. "Judy Gardner," she answered.

"Don't you mean Evans?" Nancy asked with a laugh.

"Oh, my . . . is the delivery guy back?"

"Yes, and I have to tell you . . . I'm so freakin' jealous right now I can't stand it."

Judy laughed. "Send him back."

There were two teddy bears holding hands and dressed in wedding attire. The delivery came with a card. *Marrying*. The bears were cheesy, but so stinking cute. She sent a picture of the foot-tall bears to Rick.

Ten minutes before the hour, a hand appeared around her cubicle wall; in it was a single red rose with a card.

"Another delivery?"

Rick's arm was too thick to mistake for anyone else's.

She stood and peeked around the corner to see him grinning in the silly way only he did. Boy, man, and mischief all rolled in one.

"You didn't have to."

He waved the flower and handed it to her, but didn't say anything.

The single stem smelled lovely. The small envelope held more than a piece of paper, but she looked at the card first. *Me*.

"Awww, Rick." It might be all for show, but she couldn't help but love it.

She took a step toward him and he lifted her hand with the envelope. "There's more."

Judy tilted the envelope and poured out a wedding ring. The single round stone caught the light and made her smile. A completely girlie part of her giggled. "Oh, babe."

Rick took it from her hand and placed it on her finger. The fit was perfect, the ring lovely. It was large enough to be hard to miss. She really hoped he'd taken her up on the zirconia option. Buying diamonds for a temporary ruse seemed a bit much for the pocketbook.

She held her hand out and admired the ring. "I love it."

"C'mere." He beckoned her with one finger.

His lips met hers and lingered.

"You'll have everyone in the office talking," she told him.

He shrugged. "They were already doing that anyway."

José walked by, pushed his hand into Rick's. "Damn glad my wife won't be stopping by anytime soon. You put the rest of us to shame."

The two of them spoke for a minute before Mr. Archer walked by on his way out. Handshakes and congratulations were passed around.

Judy purposely left a drawing on her desk and ignored it until after nearly everyone had left the office. Nancy was one of the last to leave. "You sure you don't have a brother?"

"Sorry, darlin'."

"Damn shame," Nancy mumbled as she left.

"I'll just finish this up," Judy said for anyone left listening. Acting as if she were on a mission, she walked around the office checking for lingering employees.

Even Debra Miller had left on time, leaving the office bare for them.

"We're clear," she told Rick.

Out of his inside jacket pockets, he removed a couple of small devices. One looked like a thick black ring. Rick removed his cell phone and clicked a few things. "Here. Hold this."

She glanced at the screen, noticed her own image standing there. "That's a camera?"

"Yeah." He tied the small camera into the ribbons of the sun-flowers and angled it toward the desk. Happy with that, and without a smile, he took the second device. This one had a wire on the end of the camera. He feathered the wire on the stems of the roses and pointed the device toward the entry to her cubicle. "This one has sound."

"Why two?" she asked.

"If housekeeping moves one, the other will pick up something."

She hadn't thought of that.

"Now, show me what you found."

Judy tucked into her chair, removed her purse from the drawer, and opened the top to show Rick where she'd found her license. "It was just lying there. No way I could miss it."

He removed the license from her fingertips, looked at it through the plastic bag. "You placed it in the bag?"

"I did."

One of his eyebrows lifted. "Nice thinking, Utah."

"Figured all the crime shows couldn't be wrong."

He looked beyond her inside the drawer. "Did you find anything else?"

She pushed her chair back. "I didn't look."

Rick grabbed a pencil from her desk and shuffled things back and forth in the drawer, though she didn't see anything out of place. "Right after I showed up, a boatload of reporters marched into the office. Some walked right by my desk."

"How many of them would know this is your space?"

"None, I guess." She shivered.

He laid a hand on her shoulder. "Let's get out of here. I'll get this to Neil. Maybe we'll find a clear print, see if Dean can come up with something."

He pressed the red *raid* button, knew he beat her once again. He ran the tip of the knife in his hand down the length of her picture. The red dress smacked of insubordination. She mocked him with the color, made him want to help her bleed all over it.

The fake blood splattered on the screen wasn't enough . . . not since he'd smashed his fist into her that first time. That was so much more rewarding than this one-dimensional screen with beeps and whistles. His talents went well beyond this game. The badge-wearing police were arresting the wrong guy, sniffing around the wrong places. So stupid.

The only thing he hadn't anticipated was the security surrounding Judy now. Toying with her before he took her out was proving much more difficult than he first thought.

The *raid* button flashed along with a sign reading *Bring the Pain.* The edge of the blade pushed against his finger, bringing blood to the surface. He watched in utter fascination as a drop of blood splashed on the magazine picture. His fascination with the image made him remember another one. She hadn't put up much of a fight, however. He hadn't meant to kill her. The thickness of her skull must have been a defect. No, he only wanted to remind Judy that he was out there. She shouldn't be smiling in any of the pictures . . . she shouldn't be in front of a camera at all. Even today, she laughed at the media and shooed them away as if they were her minions.

His finger pressed into the photograph.

She shouldn't have made what should have been the most painful time in her life memorable by getting married. What sane person got married when a killer was after them? Who did that?

A cocky bitch.

Three-star general my ass.

He no longer could identify the image under his finger.

But he knew who it was . . .

After leaving his present for her today, she wouldn't be back at her day job. She'd be the coward she was . . . hiding behind her game, behind the walls of her brother's house.

Then he'd just have to wait. Her fortress wasn't as secure as those around her believed.

Meg ran out of the house before Rick put the Ferrari in park.

Rick reached over and held Judy's knee, keeping her in the car while Meg ran toward them.

"I'm sorry. Let me just say that now and get it off my chest."

If there was a look that Meg perfected and Judy saw through better than anyone, it was the guilty innocence that came with the half smile and squinting eyes. Must have come from her mixed-up religious beliefs growing up. It was like her Jewish grandmother and her Catholic mother each took hold of one side of her body and went to confession. *You're guilty, but you don't really believe in hell so what does it matter?*

Judy shook off Rick's hand and stepped from the car. "Sorry about what?"

Meg's smile grew to a thin line and she offered a half glance over her shoulder toward the house.

Like a video on slow motion, through the doorway of Mike's home walked her father.

Though Judy never feared her dad, he wasn't a small man and she'd spent most of her life trying to please him.

"Tell me my mother is here."

When Meg didn't say anything, Judy shot her eyes to her best friend.

"Sorry. It wasn't like I could tell him not to come in."

Rick stepped around the car and placed his arm around her waist. "How bad can it be?"

Judy wasn't sure. There weren't many conversations she'd had with her dad without her mother nearby, yet here her father stood, miles from nowhere, Utah, without an ounce of a smile on his face.

"I'm so out of here!" Meg said, turning her attention to Rick. "I think your Tarzana house has my name on it. Extra rooms, extra beds, lots of cameras. Love ya, Judy, but this is a family matter and I'm not volunteering for any more drama this week." Meg leaned in, gave a big hug. "Call if you need me," she whispered.

Judy waved her friend away. "Go. Text us when you get there. This guy is still out there and I'd never forgive myself if something happened to you because of me."

"I'm good."

"In the flour container is a Glock, fully loaded."

Meg hugged Rick. "The fact I'm leaving with the promise of weapons, and you're staying here, should scare you."

Judy and Rick faced her father, his frown, and his disapproval as they both walked toward him.

Not a syllable of a hello, or a smile of any kind, her father filled the doorway with a glare centered on Rick. "You'd told me you'd keep her safe. You said nothing about marriage."

Rick's fingers squeezed as if to assure her he could handle her dad.

"Keeping her safe means being by her side, Mr. Gardner."

"So you give up her freedom for your own?"

Rick lifted his chin.

"Dad!"

"This is between him and me."

"The hell it is."

Her father shifted his stare to her.

Judy forced a breath deep in her lungs. "Inside. I don't need this in tomorrow's papers." With that, she stepped out of Rick's arm, past her father, and into the house.

Truth was, her knees knocked, but she strode into the house, dropped her purse on the table in the hall, and moved into the kitchen. She took the single-stem rose, laid it by the sink, and opened the refrigerator. Meg had opened one of the many bottles of wine Mike had on hand and left her half a bottle. Pouring the liquid into a glass, and not even bothering with a wineglass, proved how close to the surface her nerves were.

Judy heard the men walk in behind her. Instead of turning toward them, she looked out the back window, sipped her wine, and asked, "Where's Mom?"

"She stayed home."

"Refused to come?"

There was a pause, proving she had the right of it. "I've already had one child marry out of convenience or some such bullshit. I wasn't about to sit around without finding out what's going on this time."

Judy turned toward her dad then and Rick stepped closer to her side. "I'm not Mike."

"No. You're my daughter." A portion of her father's edge chipped away. "What father lets his daughter make lifelong mistakes without trying to stop her?"

Judy set her glass down and took Rick's hand. She really hoped, no matter what Rick might think about their temporary marriage, that he'd let her do the talking. "Your ability to control my life is no longer in place, Dad. If in fact we've made a mistake, it's ours to make. More importantly, it's already done."

When her father met her stare, his glare reminded her of Zach when he wasn't happy. Or maybe Zach reminded her of their dad. "You were never this difficult before you went to that damn college."

"You mean before I grew up?"

He growled.

She sighed. "I'm an adult. That might come as a shock to you, but I am."

"You sound like your mother."

"Mom's an intelligent woman. You should listen to her."

Even Rick glanced over as if she were skating on thin ice.

Seconds passed, and Rick turned to her dad. "How about a beer, Sawyer?"

"Fine." Her dad pivoted on his heel and marched to the sofa in the den.

Alone, but within earshot of her dad, Judy gripped the counter and tried to keep from trembling.

Rick grabbed a couple of longneck beers and placed them on the counter beside her wine. "He just cares," he whispered.

"I know. We just don't need any extra drama right now."

"Defuse, deflect, or destroy. I think maybe we should go with defuse and deflect."

Judy leaned into his shoulder with a laugh.

Chapter Twenty-Four

Rick encouraged Judy to shower, take a moment to decompress. The tension in the room ranked up there with his first days in the service.

Once Judy disappeared and the sound of the pipes opening up filled the vast emptiness of the huge house, Rick leaned his head back. "I care for your daughter, Mr. Gardner."

Sawyer grunted.

Rick would have liked to tell the man the depth of those feelings but didn't think Judy's dad needed to hear those words before she did. With everything going on in their life, he didn't want to add any more to hers. He wasn't sure she felt the same and didn't think the rejection would sit well with him. If he confessed his love, and she came back with some *let's be friends when this is over* bullshit, it would gut him.

Their relationship was fragile on many levels.

"You care for her?" He didn't sound convinced.

"Yes." Rick didn't look at the man, didn't want him to see his deeper feelings.

"Marriage isn't supposed to be temporary. I didn't think I had to tell my children this growing up. Thought it was a given since Janice and I never considered separating."

Even though neither Judy nor Rick said a thing about their marriage being temporary, seemed Sawyer already came to his own conclusions.

"I cared for her before our life grew complicated. There's no guarantee anything is temporary."

"What are you saying, Rick?"

Rick looked at his father-in-law, met his stare. "I'm suggesting you restrain your judgment. Judy's been through a lot and doesn't need the distraction of pleasing her father right now."

Sawyer blinked a couple of times before tipping his beer back.

Rick's phone buzzed. When he looked, he saw the video feed of Judy's office light up. The motion detector on the one bouquet triggered the device to signal him.

"An important text?" Sawyer really wasn't impressed and Rick realized just how difficult it was going to be to win the man over.

The cleaning crew was in Judy's office, wiping down her desk and emptying the trash. Rick leaned over and gave Sawyer a glimpse of the phone. "I told you I was going to watch over her. This is her office."

"You're spying on her at work?"

Rick shook his head. "We think the guy who attacked her has access to her space. We're watching for him."

When Sawyer said nothing, Rick stood and started from the room. "Mind joining me, Mr. Gardner? I'd like to show you something."

The room Russell and Dennis had taken over housed several monitors and recording devices. Rick flipped a few switches and let the monitors spring to life. The cameras outside the Beverly Hills home were obvious. The gate, the backyard, the front door. The feed into Judy's office showed them both activity as a housekeeper pushed a vacuum around the office and then out in the hall and out of view.

Sawyer looked at the other feeds. "What's all this?"

"You've met Neil." He pointed to a set of feeds on one large monitor. "This is his place." He pointed to another home. "This one is Malibu, where Blake and Samantha live. Zach and Karen's place." He flipped the feeds as he spoke. "And this is in Tarzana, my place."

Sawyer found another location housing only one camera. "And this one?"

"The Governor's Mansion in Sacramento. Not that we need to actually monitor that, but Carter and Eliza like to know that we can tap into their system if needed."

Sawyer waved his hand at all the monitors. "What are all you afraid of?"

Rick actually laughed. "Nothing. The Marines taught me many things. Being resourceful and having the knowledge to protect those you care about is a priority for us. Blake Harrison is one of the richest men on this continent. Neil is married to Blake's sister, and you already know some of the risks Michael faces."

Meg walked through one of the feeds at the Tarzana house. A light indicated the signal of the alarm being set.

"And why is your home monitored? You look like a man who can take care of himself."

Was that a compliment?

"Because normally all this is there. This is a temporary setup put in place when I was in jail." It killed him to say that. "Once we capture the man behind the attacks, this will all leave your son's home."

"Are you sure you'll find him?"

Rick leaned against the desk. "I will. I take my responsibilities seriously. Keeping my wife safe is my main priority."

———

Hannah picked up on the second ring.

"Hey, sis."

"Oh my God, Judy! You do realize that I'm now going to be placed in a chastity belt and forced to live my life in a tower because of you."

Hannah was a typical overdramatic eighteen-year-old. If Judy was honest with herself, she knew Hannah's life would be more difficult with the decisions Judy had made.

"I know. I'm sorry."

Hannah paused. "You really married him?"

"I did."

"I always thought I'd be in your wedding. I was too young to remember much of Rena's."

"We signed papers, Hannah. There wasn't a real wedding." Judy glanced at the ring sitting on her finger and admired the shine.

"So it's true . . . what Dad said about your marriage being a fraud like Mike's was?"

No. Mike and Karen had only ever been friends. From what Karen told her, they hadn't even slept together. Considering how attracted Karen was to Zach from day one, that was probably for the best. Rick was much more than a friend. "Everything happened so fast. I don't know what's going to happen or how things will end up."

"If you stay married, you better have some kind of wedding eventually."

"Careful what you ask for . . . I might ask you to wear some horrific dress that itches in all the wrong places."

Hannah laughed.

"I need to talk to Mom. Is she home?"

Hannah said her good-byes and handed the phone off. "Make him go home, Mom. Please!"

Janice offered a soft laugh. "I would like to think I have that power over your dad, but making him do anything is always a balancing act. I told him not to go. I thought by my not getting on the plane he'd abort the notion of going to California."

"Rick and I need to concentrate on us. I know that sounds selfish, but I can't deal with Dad right now."

"I understand, honey, but your dad has a mind of his own and feels it's his duty to make sure you haven't married someone just to keep him out of jail. Think about that for a minute."

Judy sat on the edge of her bed talking into the phone and pinching her nose. "The only reason Rick was in jail was because of me. It's not like he robbed a bank and I'm an airhead who shacks up with a lowlife."

Her mom laughed. "No one is calling anyone names. I don't think your father thinks Rick is guilty of anything."

"Then why is he here? It's like he doesn't trust my judgment at all. He didn't run here when Karen and Mike got married."

"Mike is a son."

"So?"

"It's different with daughters."

The conversation was making her head split.

"You'll understand when you have children of your own. For now, you'll have to trust me. Your dad and I love you, honey. We wanted to see you walk down the aisle when the right man entered your life."

The next words popped out of her mouth without a filter. "Who says Rick isn't the right man?"

There was a long pause.

"Well then . . ."

"Yes . . . well then." Judy released a long-suffering sigh. "You have to trust that I know what I'm doing, Mom."

"I've never doubted you, honey. Never."

Judy ended the conversation with her mother and forced herself to join the men.

"I love him," Judy said hours later when she and Rick retired for the night. "But I want to strangle him." She flopped on the bed and stared at the ceiling.

"I'm not sure that's the way to win him over."

Judy growled.

"Look on the bright side," Rick said. "My parents haven't shown up."

Judy glanced at Rick as he kicked off his shoes. "Have they even called?"

"My dad did."

She rolled on her side and leaned on an elbow. "What did he say?"

"Asked if I was guilty."

"Oh no."

Rick didn't seem fazed. "My parents think I'm crazy. Can't blame them. I ran to the Marines and got out nearly as quickly. I end up in jail, in the news."

"But if your dad thinks you're capable of killing anyone . . ."

Rick paused and removed his sport jacket. Concealed in a holster was one of the guns he carried. "I saw active combat, Judy. I'm capable of killing."

She shivered. "I never thought of it like that."

He slid out of the holster and laid it on the dresser before stepping toward the bed. He crawled on top of the comforter with her, leaned his head next to hers. "I wouldn't hesitate to kill someone hurting you."

"That scares me."

"I would never hurt you."

His green eyes pierced her. "I know."

He reached for her, pulled her close, and kissed the tip of her nose.

She placed a hand on the side of his cheek. "Do you realize we haven't consummated our marriage yet?"

Those dimples doubled and his lips met hers. Soft kisses coaxed her open and onto her back. They'd had so many distractions, so many obstacles, they hadn't spent nearly enough time in each other's arms.

Rick wasted little time reminding her of how talented he was with his tongue, keeping her pinned to the bed without really holding her down. She felt safe with him close. His presence was a crutch, she knew, but as vices went, Rick was worth any hangover he might induce. The tips of his fingers ran inside the edge of her pants and she moaned.

He silenced her with a kiss, robbed her of breath. When stars started rolling in her head, she pulled away. "Oh, Rick."

"Shh . . ." He kissed her neck, pulling another moan from her. "Much as I love the noise you make in bed, babe . . . making love within feet of your disapproving father would be better without the threat of him attempting to walk in on us."

She froze and squeezed her eyes shut. "You did *not* just say that."

He laughed as he unbuttoned her shirt and pressed his lips to her breast. "You like adventure."

Her hands were on his shoulders, ready to push him away. "But my dad . . ."

Apparently, her father wasn't a threat for him. He found the pert end of her breast and moved in to taste while his knee slipped between hers. "Oh!"

Rick laughed over her breast while he worked the clasp until she was free of both her shirt and her bra. His five o'clock shadow rubbed below her breast as he paid equal attention to both sides of her body.

Thoughts of her father fled and she sought Rick's touch everywhere. The scent, the feel of his skin on hers doubled when he removed his shirt and sent it to the floor. Would she ever tire of the thick dips and curves of his amazing body?

"So soft," he said as he nuzzled her hip once she was free of her pants. Hot breath moved in waves over her core. His intentions of tasting all of her smoldered in his eyes.

She shook her head on the bed, tried to control the tone in her voice. "I'll scream," she warned him. Keeping silent with a tongue-induced orgasm wasn't in her.

He pushed aside her panties, left one side dangling from her ankle, and kissed up the planes of her naked body. "No. You'll feel everything and keep quiet."

His words brought moisture everywhere.

"I can't."

"Shh." He leaned in, licked her inner thigh.

The need to moan tickled her throat, but she held it back.

"There you go."

Rick moved one of her legs over his shoulder and nibbled his way around her, each taste a little closer than the last. She couldn't hold still, the need for him to find her was so keen she nearly grasped his head to help him focus. Then he was there and Judy brought a fist to her mouth to keep from crying out. He was merciless, holding no prisoners and keeping nothing back as he teased and prodded. With her orgasm close, she pushed against him with an intensity she couldn't ever remember being so powerful before this . . . before Rick. Before coming in silence as she writhed on the bed.

He was laughing at her as he crawled up her frame, shedding the remainder of his clothes en route.

"I'll get you for that," she promised with a smile.

"Promises, promises."

Yet before she could make good on her words, Rick anchored himself between her lax legs and pushed himself home. So warm, so perfect. She wrapped her legs around him and took all he had to give.

She tasted herself on his lips. His kiss mimicked his hips.

He hesitated and looked down at her with concern. "Condom," he said. "I didn't—"

When he started to pull away, she held him tighter. "I'm on the pill. Last checkup was all good."

"I'm good, but are you sure?"

She answered by pushing her hips closer. Sex without condoms wasn't something she ever did. But making love to Rick without one . . . that felt perfectly right. "Too much talking," she whispered. "Not enough moving."

He laughed, rolled her around on the bed until she straddled him. When the bed squeaked they both froze and stared at the door.

She giggled and Rick moved her back under him, sealed his lips to hers and made love to her so slowly, so silently, and so completely, she heard angels sing.

Judy rolled over to find Rick missing from her bed. The clock at the bedside blinked five in the morning. With a smile on her face, she slipped into a bathrobe and found Rick huddled over her tablet with a cup of coffee in his hand. "Hey."

She slid her arm around his shoulders, loved how easily they fit together. His morning kiss brought a blush to her cheeks. "Good morning." He nodded toward the steaming coffeepot. "I made coffee."

"Good in the bedroom and in the kitchen. How did I get so lucky?"

"Don't ask me to actually cook anything."

"Don't blow my illusion." She poured a cup, mixed it to her liking, and let the first taste slide down her throat with a moan.

She caught him staring at her and smiled. "What?"

He licked his lips with a look of hunger.

The female in her wanted to purr. His hunger wasn't for coffee, and she knew it. "You're bad."

"I like your moans. Missed them last night."

But he'd been right about the intensity of their joining without making any noise. "I think we'll have an opportunity to moan again."

He fidgeted in the chair and directed his attention to her tablet. The game she played was on display. "What are you doing?"

"Trying to see if there are any clues here. Any patterns."

She moved to sit in his lap, and tapped the screen, collecting money from her virtual buildings. "Find anything?"

"Not really. This guy raided you a few times in the last couple of days, but then so did this woman."

"It's part of the game. Once you find a weak player, you tend to go back to them over and over to increase your stats. It's nothing personal."

"It is if the guy behind all this is playing this game. You said yourself there are diehards on here."

She sipped her coffee and pressed *revenge* button over the players that hit her in the night. "Well let's see if we can provoke a response off these people." She bombed a few defensive buildings, making the player weaker, and then raided a building or two, stealing their virtual money.

"What are you doing?"

Judy explained her strategy and repeated it with two more players. "If they're diehards, they'll come back hitting. If they don't care, they'll just stay away."

"And if they're our guy, they might just try and wipe out your base?"

She shivered. "It's a game. You can't wipe out a base. But yeah, you can have a bully on the game. Eventually they get bored and move on."

"Or they hunt down the player in real life and hurt them." He squeezed her waist. "There are crazy people out there."

She knew that now. Wouldn't look at the game the same way again. If it wasn't the only link they had to a possible suspect, she'd delete the thing now. "Any activity on my Facebook page?"

"Nothing. A few friends left comments about your red dress."

She smiled.

"Love that dress." He nuzzled her neck.

She pushed him away when her dad walked in the room and cleared his throat.

"I can take the morning off . . . drive you to the airport," Judy told her father after she showered and readied herself for another day.

Rick was in their room, giving her time to talk to her dad alone.

"I rented a car," Sawyer said, looking past her and down the hall. "Still . . ."

He blew out a long-suffering breath and turned his gaze toward her. He looked miserable.

"I'm sorry I'm disappointing you."

He shook his head. "I don't like some of the choices you're making, but I'm not disappointed."

"You look like you are."

Her dad attempted a smile, sucked at it, and let the facade drop. Judy found herself smiling.

"I like Rick," he said. "I'd like him more if he'd told me his intentions."

"Shouldn't I be the one he talks about his intentions with?"

Her words wiggled into her father's brain. "I suppose."

Judy stepped closer to her dad. "I know you're worried about me. But I'm OK. I really am."

He nodded and opened his arms.

She hugged her dad and heard him sigh. "You need me . . . day or night."

Emotion sat in the back of her throat. "I know."

Sawyer kissed the top of her head and let her go. "You go . . . I'll lock up when I leave."

"Love you, Dad."

"Love you, too, baby."

Chapter Twenty-Five

Rick sat across from Dean and Neil, their collective heads huddled in an effort to find a thread between Judy's war game pastime and the guy stalking her.

Her office had been quiet, no sign of anyone entering her space and leaving any gifts for her to stumble upon. There hadn't been any headlines of attacks . . . no evidence the police were even watching Rick.

Quiet. Too damn quiet.

"Something is here," Dean said under his breath. He had Judy's Facebook open and spent a painful amount of time tracking her friends and searching for links. Neil was working through the online game as a player and attempting to find the real names behind a few gamers.

"I think so, too," Rick said.

"Maybe the guy backed off the game. Deleted his profile." Neil typed with two fingers, then switched to a computer and continued the two-finger search.

"Doesn't fit the profile," Dean told them. "He's going to want to watch the fallout."

Rick sat back from the pictures of the crowd collected by Russell and Dennis at the courthouse and compared them to the shots of the gathering of people outside the garage when word got out about the initial attack. He then compared them with those collected outside the scene from the murder. They'd collected a handful of hours of news coverage, which Rick was going through one frame at a time. Life as a Marine was easier. Identify your target, point, and shoot. Next! "I'd never cut it as a detective," he said.

"Well shit!" Neil's voice rose with excitement, something seldom heard from the large man.

"What?" Rick inched the wheels of his chair closer to Neil's to see what he was *well shitting* about.

"What's this?" Neil pointed at the tablet with the game opened on a profile of a team member.

"A joke?" The profile name read *Major Harry Dog*. To give Harry some credit, many of the profile names were plagiarized off real people from General Grant to Hitler. Other names were obvious jokes, Dare Devil, Betty the Baker, Mominator, Lord of my Rings . . . the list went on for thousands. The list of those playing alongside Judy was limited to about sixty. Then there was the list of those beating her on the game and staying in her cache, which increased the list by several hundred.

"Read this and tell me what you think about the person behind it." Neil sat back while Rick and Dean inched in.

Rick glanced at the profile, saw a man in desert camo with a hard hat on the cartoon character. The nation's flag was Britain. From the amount of missions completed and fights won, the man had been playing for some time. "A man from somewhere in Europe who obviously doesn't have much of a social life if he spends this much time online."

Neil moved forward and opened another chat screen. "Not only is Major Harry not a man, she is in the States. My guess would be East Coast."

The times Major Harry was chatting online with fellow players were in line with the East Coast, cutting off at night saying she needed to catch the evening news. Neil scrolled up the page and highlighted a post. Sorry I missed the battle, team...left my phone in my purse and didn't charge.

Rick scratched at the hair on his chin, his brain swimming with the information. "So she is playing as a he."

"And if a she is playing a he . . ."

"Then he could be playing a she." Neil met Rick's gaze.

Dean let loose a growl. "Well hell!"

They were all back to square one.

"We should have thought about that," Rick said. At least he knew he was looking for a picture of a man.

She was still at work. Only came home with the new fuck and didn't appear worried in the least with her daily routine. She'd even been back on the game, bombing, raiding, and chatting on the loop. Just like nothing had happened.

When a notice came that he'd been attacked by her on his main profile, something inside him threatened to snap. How dare she?

He pinned up the picture he'd taken that afternoon when she went to lunch with her work friends and carefully sliced up the image of her arm. She might wear long sleeves or jackets to hide the scar, but he knew it was there.

They both knew it was there.

The knife in his hand carved the cheap wallpaper behind the picture, shredding it.

The image of her beyond the knife kept him carving. The parking garage had been too brief. Too fucking brief. To feel her tremble . . . feel her fear . . . yeah, that he wanted.

Next time she wouldn't get away.

And he'd have her all to himself.

"Mike!" Judy threw her arms around her brother and let him lift her in a huge hug.

"I thought I'd surprise you."

Her brother walking into the office building didn't make quite the same splash it had the first time. In his hand was a bouquet of flowers, his Hollywood smile framed his face with perfection.

She leaned back, glanced at the roses. "What are those for?"

"I missed the wedding."

She grinned, took the flowers from him.

He leaned in, placed his lips next to hers. "Rick said you needed fresh flowers to hide the camera."

Apparently, her temporary husband had already briefed her brother. It had been well over a week since the floral delivery and nothing had happened. Nothing. Housekeepers did their job . . . her colleagues would leave the occasional to-do list on her desk, otherwise nothing.

Judy glanced around Mike, didn't see anyone lurking, and motioned for him to stand in the doorway.

She turned away and removed the stick holding the camera from the flowers Rick had given her and transferred it to the new bouquet. While she handed the old flowers to her brother, the cell phone on her desk buzzed.

Rick's message was to the point. Toward the door.

Judy angled the disguised camera toward the opening of her cubicle and waited.

The next message from Rick was a smiley face.

Mike offered a wink when she finished. "So where am I taking you to lunch?"

Five minutes later they were sitting in the café they'd managed a meal in the last time he'd come to her work.

"I heard Dad showed up . . . alone." Mike broke off a piece of bread and shoved it in his mouth while he talked. Nothing like talking with your mouth full to prove you're family.

Judy rolled her eyes. "It took him a year to send Zach to check on your marriage. I'm married a few days and poof! Here's Dad."

"I'm a guy." Mike washed down the bread with the bottled water he'd ordered and shoved another chunk in.

"Like that matters. Whatever. Rick must have said something to make him happy. He left the next day."

"Maybe Mom called . . . talked some sense into him."

Judy sipped her iced tea. "Yeah, maybe."

Their meals came and she started in on her salad, while picking fries off Mike's plate.

He managed a few bites before bringing the conversation to her. "How are you really doing?"

Talking to Mike had always been like talking to an older sister. He was so much more approachable than Zach, and younger than Rena . . . wiser than Hannah. They had a great family, and if given the chance, she'd pour her heart out to all of them . . . but Mike always seemed to have a sensitive ear. Now that he was back in her life, she remembered that fact and let her tongue loosen up.

"I look over my shoulder a lot."

Mike paused between bites.

"It doesn't keep me from working, doing what needs to be done. But I question anyone I don't know when they walk up to me."

"I guess that's normal."

"Yeah . . ." She set her fork down. "Rick has been amazing. I thought he'd get tired of driving me around, checking in with me almost every hour."

Mike lifted an eyebrow, popped a fry in his mouth. "Karen told me he was into you before our divorce."

"Karen's a wise woman."

Mike nodded with a laugh. "She told me about your marriage." He looked around them, bringing her eyes up as well. Seemed no one was close enough to hear their conversation. "Think things will last once everything settles down?"

The night before flashed in her head . . . the way Rick had made love to her, made her feel like she was the only woman in the world. "I don't know, Mike. It's not like either of us planned this. We've been pushed together like something out of one of your movies."

His plate clean, Mike pushed it away, sat back, and leveled his eyes to hers. "You know he loves you . . . right?"

The words from her brother made her draw in a sharp breath. "I know he cares."

Mike smiled, lowered his dark sunglasses over his eyes, and tossed a few bills on the table. "Well, sis . . . let's get you back to work."

He walked her back to her office, kissed her cheek, and told her he'd see her at home.

For the next hour and a half, she thought about her brother's words . . . his observations.

She couldn't help but smile, couldn't stop the warmth from spreading over her skin when she thought maybe Mike saw something from Rick that he hadn't yet shared with her. Was it possible with all the chaos to fall in love with the right man?

Shaking her head out of the fog left in her brain from her brother, she spread the plans to the Santa Barbara project on her desk. José had left for the last half of the day, and her to-do list had dwindled to nearly nothing on a Friday.

"Miss Gardner?"

Deep in thought, she was startled by the sound of her name. Mitch, a courier who frequented the office, stood in the doorway to her cubicle chewing gum. "Hey, Mitch."

"I have a delivery for Mr. Archer."

Judy stood and reached for the package in his hand. "He's gone today. I'll take it for him."

Mitch handed her the package. A bandage on his left hand caught her eyes. "What happened?"

He glanced at his hand like it didn't belong to him, and hid it behind his back. "Accident."

Mitch was probably her age . . . maybe a little younger, and shyer than the average guy. He was taller than she was and could stand to lose a few pounds.

Walking around him, she offered a smile. "Need me to sign?"

"I have another quick delivery." He waved a package in his hand. "I'll come by on my way out."

Judy watched him walk away, and walked into Steve's office to set the package down.

She hesitated inside for less than a minute. A loud noise accompanied by the building shaking made her grasp the desk.

The door behind her slammed shut right as the fire alarms started to scream and the lights in the room started to flash.

Earthquake?

Only the room wasn't shaking. It was screaming, and flashing, and outside the door to Mr. Archer's office, she heard people running.

The deafening sound of the alarm made it nearly impossible to think.

Judy rushed to the door, fumbled with the handle, and found it unmoving.

She hit her fist against the door, heard people rushing by. "Hey!"

Someone beyond the barrier yelled the word *fire* and panic made her pull on the door harder.

Rick really enjoyed Michael's company. After being with Judy for even a short time, he started to see the man and not the Hollywood movie star he'd grown to know since working with Neil. Judy's conversations about her brother before he happened upon the Hollywood scene simply made the man more human.

"Thanks for taking her the flowers," Rick said when Michael walked into the den where he was going over the short list of players from Judy's game that hadn't yet been cleared. Dean had returned to his office and was in the process of soliciting his superiors to investigate the possibility that a murderer lurked beyond the graphics of an online game.

The chances of the detective getting anywhere with his colleagues were slim, but then again, he was on damn near family terms with the governor of the state and his wife. If anyone could get Detectives Raskin and Perozo to start looking somewhere other than in Rick's direction, it would be Dean and the Billings.

"No problem," Michael told him. "She looks good."

Rick knew he was complimenting more than her looks. Not something many brothers would notice anyway. "She's resilient."

Michael leaned against the counter in the kitchen, lifted his chin. "She's tough. Helps that you're here to be her rock."

Rick offered a nod. "I've assigned Russell to accompany you around if needed while you're home." It wasn't like Rick could play bodyguard while watching over Judy.

Michael shrugged. "I don't have anything big planned."

Rick knew that Zach had asked Michael to find a way to get home for a while. Safety in numbers along with a high-profile actor on the other end of a camera was a great way to keep a constant alibi for all involved.

"You sure this isn't cramping your latest film?"

"Family comes first," Michael told him.

Translated . . . that meant Michael had told his producers to work without him for a while. The fix was temporary.

Rick felt an answer was close. Now that they'd narrowed their search to players on the game, he could practically taste a break in the case.

The cell phone in his pocket buzzed at the same time the phone in the house rang.

Michael moved to answer the home line and Rick looked at the video feed from Judy's office. At last glance, he saw her sitting at her desk working, only now she wasn't there and the cubicle was empty. So why was the monitor sensing movement?

He stood to move to the room housing his monitors when he heard distress in Michael's voice.

"He's right here."

Michael handed the cordless to Rick. "It's Neil. He says something's happening in Judy's office."

Rick knocked down the immediate feeling of panic and grabbed the phone. "Talk to me."

"Have you looked at the monitors?"

Rick nearly ran to the monitors and clicked them all on. Judy's office sat center stage. Her space was empty, but employees ran by the opening of her cubicle. "What's going on?" He turned up the volume, noticed the strobe light flashing behind where the cameras were hidden.

"What's happening?" Michael asked behind him.

"I don't know."

"The fire alarm is blaring," Neil told him. Sure enough, the only sound on the monitor was that of the fire alarm and of panicked employees running by.

"False alarms go off all the time. Why the chaos?" Rick asked.

"Hold on."

While he waited for Neil to get back to him, Rick took the cell in his hand and speed-dialed Judy's number. As it rang, he heard the ring through the monitors. Had Judy left her cell phone behind as she exited the building?

His gut started to twist.

"There was an explosion," Neil told him when he got back on the phone. "Fire is responding."

A diversion . . . chaos . . . Judy would easily get lost in the shuffle. "I don't like this," Rick said.

"Neither do I."

One glance at Michael, and the two of them ran for the door.

Chapter Twenty-Six

"Help!" Judy yelled over the blaring alarm, pounding her fists on the door.

The hall outside the office sounded painfully silent, like the building had been evacuated and she was left behind. "Hello!" She pounded again.

She turned toward the desk and moved to the phone right as the door to the office opened.

White smoke billowed in from the hall. "Miss Gardner?"

"Mitch?" Thank God he had heard her.

"There's a fire. C'mon." He practically pulled her from the office, running away from the elevator and toward the back of the office where the smoke didn't seem as thick.

"What happened?"

"Not sure. Sounded like an explosion. I got turned around, heard you yelling."

A strong cough ripped from her lungs as smoke threatened their path. "We have to get out of here."

Mitch, who she never saw as a hero type, guided her out of the office down a back stairway she hardly knew was there. Smoke filled the stairs close to the third floor, but he kept them moving forward.

"This doesn't feel safe."

"C'mon." He pushed through the second-floor offices and ran

through smoke. He handed her some kind of cloth and helped her cover her mouth to keep from inhaling the smoke-filled air.

They moved in what felt like circles. Judy's breath came in short pants that brought up a cough. The cloth wasn't doing a good job of filtering. Each breath felt more difficult than the last.

"We need to find the stairs." Her head swam.

"This way."

Only this way wasn't toward the stairs. At least she didn't think it was.

Mitch's grip on her arm was viselike and more menacing than she expected from the shy delivery man.

She removed the cloth from her lips. "We need to go back the other way."

Mitch pulled her with him.

"Mitch!" She didn't know of an exit where he was headed.

"I know where I'm going, Judy." His angry voice shook her. Sounded familiar.

She hesitated, noticed the smoke thinning. She sucked in a breath through the cloth and looked at it.

A pillowcase?

She froze, twisted out of Mitch's grip.

He turned, looked at her, and she knew.

She acted as if she was going to run, turned into him with her elbow aiming for his torso. They connected and she ran.

A wall of smoke filled her vision, right as a freight train ran her into the ground.

"Stupid bitch."

———

Rick and Michael arrived along with the media.

Outside the building, employees gathered in sections, too many unrecognizable faces from every floor. Dressed in full firefighting gear, the fire department personnel filed into the building, pulling hoses. Smoke pushed out of what appeared to be the third floor on the west side of the building. Judy's office was several floors above toward the east.

Michael turned in circles. "Do you see her?"

Rick peered over the heads of people gathered. "No."

"I'll search over there." Michael pointed to a thick crowd of people standing on the opposite side of the street.

"OK."

Michael jogged away and Rick searched the crowd around him for a familiar face.

The police started to arrive and usher the people away from the building and still Rick didn't catch a glimpse of Judy.

When a familiar face met his, he took hold of Nancy's arm and turned her around. "Nancy?"

"This is crazy," she said turning toward the building.

"Have you seen Judy?"

Nancy shook her head. "No. We heard the explosion and ran. It was nuts in there."

"Where was the explosion?"

She pointed toward the smoke. "Either the third or fourth floor. Not ours."

That was something, at least. "If you see Judy, tell her I'm here."

He'd already lost Nancy's attention when a second explosion, several floors above the fourth floor, rattled the building and sent people screaming away from the building.

Running toward him through the crush of people was Neil. He looked like a linebacker pushing through a bunch of tight ends.

Rick didn't give him time to ask. "I haven't seen her."

From behind them, Michael joined the conversation. "Her boss didn't see her leaving."

Behind Neil's shoulder, the police were starting toward them. Probably to move them out of the area. He bumped his friend with an elbow. "Distract them. I'm going in."

She weighed nothing tossed over his shoulder and lifeless as he hid his path with smoke canisters and well-timed bombs. To think the Army didn't think he was fit enough for the job. Stupid fuckers.

The path joining the buildings was an abandoned corridor in the garage. If the homeless population knew of its existence, it would be littered with rotting garbage and the stench of urine. But for whatever reason, the vagrants in the area didn't know it was there. He did.

He relieved the baggage from his back and opened the door to the adjacent building's empty corridor. With the path clear, he tossed Judy back over his shoulder and down two flights. He twisted a familiar set of halls, the space becoming increasingly dark and obviously unused.

From the look of the old boiler room, it had been abandoned at least a decade before. The space was perfect. Noise from an old shaft that housed the newer ventilation and heating system drowned out much of the noise that would come from the room. Not that he needed to worry about that. Judy's building would be evacuated, and with the weekend now in full swing, there wouldn't be any meandering employees around to stumble upon anything.

He dumped her on a pile of blankets he'd placed there earlier, careful with her head only because he didn't want to ruin his fun by killing her too early. He'd been looking forward to this for weeks.

The chloroform he'd placed on the cloth she'd willingly taken to her mouth was starting to wear off. He wasn't quite ready for her to be completely aware of where she was, the fun they were going to have, so Mitch found his little helper and cooked up a small cocktail for his guest.

He drew up the solution and flopped down beside her. He wiped the vein in her hand to attention, pierced her skin. She jerked away, but he kept hold of her.

Judy's eyes opened, the panic sparkling from her lashes wouldn't be forgotten anytime soon.

He pushed the plunger with her first struggle, slipped the needle away, and waved it in front of her eyes.

"W-what do you . . ." Her words were already slurring, her gaze unfocused.

He let her arm go only to feel the dead weight of it hit his thigh. He pushed his fingers to her lips. "Shh."

She moved her head to the side but didn't have the ability to turn it again before her lids closed and she slumped over.

Mitch stood, rubbed his hands together, and smiled.

Meg pushed through the crowd, Lucas and Dan at her side. She'd just made it back to the house when Lucas and Dan showed up at the gate, informing her about the explosion.

They had to park blocks away from the chaos and run toward the mess of police and fire trucks. As they pushed through the people, they looked for Judy but didn't see her.

The clearly defined police line left anyone there to watch on the opposite side of the street. Several trucks sprayed water on the flames billowing through one of the top floors. The media was setting up cameras and reporters were applying lipstick before they stepped on their stage.

She had to have gotten out.

Dan pulled her hand, pointed toward a mass of people and several camera crews. "Isn't that Michael?"

Her relief was temporary as they moved closer and didn't see Judy at her brother's side. One look in his eyes and her head swiveled toward the building. "No."

Michael's arm wrapped around her shoulders and the cameras around them snapped pictures. He leaned close to her ear. "Rick is inside searching. Neil is casing the surrounding buildings."

"Is there anyone trapped in there? Do we know?"

Michael shook his head. "We don't know. From what I can tell, there was plenty of time for everyone from her floor to escape."

"Then where is she?"

Michael's hand squeezed her shoulder. "The first explosion was on a lower floor. The second was close to the roof."

"Do we know what caused the explosion?"

"No one knows."

A reporter pushed closer, shoved a microphone in their faces. "Michael, have you heard from your sister since the fire started?"

"Go away," he told the reporter.

Dan and Lucas moved around the two of them.

"Was your sister in the building today?" another reporter asked.

"No comment," Dan said as he placed his body between Michael and the reporter.

"Friends of yours?" Michael asked Meg.

She nodded and stared beyond the reporters to the activity outside the building. Seemed the fire on the lower floor was contained and the efforts were focused on the top levels.

Even though the reporters still asked questions, Michael ignored them, his eyes constantly searching over the heads of the crowd.

Waiting for minutes felt like hours. Each one that passed felt more dire than the last.

Neil found them, and pulled them away from the crowd.

They huddled next to a building, Lucas and Dan pushed the reporters back.

"Rumors are already flying. The police think the explosions were deliberately set."

"What? Why?"

"We don't know. The only rumor I confirmed was two smoke canisters found in a ventilation shaft and one outside a parking lot."

Meg started to feel her lungs restricting as panic for her friend set in. "Someone did this on purpose?"

"Looks that way." A heavy amount of uncertainty sat behind Neil's eyes. Meg hadn't known the man long, but he always seemed to guard his emotions.

"Oh, no. You don't think . . . that Judy . . ."

"Don't jump to conclusions."

Meg shook her head. "Why? You have. We have to find her." She sucked in a breath to find it lacking of oxygen, struggled with the next one.

Michael took hold of her shoulders and helped her sit while she fumbled with the inhaler in her pocket. Two puffs later and the stars in her head stopped spinning. "I'm OK," she insisted.

"I'm going back over to see if there's any more information," Neil told them. He directed his eyes to Michael. "Call Zach and Karen."

Worry punched her gut harder when with a face full of soot, Rick found them and dropped beside her on the curb. "I made it as far as the second floor." He coughed. "Too much smoke."

They all stared at the building, praying that Judy would walk out of it, or up to them and ask what they were all worried about.

Only she never came.

Chapter Twenty-Seven

Every high is followed by a hangover. The only hangovers Judy had ever experienced were the alcohol-induced stunners nearly every college student experiences somewhere in their four years at school.

So when she woke, and her head split in two the moment her eyes opened, she identified the roll of her stomach and the cotton lodged in her throat with a groan. She attempted to ball into a fetal position and remember the night before, but found her hands bound by a rope on each side of her body.

She blinked a few times, tried to focus. Stone floor, rusted old machines she couldn't immediately identify. The sound of a blower forcing air into a shaft filled the otherwise silent room. No windows . . . no doors that she could see, and only a few bare lights that looked like they'd wink out at the first opportunity.

She shook her cloudy head, tried to focus on the bare bulb above.

He'd waved a needle at her, laughed, and for a brief moment, she thought she was dreaming, then there was nothing.

"Oh, God." Moving her head took serious effort, bringing pain from cramped muscles. She pulled against the rope holding her, felt her own fatigue. She was still clothed, though the cold depth of the floor was seeping into her bones and making her shake.

Or maybe that was pure fear.

The doubled lines of everything around her started to focus. Judy didn't see him at first, thought maybe he'd left her there.

The hope of that quickly faded as he stepped from the shadows wearing a full set of military fatigues, complete with boots, face painted to blend in with the dank quarters.

Through the black and gray makeup, his sneer met a gleam in his eye.

She pushed her body back from him, noticed her feet weren't bound, giving her some mobility.

Slow, steady steps brought him to her. He knelt just out of reach of her legs. "Nice of you to wake, General."

"Let me go."

He laughed. "After all the effort I've taken to get you here? I don't think so."

He looked nothing like the awkward twentysomething that brought special deliveries to their office. There wasn't an ounce of uncertainty on his face, or in the way he held himself on the balls of his feet.

"Why? Why are you doing this?"

He blinked a couple of times, as if the question confused him. "Capture the enemy. Much better than just destroying them." Without words, he stood again, retreated to the corner of the room, back in the shadows, and just watched her.

Whatever his plan was, he wasn't rushing it. He acted as if he had all the time in the world.

She looked around the room again, didn't recognize any of it. She thought of her father's hardware store, the plumbing aisle filled with valves and pipes. Only the pipes she saw weren't from anything in the last twenty years. A boiler, maybe . . . which would mean they were in a basement of something. From the size of the room, the height of the ceiling, she thought it might be a large apartment complex.

She shivered, wondered if anyone above knew a psychopath lurked beneath.

Her pasty lips stuck together when she attempted to find moisture. She'd never directly dealt with someone who was clearly twisted, wasn't sure if she could talk sense into him or not.

His dark eyes watched from the shadows, unnerving her. Perhaps that was his goal?

"Mitch?" She attempted to use his name. "It is Mitch, isn't it?"

He didn't answer.

The next breath she pulled in made her shiver. The room was cold and an occasional draft blew in from behind her.

"I'm not your enemy."

Silence.

Then she heard a squeak from the corner of the room followed by something with tiny legs running.

Rats.

Things like that never really bothered her . . . not in a girlie, *squeal and jump away* kind of way. But she was half-lying on a cold floor without a way to escape the things.

From the corner, Mitch started to laugh, and Judy knew her lack of concern for rats was about to change.

———

It was past ten. Judy was officially missing.

Didn't bother Rick in the least that he paced like a caged animal outside the office building while arson detectives did their job. The only injured people in the building were from the floor where the first bomb exploded. No doubt now it was set . . . along with smoke bombs placed in various parts of the building.

The whole thing was a diversion . . . a distraction to remove

Judy. He knew it the moment he heard about the blast. Now it was confirmed.

In a van parked beside that of the media who'd finished their live shots for the late news, sat Russell and Dennis, who were searching the feeds generated from the office before the explosion.

The first sign of Detectives Raskin and Perozo resulted in Neil holding Rick back as they approached.

"You son of a bitch. Spent all your time on the wrong guy and now she's missing."

Raskin held up his hand. "Everyone is looking for her."

The hell. Like that's enough!

Dean stepped in and pulled the detectives out of the way.

From the van, Russell called Rick over. "What do you have?"

"This is the last few minutes before the explosion."

They'd seen it before, but it didn't have sound.

Judy stood with her back to the camera, bent over her desk.

A kid, midtwenties at best, filled the cubicle doorway. "*Miss Gardner?*" The sound was muffled.

"Can you turn that up?"

Russell upped the volume.

"*I have a delivery for Mr. Archer.*" The kid had a box in his hand. Looked away for a moment and then back again.

"*He's gone today. I'll take it for him.*" Nothing looked out of the ordinary with the exchange.

"*What happened?*" Judy's sweet voice stroked Rick's heart.

The kid jumped back, pushed his hand behind him. Nervous. *He's anxious.*

Rick peered closer . . . watched Judy leave her cubicle with the package while the kid promised to come back to have her sign for the package.

"I don't see much here, Russell."

"Wait."

The footage was void of anything, and within seconds the explosion was heard and screams of people reacting to it filled the footage. Strobe lights and fire alarms blared.

Mitch moved into the frame as he passed the people running toward the stairs. Judy wasn't seen in the mass exit. Neither was the kid.

Rick clenched his fists. "Rewind that to get a clear shot of this guy."

"Got it."

Rick sent a whistle in the air and captured Michael's attention. He motioned the man over, pointed at the image on the screen. "Ever see this guy when you've visited Judy?"

He shook his head. "Can't tell you." Michael turned around, waved to a few people he had been standing next to.

Rick recognized Judy's boss. Debra Miller sat huddled under someone's oversize coat.

Michael directed the woman's attention to the screen. "Do you know this guy?"

Debra looked closer. "A courier. I think. Delivers stuff but doesn't work for us."

"Know his name?"

She shrugged. "My secretary handles deliveries."

Much as Rick hated to bring in Raskin and Perozo . . . they had an entire police force to tap into where he and Neil didn't. "Dean?" Rick called his friend over. "I need to know who this guy is."

Dean stood beside Raskin and Perozo as they watched the footage.

"He doesn't leave the building." Dean stated the very observation the rest of them had made.

"Neither does Judy."

If I show fear, he'll exploit it. That was obvious when he'd spread peanut-butter-covered bread close to her . . . taking great pleasure in smearing the sticky stuff above her knee. Why had she picked a skirt today?

She couldn't determine the time, but her stomach growled and her eyes were having a hard time staying open. If not for the fear of closing them, and the need to pee, she would be asleep already.

The first rat took the peanut butter offering, bringing her wide awake in a heartbeat. Her back stiffened against the old metal box she was propped up against. From the corner, she watched Mitch eating the bread as if it were popcorn.

She shoved the rat away with her foot, and found another one willing to come in close for the food. Her first scream moved them along . . . but the second didn't do much other than make them pause before finding the food.

Her eyes locked on the four foot-long varmints fighting over the food when she felt something brush against her hand. It jumped, landed on her lap, and Judy lost it.

The rat squealed, its tiny feet clawed into her bare thigh. Her screams didn't stop the tiny beast as it scented the food and ran in circles. A flash of light blinded her.

The bastard was taking pictures of her.

Only with the bright light, the rats scurried into the dark.

"Priceless," Mitch managed.

Judy kept screaming. Someone had to be nearby . . . someone would hear her.

Mitch lifted his voice to match hers. Yelled the word *help* at the top of his voice.

"Do you think I'm that stupid, General? I assure you, I'm not." He advanced then, dropped his hands to her ankles, which were covered by her long boots, and kept her from kicking him. With a free hand, he covered the peanut butter and smeared it up her thigh.

She couldn't stop the few tears that spilled, but she didn't cry out when he pinched her by squeezing her bare skin.

"It was only a game," she told him.

His hand slid higher, his face grew dark.

Judy forced her eyes to his, clenched her back teeth together, refusing to respond.

"Is this a game, General?" Higher he went.

He loved her tension . . . enjoyed her pain.

Judy sucked in a deep breath and willed her limbs to relax. She even forced a smile past her drying tears.

His eyes searched hers and he shoved his hands between her thighs.

She squeezed her toes inside her boots and never stopped staring at his dark eyes, didn't let him see her fear.

He jerked away, his hand leaving her only to rap his fist against her jaw. She went with the punch just as Rick had told her to. The taste of blood trickled in her mouth.

Instead of provoking another punch, she kept her eyes to the side of the room.

Mitch stood and moved back to his corner.

Dean and his posse of detectives were waking up the courier company that delivered packages in an effort to learn more about Mitch.

As they did this, Neil and Rick found a link on the game.

Dainty Destroyer was the gamer tag of a woman who called herself Michelle. Only when Neil and Rick looked over the Facebook page where Michelle spoke with Judy up until the first attack, they didn't find any evidence that Michelle was a woman. There weren't any pictures on the profile . . . just random postings of flowers and cats. She did respond with a comment or two on Judy's page where Judy had posted pictures of her graduation. I didn't know Michael Wolfe was your brother.

Judy's response was a simple Shh, don't mention that on the game.

"How fast can we get an ID on this person?" Rick asked Neil.

"Through the right channels? Monday?"

Rick simmered. "Through the wrong channels?"

Dennis had an earpiece in. Their resident hacker clicked away. "Working on it."

Dean stepped up to the van. "They're letting us in."

Rick waved a finger in Dennis's direction. "Keep looking."

Rick stood shoulder to shoulder with Dean as they marched past the police line, ducked under the tape, and jogged into the building. They started at the site of the first explosion. Looked like an equipment room of some kind. Burned-out monitors, lots of trashed wires.

"Guess what this was?"

Rick glanced above him, noticed a lack of cameras, stepped outside and found a few burned-out ones. "Surveillance."

"So the guy took out the cameras first."

"Only he wasn't expecting ours."

"Right," Dean said as they started up the main stairway. At the seventh floor, Dean gripped the banister and waved Rick along. "Go. I'll catch up."

Rick ran the rest of the way, felt the burn in his lungs, and ignored it as he pushed into Judy's floor. Emergency lights were the only thing working, giving very little light to a space he'd only ever seen filled with people.

He stepped into Judy's cubicle, stood exactly where she had when the courier approached her. Rick turned, mimicking their conversation, and stepped around the flimsy office wall and a few steps down the hall to Mr. Archer's office.

The door was open. Rick removed a flashlight from his pocket and followed a line down the frame, noticed something lying on the floor below the jamb. He bent down, noticed a metal fragment and searched for where it originated. By the lock, the door was scarred, as was the threshold. As if the metal on the floor somehow kept the door from opening. Rick glanced around the office, noticed the package Judy had taken from their suspect.

He heard Dean sucking in a breath from outside the door. "Careful," he warned. "Looks like the door was locked from the outside." He shone his light on the floor for Dean to see.

While Dean investigated that, Rick walked over to the desk and laid his light to shine on the package.

It was addressed to Mr. Archer but didn't have a return address. Using a letter opener, Rick tilted the box over and dug into the tape sealing the package.

Dean moved beside him, held his breath.

Rick opened the box, noticed several papers inside.

Before the first one slid onto the desk, he recognized a photo of Judy's red dress . . . her hat as she ducked into the limo.

"Damn it."

Dean used a pen on the desk and spread the images out. They were all of Judy. Several were cut up.

The phone in Rick's ear buzzed.

He clicked on. "Talk to me."

"We have an address."

Rick bolted from the room.

Chapter Twenty-Eight

Rick and Neil rolled up to the property that held two living spaces divided by a chain-link fence. The front house had lights blazing and evidence of children's toys scattered in the yard. The back house, the one they focused on, appeared empty. Seconds after they skidded to a halt, Raskin and Perozo moved in behind them.

The detectives left their blue lights flashing on the car while Rick ran toward the back of the house. The place was dark, no car in the drive. Holding his weapon in front of him, Rick nodded toward the back of the structure.

Neil moved around the house.

"Back off," Raskin told Rick, his own weapon pointed toward the ground.

In his ear, Neil said, "It's dark back here. Don't think he's home."

"Roger." Rick ignored the detective and rapped his finger on the door. "Hey, Mitch?" Rick yelled at the closed door.

There wasn't a response.

"Still nothing," Neil reported. "What are the chances he booby-trapped this place?"

"What are the chances Judy's inside?" Rick asked.

Raskin heard Rick's question, motioned toward the front house, where a woman and a child peered through the kitchen window. "I need to get them out of there."

Rick nodded. "Go."

Less than a minute later, the family from the front house were shuffled away. Perozo huddled next to the neighbor's car. "They haven't seen him since this morning."

She's not here.

"Back up," he told Neil in his mic. "Just in case."

"We need a search warrant," Raskin managed from the side of the front house.

Every minute Judy was missing was one too long.

"You need a search warrant." He wiggled the handle, just in case it wasn't locked. It was. "I don't." Rick lifted his foot to the door, busted through the lock. The door crashed against the frame.

When no explosion ruined what was already the worst day of his life, Rick led with his gun aimed into the room. He flipped a light switch on the wall and stopped cold.

Judy was everywhere.

Images tacked, stapled . . . strung around the room.

"Holy hell," he heard Raskin say behind him.

Mitch Larson had only lived in the converted garage for a few months . . . that was according to the tenants of the front house. He didn't have parties, came at strange times but never seemed to have anyone around so the people in the front house didn't pay him much attention.

Seeing Judy on every wall, every surface, told Rick how sick the man who had her was. It also gave him hope she was still alive. Because as much as he was beating down any possible emotion that resembled grief, it lingered above his head like a cloud. Statistically, Judy was already dead.

When his mind went there, he pushed it away.

Hold on, baby. I'm coming.

They were closer. Though she wasn't sitting in Larson's rented space, they were closer to knowing the man who had her.

Police filled the space, lights flashed outside the residence like white noise from rain.

Several images kept playing in his head, pictures of Judy with the word *General* written over them in a juvenile hand, images of her home . . . the office building where she worked. There were even a few shots of her outside of Zach and Karen's house taken the night of the fundraiser. Pictures taken by a private camera and not something printed in the local paper or gossip magazine. So Mitch had been watching her since then.

The images of her prior to coming to California were taken off the Internet, mainly with Michael in the shot and generated by the media.

The office building shots caught his attention. They didn't hold images of Judy, just the building. The bastard had even taken pictures of the place he attacked her the first time. Question was, did he take the shots before or after he'd attacked her?

Outside Mitch's place, Dennis and Russell were inside the van with Neil . . . all working hard to find out any information they could about Mitch Larson.

Rick's gaze met that of a picture taken of Judy and Mike outside the café close to her office. She wasn't wearing what she'd left the house in today, so the picture had to have been taken long before. In his ear, he heard Neil's voice.

"He's wannabe military."

The information didn't come as a surprise. "How wannabe?" he said into the mic, ignoring the detectives around him who were swiping for prints and photographing the scene.

"Enlisted only to feel the sting of rejection six months in. Army. Had a psychotic break while on a training mission." Neil delivered the facts without emotion.

Rick diverted his attention away from the photographs. "What kind of break?"

"Challenged a superior officer. Female. Went through a series of tests and was discharged."

"Dishonorable."

"Is there another way six months in without an injury?"

"What else do we know?" Rick turned back to the images, knew something was there . . . he just needed to find it. Only the pictures were floor to ceiling and many were carved into while others had dried blood smeared all over them.

"He's crazy, not stupid. Excelled in intelligence and details. First clue he wasn't balanced was his desire to get close to his enemy. Guns aren't his thing."

Rick thought of the scars on Judy's arm. "He likes knives."

Neil paused. "Yeah."

Rick knew a trip to the dentist was inevitable with how much he was grinding his back teeth. "Get close to your enemy. Feel their pain, their fear."

Neil waited a second . . . maybe it was two. "We're going to find her, Smiley."

More images of the office building filled the wall of Larson's bedroom.

The sick fuck slept in here . . . imagined whatever it was he was doing to Judy right now.

He had no intention of bringing her back here.

The room was littered with Judy's image. Some were taken at the Beverly Hills home where even now her brothers and friends waited for any word on her well-being.

It was well past three in the morning, so no one was at the office except the lingering fire department and police that would guard the place until first light. Until arson could poke around with fresh eyes and a new outlook. None of them were actually looking for a missing wife.

Only Rick. He was looking for his wife.

The woman he married and swore to protect.

The thought of telling her father he didn't find her in time ate at him. The thought of her lying lifeless . . . finding her dead and abused.

Rick closed his eyes and blew out a slow breath.

No.

He opened his eyes again, tuned out the noise around him, and focused. The wall in Larson's bedroom showed images of Judy everywhere. Rick looked beyond the woman he loved . . . looked at the world surrounding her.

The office building loomed in many images.

The parking garage. Empty. Dirty.

The office.

Empty halls of concrete and grime. Every tenth image was of an abandoned space. In many were pictures of Judy cut out and standing, sitting in the space.

Cut up.

Bloody.

Rick touched the device in his ear. "Is there a basement in the building Judy works in?"

Neil said one word. "Checking."

A few second later he heard him reply. "New building. No basement."

Raskin tapped Rick's shoulder. He jumped.

"I owe you an apology."

Rick glared at the man. "You owe me more than that."

Raskin offered a nod, turned back to the images in the room. Both of them worked to find her. Rick felt that now.

Dean stood in the corner of the room, fatigue sat behind his eyes like a drug.

None of them did anything other than drink bad coffee and keep looking for something . . . anything.

"Rick?"

Neil's voice sounded hopeful.

"What?" Those around him, including Raskin, turned to look at him.

Rick held his ear, making it clear he was talking into a mic. "What?" he asked in a calmer voice.

"The building adjacent has a basement. Two floors under the main structure."

Rick waited for the boom.

"Abandoned . . . secluded . . . easily reached by way of the garage."

The hope in Rick's chest expanded. He looked around the room again, couldn't help the half smile on his face.

Rick turned from the room, made it a few feet before Raskin stopped him. The man leveled his eyes to his. "You know something."

The smile on Rick's lips dropped. "And you owe me."

The tension in the detective's jaw was palpable.

"Damn it."

For a minute, Rick didn't think the man was going to let him go without an argument. "Look around. The answer is here."

"Tell me," Raskin demanded.

"I need fifteen minutes."

Raskin glared.

"You married?" Rick asked.

Raskin let him go, nodded toward the door. "Get out of here, Evans. We'll call you when we have something new."

The short nod Rick offered would have to be enough. He lowered his head and walked out the door. Once clear, he jogged to the van that was idling and waiting.

Neil handed Rick a tactical weapon when he closed the door to the van. "They never left the building . . . not really."

The ten-mile high-speed drive back to Westwood was the longest in Rick's life.

———

"I need to pee." The physical need outweighed the need for silence. The rats had lost interest after the flash of the camera scared them away.

It appeared she woke Mitch with her words. "Think prisoners of war tell their captors of their bodily functions?"

Judy did her best to keep a straight face. "There isn't a war, Mitch. This is your idea of a good time. And I need to pee. Good news for you, a lack of food and water means I won't have to again for a while."

Mitch grinned, lifted a bottle of water to his lips.

Judy had long since lost the ability to salivate. Between the smoke from the building and the drugs still swimming in her system, she was as dry as they came.

It didn't seem like her words were doing anything for him. She closed her eyes and tried to ignore the need.

"What are you doing?" he asked.

She kept her eyes closed. "Trying to go with an audience. Haven't done that since I was three."

He pushed against the wall, made his way to her side.

She refused to look at him when he reached for her left hand, undid the knot tying her down.

Biting her bottom lip, she refused to respond.

First order of business, get out of the ropes, second was to go. She couldn't remember ever having the need quite as keen, but it was there now.

Mitch gripped her wrist before removing the rope on her right arm. Circulation made her arms tingle as he lowered them to her sides.

"Fight me," he said, "and I'll cut you."

She felt a blade at her throat. He was going to cut her anyway . . . eventually.

"I just need to go to the bathroom, Mitch."

Pulling both her arms, he shoved her to her feet, where she stumbled into him, felt his knife jab into her arm. The bite of the blade made her cry out and back away.

Mitch wrapped one of her hands to a bare pipe several feet away from where she'd been for the past several hours.

He took a step back, but never stopped watching her.

"Go."

The need was so great, but his eyes never left her.

"You're watching."

He glared. "Get used to it. Mine is the last face you'll see."

She understood that . . . if he had his way.

Judy moved around the rusted old boiler and knelt in the corner. She thought of the trips up to the cabin . . . how camping and peeing in the forest were just a part of the experience.

She missed the cabin . . . her family. Rick would love it up there . . . in the mountains above her childhood home.

He was looking for her now. Probably beside himself trying to find her.

Her family was worried, fearful they'd failed her in some way.

She managed to empty her bladder and sat huddled in the corner long after she needed to.

If she was ever going to see Rick . . . her family . . . again, she needed to be smarter than her captor.

Mitch had a knife.

"Knives are easier to outrun than a bullet." Rick's words swam in her head.

Mitch was also crazy. Reasoning with crazy wouldn't work. Observing the crazy's actions, motivations, and intentions . . . that she could do.

"You're done," he said while he took the few steps toward her that separated them.

If she was going to act, do anything to save herself, it would have to be when her arms weren't tied up. It would have to be when she wasn't drugged . . . have to be before she was too weak to do anything.

It was going to have to be now.

She did her best to act resolved to him removing the tie on her arm and walking back to where she'd sat for the last twelve hours.

Just when she thought there might be an out, Mitch surprised her. "Grab that bar," he demanded.

The bar he pointed to was above her head . . . nearly out of reach. "Why?"

Mitch lost any patience he might have had. "Do it!" His voice boomed and echoed.

She jumped, not sure if she should comply or fight.

He moved closer and Judy grabbed for her tied-up hand. She had her cold fingers inside the rope but didn't manage to do anything but scrape her fingers before Mitch was on her. Her kicks fell on air or his thick boots, which didn't slow him down.

She stopped when his knife scraped a line up her neck. Every sucked-in breath met the blade.

"Grab the fucking bar, General."

The desire to fold in and protect her body made it nearly impossible to comply.

He tilted the knife so only the tip sat at her neck. He pushed it in like a needle. His body pushed hers against the boiler, a valve shoved into her side.

"You're testing me." He moved the blade, cut deeper.

Judy closed her eyes and lifted her hand, gripping the bar.

He secured the rope dangling from her wrist, tied her to the bar above her head. The blood that had managed to make its way to her fingertips fled. He moved her other hand next to the first. She was nearly on her tiptoes, dangling. She wasn't sure what was going to give first, her wrists or her shoulders.

Nothing Rick had taught her about protecting herself was going to work like this.

"Now isn't that better?" Mitch's voice upped an octave. She realized then that he used the higher voice when he was delivering packages. His assertive voice was so much harsher. Still, she'd curse herself for the rest of her short life for not recognizing it. For not knowing he was the man who attacked her in the garage.

Judy looked at her hands holding on to the bar. One slipped and she felt her muscles strain.

"You don't like it." Mitch cocked his head to the side. "And here I thought you wouldn't mind standing for a while. That floor is cold."

She was trying not to show her fear but knew she failed.

He stood back and looked at her like she was a painting on a wall. From his pocket, he removed his phone and focused it on her. "How about a smile."

"Fuck you."

He winked. "Not yet . . . but soon."

She cringed.

"Now smile."

She lost her grip on the bar and tried to catch hold again. Her toes pushed off the floor and she managed to grab the bar again.

Mitch moved closer. "Let me see if I can convince you to smile."

She focused on his knife as he moved it under her shirt and started to cut away at the buttons holding it together.

She whimpered and he kept popping buttons until her torso was exposed to his eyes, his blade.

"You ready to smile, General?"

He stood back, lifted the phone again.

Tears ran down her cheeks while she forced a smile.

Light blinded her.

He stood back and looked at the picture. "Now isn't that better?" He twisted the phone for her to see it. The image didn't even look like her anymore. Smudges of mascara streaked her cheeks, while the swelling and bruising of her jaw accompanied the drops of blood on her neck. Her hair was matted, her skin was pale, and she looked like a dangling carcass with a caricature smile.

Mitch sat back, looking at pictures on his phone, then he stared at her, lost in his own thoughts.

Every second felt like hours.

She bent one knee, trying to find something behind her she could wedge against to relieve some of the pressure on her arms.

The bar above her creaked and snapped Mitch out of his self-induced trance. "You can't get away," he told her.

"I can't feel my arms."

He puffed out his bottom lip like a two-year-old. "Well, we can't have that."

The knife slid up her sleeve, exposing her arms. He looked at his earlier handiwork and traced the edges of her scar with his knife. She tried to pull away as he made sure she felt her arms.

He laughed, and she screamed with every cut.

Chapter Twenty-Nine

Neil and Rick sprang from the van before it rolled to a complete stop. Night vision goggles, heat-sensitive radar . . . they had what they needed to go in quietly and find their target. Good thing it was pitch-black outside or they would appear just as crazy as the guy who kidnapped Judy.

They started in the garage, found the entry to the adjacent building, and easily disabled the lock. In single file, and without words, they moved down the short hall before they found the stairs leading down. A *Do Not Enter* sign was plastered over the door, but it was obvious the door had been used recently. Someone had actually oiled the hinges, making the door silent as it opened.

Rick clicked on the night vision and the hall in front of him offered a green view of the empty basement. The sound of a fan blowing accompanied their footfalls. The first fork in the hall split them up. Without words, Neil took the right and Rick continued forward . . . closer to the noisy fan.

A door on his left made him pause. The rusty lock and unoiled hinges had him moving on. The corridor veered left. Without a direction, he took it, found a storage room filled with old chairs, desks, and various office supplies. The space was dusty from its obvious lack of use. The only thing there was evidence of was rats in the corners.

Back in the hall, he continued toward the fan.

In his ear, Neil said, "Moving northeast."

"Copy."

Each step in the basement met with disappointment. If Judy wasn't there, where was she?

Rick pushed back the desperation inside him. *C'mon, Judy.*

He rounded what looked like the end of the building. An arrow pointed to the boiler room.

Judy's piercing scream filled him with both dread and relief.

He ran now, switching the safety off his rifle.

———

Judy wasn't sure if pure adrenaline or unadulterated fear gave her strength, but when Mitch started back at her with the knife, determined to hurt her even more, she gripped the bar over her head and bent her elbows like she did when she worked out.

With bent knees, she connected with the man's chest.

He stumbled back and she kicked both feet toward his face with a scream.

Mitch hit the floor, blood spilled on the side of his face.

The pipe above her started to give with her weight and she tried to bounce the rust free.

Mitch scrambled to his feet right as the bar gave way, dumping her on the ground.

Blood rushed to her arms with pins and needles.

A blurry mass rushed her, knocking her to the floor. "You're going to regret that." Mitch's arms squeezed around her so hard she fought to breathe.

"Let her go!"

Judy almost didn't recognize Rick's voice.

Suddenly, Mitch pulled her in front of him, dragged her to her feet, his knife at her throat. Her hands gripped his to prevent him from killing her.

Rick had his weapon pointed directly at them, a lethal stare boring into the man holding her.

"I'll cut her."

Rick's beautiful green eyes found hers. Her trust in him didn't waver. "Shoot him," she pleaded.

Mitch pulled her closer, ducked behind her head.

"Going to risk killing your own wife?" Mitch moved to the back of the room. She had no idea if there was an exit that way or not.

Rick's weapon traced their movement. His eyes moved from hers and pinned on Mitch.

"Take the shot."

The tension in Mitch's hand was so tight she knew she wouldn't survive the cut. The knife drew blood.

Noise behind Rick gave Mitch pause.

Judy pulled his arm, prayed her strength would hold, and twisted her head so it wasn't blocking his.

Noise exploded inside the room. The man behind her fell to the ground, nearly dragging her with him.

Judy stepped out of the mess and directly into Rick's arms.

Rick buried Judy's head against his shoulder and held her.

Behind him, Neil and Detective Raskin stepped closer. From the look of Mitch's body, he'd suffered more than one bullet.

Rick gently dislodged Judy from his shoulder and felt down both sides of her arms, her body. "Were you hit?"

She looked down at her mess of clothes and shook her head. "No."

Thank God. He pulled her into him again and her arms gently wrapped around his waist.

"We need an ambulance," he heard Raskin say into his phone. "And the coroner."

Neil laid a hand on his shoulder. "I'll call the family."

"Tell them I'm OK," Judy whispered. "Just a few cuts."

Rick noticed more than a few. "Let's get you out of here."

They walked toward the corridor. Detective Raskin shrugged out of his jacket and handed it to Rick to place over Judy's shoulders. Without words, Rick led Judy out of the basement, half carrying her away from her prison.

———

"All charges have officially been dropped." Dean delivered the news Monday afternoon.

Judy held Rick's hand over the table and squeezed it hard. In the other rooms, her entire family moved about the Beverly Hills estate.

Judy didn't want to discuss the kidnapping, or the man responsible for it, in front of her parents. All of it had been traumatic enough . . . for all of them.

"Do we know why he targeted me?"

She and Rick had their theories, but nothing had been confirmed.

Dean glanced at Rick, then to her. "How much of this do you want to hear?"

"All of it," she told him. "He can't hurt me now."

No, Mitch Larson wouldn't ever hurt anyone again.

"I'm sure Rick told you about the pictures." She couldn't imagine her image all over the man's home, even after Rick told her about them.

"Yes."

Rick offered a smile of encouragement.

"Along with the pictures were long-winded rambling narratives blaming you for his dishonorable discharge from the military."

"But—"

Dean waved a hand in the air. "Of course you didn't have anything to do with it. He also used your name and that of the female officer who his real grievance was with, interchangeably, in his letters. He had pages of notes from that online game. He had three accounts, including that of a woman you friended on Facebook."

Judy pictured the profiles in her head when Dean listed the names Mitch Larson had used. The dots connected and linked him directly to her.

"So when I kicked his butt on the game, he found his target," Judy concluded.

"It appears that way."

She squeezed her eyes closed. "How stupid and naive of me."

Rick brought their joined hands to his lips. "This wasn't your fault."

"I know. But I made it easy for him." She turned her attention to Dean. "How soon can I scrub my profiles from the Internet?"

"Detective Raskin is working with the Internet department to back up the files for their use. Shouldn't be but a couple more days."

"I want it all gone, everything I can get off the Internet. No more online games. Monopoly might be boring, but it's safer."

Dean pushed away from the table, shook Rick's hand. "If you need anything . . . you know where to find me."

Judy offered a hug. "Thanks for everything."

"Be safe," he told her before he left the house.

It took a month for her family to return to their normal lives. If it wasn't for the promise of going to Utah for Thanksgiving and a week at Christmas, her parents wouldn't have ever left.

Judy met with Debra Miller after the family dispersed.

They sat across Michael's kitchen table, drinking coffee. "I'd like you to come back," Debra told her.

Judy smiled into her cup. "I don't honestly know if I can." She was stronger than she thought she'd be, but walking back into the office . . .

Debra tapped a perfectly manicured nail against her cup. "I won't pretend to understand how you feel. Get through the holidays before you give me your answer."

"I'm just an intern," she reminded her. "You don't have to feel any guilt about what happened."

Debra actually laughed. "I don't. Misdirected guilt isn't fueling this conversation, Judy. I like your designs . . . like your passion. José was promoted and we're in need of someone to replace him, not to mention I'd like you around to help with the Santa Barbara project."

"You're offering me a job?"

"I'm offering you an opportunity." Debra sipped her coffee. "Besides, I can't help but notice the delicious men you surround yourself with." She winked over her cup.

Debra Miller was a very attractive, put-together woman. Judy doubted she struggled for male companionship.

Judy walked her out of the house as Rick was pulling into the drive.

He removed his helmet and left it dangling from the handlebars of the Ducati. He shook Debra's hand.

Debra glanced over her shoulder and lifted her eyebrows. "See what I mean?"

Judy laughed and Rick smiled, though she knew the joke was over his head.

"Call me after the first," she said.

"I will."

Judy and Rick watched her leave before moving inside. "What was all that about?"

She rinsed the cups and put them in the dishwasher. "She offered me a job."

"Really?"

Judy gripped the counter, looked in the backyard. "Yeah."

"What do you want to do?"

She shrugged. "I don't know. I have until January to make my decision."

Rick moved around the counter and pulled her into his arms, kissed the top of her head. "She'd be lucky to have you." Rick was always saying stuff like that.

They'd fallen into a comfortable pattern of living. Meg had moved the offices back to the Tarzana house while Rick stayed at Mike's with her. But Mike was wrapping up his latest film and would be returning home for a few months. It was time to consider where she and Meg were going to live.

It was time to determine the longevity of her relationship with Rick. She loved the man but couldn't risk telling him her feelings. After everything that had happened, they hadn't had time to analyze their life together . . . or apart.

Emotionally, she wasn't sure she was ready to consider life without him. To his credit, he hadn't once alluded to wanting a different path than the one they were on.

Rick put her at arm's length, kissed her briefly. "We're leaving in half an hour."

"We are?"

"Yep . . . a date. Nothing too fancy."

She narrowed her eyes. "Well, I need to get ready then."

Thirty minutes later, they left the house in Mike's Ferrari. "You know . . . eventually my brother's going to want his car back."

Rick laughed. "I know. Means I need to get behind the wheel as much as possible while I can."

They talked about traffic, her job offer, what was happening with Zach and Karen and the extra teen that made it into their home in the last month. When Rick pulled into the parking lot to the tram leading to the Getty, Judy actually clapped her hands like a kid. "You remembered."

He put the Ferrari in park, came around to help her out of the low car.

"Don't expect me to know any of the artists. Take me to the Rock and Roll Hall of Fame, and I'm your man."

She snuggled into him on the short ride to the top of the hill. "The art isn't what makes this place special for me," she told him. "It's the building I love."

And she did. Arched ceilings, verandas, and endless angles and curves that highlighted whatever art the museum wanted to display. She dragged him from one end to the other, pointing out everything her eyes saw that his didn't.

The sun was starting to set and he pulled her toward a single table with two chairs that overlooked the city.

"What's this?" she asked.

He pulled out one of the chairs, removed her purse from her arm, and set it down. "I might not have any idea about art, but I do have some class."

"This is for us?" She looked around and saw a waiter standing close by. The sun was low, but not quite setting.

"We know some powerful people, babe. I for one am not opposed to asking them to pull some strings."

The waiter approached and filled their glasses with sparkling wine.

Rick lifted his glass to hers. "To us."

She smiled, clinked his glass . . . but didn't drink. "Rick?"

He placed a finger in the air, quieting her. "It's taken me all day to work up to this moment. So I need you to just listen."

He was fidgeting and set his glass down.

She set her glass down, folded her hands in her lap. Rick nervous was a delight to watch. The man always had such confidence in everything he did. This side of him made her think of young boys handing apples to their favorite teacher.

His green eyes met hers. "I love you."

The giddy smile on her face fell and tears welled.

"The thought of my life without you makes me ill. I've almost lost you twice and . . . I can't. I can't lose you again."

She swiped a tear from her cheek, kept listening.

"I want my ring on your finger, and everything that comes with staying your husband for life. I want the good times, the bad times . . . though a few less bad times might be nice for a while. I want a mortgage and a family car. I want all of that with you."

It took both hands to clear her vision. "Oh, Rick." She walked around the table and sat in his lap, melded her lips to his, tasted her tears in their kiss. "I love you, too. After everything we've been through, not a lot scares me . . . but thinking of my life without you leaves me empty. I want to show you the ridiculously small town I grew up in, introduce you to all my crazy relatives."

"Crazy?" he asked with a silly grin.

"*Eclectic* might be a better word." She thought of her aunt Belle. "Well, maybe a little crazy."

Rick laughed. "I've met your parents. I'm not scared."

"Me either. Not with you . . . not about us."

His arms wrapped around her. "Is that a yes?"

"Was there a question?" she teased.

"Marry me."

"Still not a question."

He found a sensitive spot on her waist and tickled her.

She squirmed in his lap.

"Will you marry me?"

With hands framing his face, she stared at her future. "Yes. I'll marry you."

He tossed his head back and laughed, picked her up and swung her around before kissing her again.

Epilogue

Snowcapped mountains made a perfect backdrop for the sunny Saturday following Thanksgiving.

Hannah rushed into the room; her floor-length dusty rose gown hugged her model-perfect body like a second skin. The college boys wouldn't stand a chance. "They're all ready. Dad's on his way up."

Judy adjusted the half sleeve of her wedding gown and tugged on the gloves that ended at her elbow as she stood. Meg pulled the train out behind her and Rena handed her the flowers.

Her mother kissed her cheek. "You're lovely."

"Thanks, Mom."

"I'll see you down there."

From the looks of the packed parking lot, everyone in Hilton, Utah, was packed into the pews below. She did love her hometown, couldn't imagine getting married anywhere else . . . but living there wasn't something she wanted. Thankfully, Rick wanted to stay in LA for a while, see where it took both of them. Secretly, Judy knew Rick was hoping she'd take the job at Benson & Miller Designs. Judy wanted to wait for the new year to make that decision. Right now, she wanted to exchange real vows with the man she loved in front of everyone important in her life.

"Are you nervous?" Hannah asked.

Judy placed a hand over her stomach. "Excited."

"I almost fainted when Joe and I got married," Rena told her.

"Don't tell Aunt Belle that, she'll really think you were pregnant when you said *I do*."

A knock on the door made her stomach flutter. Maybe she was a little nervous.

Her father, dressed in a sharp black tux, his hair combed back and his chest puffed out like the proud man he was, entered the room. One look at her and some of that pride shifted. She saw tears behind his eyes and had to open hers wider to avoid tears of her own.

Meg handed her a tissue. "None of that. Oh, jeez. Stop."

Judy fanned her face and blinked away the moisture.

Sawyer moved to her side, took the tissue from her hand, and patted the corners of her eyes. "Guess this means my little girl is all grown up."

Judy offered him a smile. "Yep."

Sawyer tossed the tissue aside, offered his arm. "That sucks."

She laughed, leaned into him. "I love you, Daddy."

"I love you, too." The wedding march filled the hall and the girls lined up in front of them.

The good people of Hilton loved a good party, and weddings were at the top of their list.

Rick stood in a formal black tux, his parents, who she'd met over the Thanksgiving holiday, sat in the front row to watch the ceremony. They'd welcomed Judy with a wariness to them that she was determined to overcome.

Judy looked past her in-laws and found Rick's gaze as she walked toward him. In front of the minister, she kissed her dad's cheek before taking Rick's hand.

"Wow," Rick said under his breath when he stepped next to her. "You're beautiful."

"You clean up well yourself, babe."

Rick laughed at the nickname. "A lifetime of calling you *babe*. Love it."

"I love you," she said with a never-ending smile.

"Love you back."

She nudged him and Neil lifted an eyebrow. "You two ready to get this going?" Neil asked.

Rick and Judy both chuckled and turned their attention to the minister.

Acknowledgments

It is time, once again, for me to thank those who helped me get to this point in a novel.

For my online gaming friends who enjoy a good war without taking yourselves too seriously . . . you know who you are.

For my fellow boot campers who keep me motivated to move more than I ever would on my own. Love you guys.

Let's not forget my street team and your never-ending support of everything I write. I absolutely cannot go without mentioning Ashlea, who has already dubbed Rick her book boyfriend.

For my critique partner, Sandra . . . yes, yes, I know . . . Michael needs his HEA. Just hang in there, *babe*!

My editor, Kelli, who laughs at all my jokes. To the entire Montlake team. You guys rock.

As always, to Jane Dystel and everyone at Dystel & Goderich Literary Management. I couldn't ask for a more supportive team. xoxo

Let me round my way back to the woman I dedicated this book to . . . Aunt Joan. I'm not sure you know how special you are to me. When I first moved to California, your support and presence in my life was completely unexpected and never more appreciated than in that difficult time. You love unconditionally and with your whole heart, and I'm blessed you're in my life.

I love you.

Catherine

About the Author

New York Times-bestselling author Catherine Bybee was raised in Washington State, but after graduating high school, she moved to Southern California in hopes of becoming a movie star. After growing bored with waiting tables, she returned to school and became a registered nurse, spending most of her career in urban emergency rooms. She now writes full-time and has penned the novels *Wife by Wednesday*, *Married by Monday*, *Fiancé by Friday*, and *Single by Saturday* in her Weekday Brides series and *Not Quite Dating*, *Not Quite Mine*, and *Not Quite Enough* in her Not Quite series. Bybee lives with her husband and two teenage sons in Southern California.